Raymond Haigh was born, educated and has lived in Doncaster, South Yorkshire, all his life. He is married with four children and six grandchildren.

DARK ANGEL

The Prime Minister and the Home Secretary are scared — very scared. Terrorists, riots, the plague sweeping over the country, these are not the cause of alarm. Their concern centres on the documents held by a biochemist, which implicate the Government in a grave crime. Now, the biochemist is missing, as well as his wife and child. Government agent Samantha Quest is searching for them — but soon she is also being watched and hunted. A trail of death follows. Can Quest find the missing family and protect them from powerful men who will stop at nothing to conceal their crimes?

Books by Raymond Haigh
Published by The House of Ulverscroft:

COLDER THAN THE GRAVE
CRIPPLEHEAD

RAYMOND HAIGH

◆

DARK ANGEL

Complete and Unabridged

ULVERSCROFT
Leicester

First published in Great Britain in 2006 by
Robert Hale Limited
London

First Large Print Edition
published 2007
by arrangement with
Robert Hale Limited
London

British Library CIP Data

Haigh, Raymond, *1937 –*
   Dark angel.—Large print ed.—
   Ulverscroft large print series: adventure & suspense
   1. Missing persons—Great Britain—Fiction
   2. Political crimes and offenses—Great Britain—Fiction
   3. Suspense fiction 4. Large type books
   I. Title
   823.9′14 [F]

   ISBN 978–1–84617–708–8

Published by
F. A. Thorpe (Publishing)
Anstey, Leicestershire
Set by Words & Graphics Ltd.
Anstey, Leicestershire
Printed and bound in Great Britain by
T. J. International Ltd., Padstow, Cornwall

This book is printed on acid-free paper

1

Samantha leaned forward to get a better view of the house through the windscreen of the Ferrari. Its rough-hewn stone had been cleaned, giving the place a deceptively new appearance, but carved lintels, tall sash windows and a blue slate roof were whispering late Victorian.

She slid the pistol from its holster under the dash and ejected the magazine. Only six rounds. Tiredness was making her overlook things she ought never to forget. Pushing the clip back with the flat of her hand, she checked the movement of the breech, then slid the weapon into her crimson Gucci bag. It wasn't likely she'd need it here, but these were dangerous times, and trouble came when it was least expected.

Climbing out of the car, Samantha smoothed a crease from the skirt of her crimson Versace suit, then crossed the driveway. A flight of steps led up to a vestibule where substantial double doors had been hooked back to reveal an inner door and sidelights. Afternoon sun, trapped within the house, was glowing through panels of stained glass. She pressed the bell, then turned and glanced back over lawns starred with crocuses; bordered by clouds of snowdrops. It was a very desirable residence.

The whine of a vacuum cleaner faded. She caught a woman's voice saying, 'Leave it, Maria; I'll get it,' and the door swung open.

Surprise registered on pleasant features. Samantha said, 'Mrs Hadley?' then held the woman's gaze on its journey up from her crimson Sergio Rossi shoes.

'That's right, and you'll be Miss Quest.' Embarrassed now, the woman stood aside and gushed, 'Do come in. Forgive me for staring, but I was expecting someone a little older and . . . '

Samantha smiled and raised a questioning eyebrow as she crossed the threshold.

Mrs Hadley let out an embarrassed laugh ' . . . and not quite so fashionably dressed. That suit and bag and shoes: they're simply stunning.' She turned to a dark-haired girl with gentle eyes. 'Leave the hoovering now, Maria, and be a dear and bring some tea up to my sitting-room.' She glanced back at Samantha. 'Earl Grey or Assam?'

'Earl Grey would be fine,' Samantha said, then followed the slightly built woman as she led the way across a hall and up a wide flight of stairs. Neatly cut grey hair, grey woollen dress, black sensible shoes, no make-up; she seemed to be trying to play down the fact that she was still an attractive woman.

Samantha glanced through open doorways. Ceilings were high and cornices deep; and the plain carpets and restrained decorations weren't concealing the grandness of the house.

Mrs Hadley led her into a room above the entrance where tall windows looked over trees and fields and rooftops towards Bradford city, misty in the valley below.

'Quite a view,' Samantha said.

'Isn't it. That's why I chose this room for myself.' She laughed. 'We all need a little hideaway, don't we? Won't you sit down?'

Samantha relaxed into a wing-backed chair upholstered in blue and cream striped silk to match the sofa and the curtains. Looking across at the woman, she asked, 'How did you get my number?'

'Emma Turner. She recommended you very highly. I meet her at the Carmelite convent at Kirk Edge. She visits her daughter and I visit the mother superior. I think you know her daughter, Ruth? She's a novice.'

Samantha nodded; said nothing.

Soon embarrassed by the silence, Mrs Hadley let out a girlish little laugh, and said, 'Ruth certainly remembers you. She said you went to see her on Christmas Eve in a fabulous silver fur coat. She said you looked like a dark angel swathed in mist.' She laughed again. 'Ruth tends to use rather flowery language.'

Samantha smiled, recalling the visit and the floor-trailing coat made from the pelts of Siberian wolves. 'You said you'd a problem I might be able to help you with, Mrs Hadley?'

'Do call me Alice,' the woman said. Then she frowned and looked down at her hands. 'It's my brother; well, my brother and his wife and their little girl, really. They were supposed to visit us over Easter, but they didn't turn up and I keep phoning but no one answers.'

'He lives locally?'

Mrs Hadley shook her head. 'Oxford.'

'So, your brother and his family don't turn up a couple of weeks ago and we're suddenly talking three missing persons?'

Mrs Hadley met Samantha's gaze and let out an embarrassed little laugh. 'It sounds rather pathetic when I try and put it into words but . . . ' She faltered, suddenly unable to think. Dear God, those eyes: green and still and penetrating. And so off-putting.

'I'm expensive, Mrs Hadley. Have you tried the police? They could check it out and it's what you pay taxes for.'

'Bruce — that's my husband — contacted the police in Oxford and they looked the house over. They even took ladders and looked through the bedroom windows. They said everything seemed in order; all the doors were locked and there were no signs of a break-in or any trouble, and the car had gone. Bruce phoned the university, and they said they'd no concerns.'

'University?'

Mrs Hadley tut-tutted at herself. 'I'm sorry. I'm not telling this very well, am I? My brother's Professor Prentice; Nathaniel Prentice. He's an authority on microbes and viruses and that sort of thing. He's supposed to lecture at Oxford University, but he seems to spend more time on research and advising the government.'

'So, the police found nothing and his colleagues weren't concerned?'

'I knew this would happen,' Mrs Hadley sighed. 'You're reacting just like Bruce. He thinks I'm being silly, but Nat's hardly at the university, so how would they know whether he's missing or not?'

There was a faint tapping at the door, Mrs Hadley rose and opened it, and the dark-haired girl came in carrying a mahogany butler's tray. She let the legs swing down, then placed it on the oriental rug.

'That's very sweet of you, Maria. Thank you.'

Maria flashed her mistress a genuine smile, then left the room.

'What about other relatives?' Samantha asked. 'Have you contacted them?'

'There's only my sister, Lilith. She lives in a little village about ten miles from Nat. When I phoned she said she'd not seen him for a couple of years. He isn't very family minded, and Ling doesn't care to visit Lilith.'

'Ling?'

'Nat's wife. She's Chinese. Lemon or milk?'

'Lemon, no sugar.'

Mrs Hadley deftly forked a slice of lemon into the cup, then crossed the rug and handed it to Samantha. 'How about a cake? Maria got these from Bentons this morning. They're rather tempting.'

'Thanks, but no,' Samantha said, then asked, 'Could they have slipped away on holiday?'

'Nat didn't bother with holidays, Miss Quest.' Mrs Hadley sipped her tea. 'And Ling would have remembered to phone me and cancel the visit. I don't think it could be that.'

Samantha glanced around the room, trying to work out how to say no to the woman without offending her. Having it known she

6

did private investigation work was a useful cover; a safety net if she decided to resign from the service. And that was something she might do. They were fighting a war that couldn't be won. She needed a break from the endless killing, the constant threat of discovery and retaliation. This missing-persons hassle was something she could do without.

She brought her gaze back to the woman who was sitting, cup and saucer on her knees, looking across at her expectantly. Sighing, she said, 'Don't you think your husband might be right, Mrs Hadley?'

'Right?' She gave Samantha a bleak look.

'That you're probably worrying about nothing.'

'I hoped you wouldn't be like this.' Hurt and disappointment were shaping the woman's pleasant features now. 'I could tell the police thought I was a neurotic woman, and Bruce just laughs at me. My brother's never bothered with holidays, Miss Quest. And these last few years he's been very loosely attached to the university. They wouldn't know whether anything was wrong or not.'

Samantha studied her. A pretty and charming woman, she was probably accustomed to being indulged, but she wasn't stupid. Making her voice gentle, she said,

'What was it that really made you worry, Mrs Hadley?'

Alice Hadley cringed inwardly. Dear God, the way the woman looks at you, searching into your very soul. And the stylishly cut black hair and beautiful clothes; the scarlet lipstick and discreetly made-up eyes: so overwhelming. Alice took a nervous little sip at her tea, then gazed down at her cup and said, 'You'll laugh at me.'

'Trust me,' Samantha murmured huskily. 'Nothing you could possibly say would make me laugh at you.'

Mrs Hadley forced herself to meet Samantha's gaze. 'It was a dream: a dream I had about a week ago. In this dream we were all in the kitchen at home, our childhood home, that's always home in our dreams, isn't it? Lilith was sitting next to me and we were looking across the big table at Nathaniel. Somehow I knew Ling had run away and their little girl was hiding somewhere. He was staring at us, wide-eyed, trying to tell us something, and I said, 'What is it, Nat? What's happened?' And when he opened his mouth, flies poured out: a black buzzing cloud of flies that covered the table and windows and walls. When they began to crawl over my face I started to scream and woke up.'

The sound of a vacuum cleaner being used on the landing beyond the door grew louder, then faded. Samantha glanced up at the high mantelpiece, saw a small statue of a monk holding a staff, robes flying as he strode out.

Looking back at the grey-haired woman, she said, 'We don't know where our dreams come from, Mrs Hadley, and we've no means of finding out what they mean. They're best ignored.'

Alice Hadley's face softened into a smile. 'You've read St John of the Cross: *The Ascent of Mount Carmel?*'

'Just odd snippets.'

The woman's smile faded. 'I take it you think I should just forget it, then?'

'I'm driving down to Cheltenham tomorrow. I could break the journey and take a look at things.'

'Would you? You've no idea how relieved I'd — '

'I'm expensive, Mrs Hadley. When I take a job I charge for a full week, whether it takes a week or not. After the first week I charge by the hour.' She gave her the weekly and hourly rates.

Alice Hadley took a deep breath. The hand-sewn suit that fitted so perfectly, the bag and shoes, the silver sports car parked on the drive; it all suddenly dropped into place.

'Peace of mind is more important to me than the money, Miss Quest.'

Samantha opened her bag, reached beneath the cold hardness of the gun, and withdrew a pad and pen. 'Give me their address.'

Alice Hadley obliged, then said, 'It's rather isolated: down a lane on the outskirts of Oxford, surrounded by fields.'

'And your sister, Lilith?'

'Her name's not really Lilith, it's Helen. She's a sculptress; quite well known. Done a lot of big commissions. She began calling herself Lilith when she married a Welsh Druid called Elliot and got involved in that Wicca business.'

'Witchcraft?'

'I suppose so.' Alice shuddered. 'I've heard her talking about the *Book of Shadows*, and she and Dylan, that's her husband, are members of some cult that performs rituals. Bruce thinks it's all a bit of a joke, but I find it rather frightening. I warned Nat's wife to keep the little girl away from her.'

'And did she?'

'She didn't need the warning. The one time we were all together, Ling kept hold of Wei and wouldn't let her have anything to do with her. Lilith scares *me*, Miss Quest, and I'm her sister. I have masses said for her, every week, by the Sacred Heart Fathers in Dublin.

Mother must be turning in her grave.'

'And what's your sister's address?'

'Sorry,' Alice Hadley said. 'I do tend to ramble on. It's Merton Farm, Green Lane, Fetton: that's a little village about ten miles south of Oxford. It's just beyond the village, set a long way back from the road.'

'What about friends?' Samantha asked. 'Did your brother and his wife socialize?'

Alice Hadley laughed. 'My brother's a work-obsessed academic; an emotional illiterate. I don't think he'd understand the true nature of friendship. That's what made his marriage all the more surprising.'

'And how did he meet his wife?'

'He lectures, up and down the country and in the States. When he brought Ling to see us after the wedding, he said they'd met at a seminar in Leeds. Seems she worked as a translator.' Mrs Hadley laughed. 'I must say, we were rather shocked. It was so out-of-the-blue. Ling's face is quite beautiful; and her figure's emphatic. Nat wasn't young: he must have been forty then. She was quite a catch.'

'Who caught who?' Samantha murmured.

'I'm not sure I know what you mean?'

'Beautiful young woman meets not-so-young academic who could use a couple of terms in charm school. What was in it for her?'

'You're very cynical, Miss Quest. She could have been in love.'

Samantha raised an eyebrow.

Alice Hadley laughed. 'Bruce and I thought she was looking for status and security. Whatever it was, we both came to really like her. She's dignified and courteous and took Nat in hand. She got him to shave his beard and dress smartly; put some of the junk he'd been hoarding in the spare bedroom, and did a little decorating, all by herself. And she hangs on his arm at those dreary university functions; improves his image with fellow academics and students no end. Nat got the best of the bargain.'

Samantha held her gaze and said nothing.

Uncomfortable in the silence, Mrs Hadley said, 'Oriental women are so fortunate, don't you think? They don't seem to have our repressions about the body; the same feelings of shame and guilt.'

'Shame and guilt?'

Mrs Hadley blushed. 'About . . . you know . . . things. I mean, I could never understand what men see in all that grunting and thrusting.'

'Grunting and thrusting: that's a new one,' Samantha said. She couldn't stop her lips curling into a smile, and they both burst out laughing.

12

Mrs Hadley clapped her hand over her mouth, girlishly admitting how outrageous she felt she'd been. 'It's all people talk about these days,' she said, when they'd stopped laughing. 'It's never meant much to me, but I've always suspected Ling's not shy when it comes to pleasing Nat. That's how she's been able to manage him.' Alice Hadley was blushing heavily now.

'You mean she's sexually uninhibited?'

'Please, Miss Quest, don't misunderstand me. Ling's always dignified; always completely respectable. It's just the way she sometimes looks at Nat, and the way he touches her. A woman's intuition, I could tell . . . ' Words tailed off in a confusion of embarrassment.

'And they don't have any friends?'

'They probably socialize a little with Nat's colleagues, but I only know one name: Dr Weaver. He's a mathematician who's working with Nat on some government project. His daughter baby-sits for Ling. They live on Boar's Hill, just outside Oxford. I remember it because I pass the house when I visit the Carmelite priory at the end of the lane.

'You seem to visit a lot of convents and priories.'

'I attend meetings there. I'm president of the local Carmelite secular order: it's a group

13

of lay people around Bradford who want to live a life of prayer and contemplation.' The woman's face was earnest now. The spiritual life was clearly her great passion.

'Is there anything else you can tell me, Mrs Hadley, anything at all? The simplest details can sometimes be the most helpful.'

'I don't think so. If anything comes to me, I'll phone it through.'

'A photograph would be useful.'

'Of course.' Alice Hadley rose, crossed over to a cupboard beneath a bookcase, and returned with a leather-bound album and a big chocolate box. When she lifted the lid of the box, she revealed a large group photograph crammed on top of a jumbled collection of snap shots.

'Peter Clayton, the Home Secretary,' Samantha murmured.

'Election night,' Mrs Hadley said. 'Bruce is his agent and he manages his local constituency office.' She pointed with her little finger at a tall amiable-looking man with black curly hair. 'That's Bruce, my husband, that's Liz, Peter's wife; the mayor's the little woman with the big hat and chain of office. It was quite a victory. The rioting after all the terrorist bombings and the big immigrant vote made it very marginal. Peter had hoped for a safer seat, but Bradford North was the best they could find.'

She picked up a photograph of an attractively plump girl from the pile. 'This is our daughter, Jessica. She did politics philosophy and economics at Durham. Peter got her a job as a researcher for Tim Saunders, the Internal Security Minister. And this' — she passed Samantha a photograph of a statue on an altar — 'is my chapel. Bruce had it built for me, at the back of the house, a couple of years ago. It was a wedding anniversary present.'

'Our Lady of Mount Carmel,' Samantha said, becoming a little concerned at all the time this was taking.

'That's right. Are you a . . . ?'

'My mother was an Irish Catholic; my father a Russian Jew.'

'Really!' Mrs Hadley said. 'How exotic. Are you very devout?'

Samantha laughed softly. 'Not so you'd notice, Mrs Hadley. I just wander the wasteland between hope and belief.'

'That sounds rather desolate. And surely you mean hope and despair?'

'I meant hope and belief, but you can throw in a little despair, if you like.'

'You seem awfully cynical, Miss Quest.'

'I try not to deceive myself,' Samantha said huskily. She nodded towards the box. 'Your

15

brother and his wife: can you find me a photograph?'

'Sorry! I do chatter. Here's one of Nathaniel after Ling had persuaded him to shave his beard. It's a good likeness. And this is Ling with Wei. Bruce took it at Christmas. They came to see us on Boxing Day. Ling enjoys visiting us, even if Nat doesn't.'

Samantha studied the photograph of a rather florid middle-aged man. The family resemblance was strong. The Chinese woman wearing an embroidered silk gown was quite beautiful; the black-haired child small for her age. She glanced up at Mrs Hadley. 'May I keep these?'

'Of course. I think I can find you some more. There's a few in the album.'

'These are fine,' Samantha said, anxious to be away. She slid the note-pad and photo-graphs into her bag, then rose to her feet.

'When will you start?'

'I'll drive down tomorrow. If you hear from your brother, call me on the number Emma Turner gave you. I'll keep you posted.'

Alice Hadley stood aside and watched Samantha move out on to the landing and head down the stairs. The crimson suit seemed to flow over her body, the hem of its tiny jacket flaring out over her hips. And how on earth did she manage to walk so elegantly

16

in those impossible shoes? She was relieved she'd not involved Bruce. It wasn't wise to expose rather impressionable middle-aged men to this kind of stimulation.

Samantha glanced back at her. 'Your husband, Mrs Hadley, what does he do for a living?'

'Manages the family business; five generations. Stone quarries. Supplied the stone to build this house and most of Bradford.' She laughed. 'Doesn't take up much of his time. Working for the party and running Peter's constituency office seem to make bigger demands.' She moved ahead as they crossed the hall and opened the vestibule door. 'Peter and Liz are dining with us tonight. They're old friends.' She smiled at Samantha, obviously proud to be on such intimate terms with the Home Secretary and his wife.

Samantha stepped out, then glanced back. 'Does anyone know you've engaged me, Mrs Hadley?'

The woman shook her head. 'I was alone in the house when I phoned you last night. Thoughts were going round and round in my head and I just had to do something.'

'It might be best if we keep it strictly between ourselves. Your brother and his wife might suddenly turn up and you'd feel rather silly if you'd told people. Does your husband know?'

'He wasn't in when I went to bed, and he'd left before I came down. I've not had the chance to talk to him about it.'

'Best not tell him, either.'

Mrs Hadley followed her out on to the steps. 'Would you like to see the chapel before you go?'

'Kind of you to ask,' Samantha said, 'but we've been talking longer than I expected and I have to get back to Barfield.' Seeing the disappointment in the woman's face, she added, 'Light a candle for me. And show me the chapel when I call again.'

Mrs Hadley brightened. 'I'll pray for success. In fact, I'll phone round the Carmelite group and ask them all to pray.'

As Samantha turned the Ferrari down the slope that led to the gates, she caught a glimpse of a tiny chapel with lancet windows and a steep roof. Guilt appeasement or love-offering? Maybe old Bruce had been doing a little illicit grunting and thrusting. It all seemed too wonderful to be true.

Sighing, she braked, swung the car through the gates, then accelerated hard down the hill towards Bradford and the motorway. Perhaps tiredness was making her even more cynical than usual. Maybe the chapel really was a token of Bruce's undying love for Alice.

2

Marcus watched the pleasure boat emerging from the arches of Lambeth Bridge. Another couple of weeks and leaves on the trees in front of Thames House would be hiding his view down the river. Turning, he gazed upstream. The low evening sun was sparkling on choppy water. He really ought to get home. It had been days. It wasn't good to leave Charlotte alone on the farm like this. Bloody terrorists. Northern Ireland had been bad enough, but these crazy fundamentalists were beyond the pale. At least the Micks phoned in a warning when they planted a bomb. And to cap it all, Quest was asking for extended leave.

He moved back to the cluttered desk, switched off his laptop and folded it shut. He'd have to grant it. She was on the edge again. If he said no she'd resign, and he needed her. He began to select documents from the piles on the desk and drop them into a battered attaché case.

Strange, he reflected, that such a beautiful and elegant woman could be so utterly ruthless; such an efficient little killer. Hate

19

drove her, of course; he'd realized that long ago. Parents killed by terrorists in Israel; the rest of her family blown to smithereens by Al-Qaeda in Berlin. But he didn't want her demanding leave right now. He needed her on the end of a phone. He needed to know she was . . .

There was an imperious rap on the door. Glancing up he watched it swing open, then cool grey eyes were looking across at him.

'Ma'am?'

'Glad you're still here, Marcus. I've just escaped from the PM, the Home Secretary and that new Minister for Internal Security. They want us to locate some professor's wife: Chinese woman called Ling Prentice. Husband's a biochemist; lectures at Oxford.'

'Name rings a bell. Why us? Surely the police or Serious Crime could handle that?'

'I got the impression someone's already been looking and they've had no success. The PM was emphatic: the woman has to be found, and quickly. They were all filing in for an emergency cabinet meeting, so I didn't get the chance to ask questions.'

'But missing persons, Ma'am? That's not our — ?'

'I'll try and find out why it's so important, Marcus,' Loretta snapped. 'In the meantime could you put someone on it and make it clear we've got to have a quick result.' Deftly changing the subject to avoid further argument, she asked, 'How are you travelling to that Edinburgh meeting?'

'Thought I'd drive up tomorrow. I really must get home tonight. I've not seen Charlotte for days.'

'Think I'll fly up then. Perhaps you could drive me back and we could swap impressions?' She gave him a tight little smile.

'That would be pleasant, ma'am.'

Loretta Fallon reached for the door handle. 'Put someone decent on the search, Marcus. It might seem trifling to us, but the politicians were very agitated, and a quick result wouldn't do the department's image any harm, especially if someone else has botched the job.'

'I'll do my best, ma'am.'

She graced him with another smile, then walked out.

Marcus slammed down the lid of his attaché case and clicked it shut. Damned woman would have been more honest if she'd said, 'It won't do *my* image any harm.'

He took his jacket from a hanger, then crossed the expanse of brown carpet and took a last look up the river while he slipped it on. The pleasure boat was disappearing under Vauxhaull Bridge, reflected sunlight blazing on its wake. Things had certainly changed since Loretta took over. Old Merryweather had known how to handle the politicians, always managing to tell them what they wanted to hear, making the most gigantic cock-ups seem like hard-won battles against some nameless foe.

He had to get home. How many nights had it been? Three, four: Christ, it had been five! Heading out of the office, he marched off down the corridor. The department, MI5, had been a gentlemen's club when old Merryweather was in charge. Everything had been a bit of a caper then. Fallon had driven out the joy; made it all so deadly serious.

Marcus pushed the button for the lift. Strange thing was, he found her quite a turn-on. Well into her forties, she was no spring chicken, but she was tall and slender and full of energy. Always dressed in those navy-blue suits with long pencil skirts and white silk blouses. It was like a uniform. Never wore high heels. Probably didn't want to draw attention to her height.

The lift doors hissed open. Stepping inside, he pressed the button for the basement car-park. Couldn't say her face was even pretty, but those cool grey eyes radiated intelligence, and the generous mouth was rather sexy. She ought to dye her hair to hide the grey; get rid of that black ribbon and let it fall around her face. Make her look ten years younger.

And who could he allocate this wretched missing-persons job to? Oxford was Alex's patch, but he'd gone undercover into that transit camp near Bognor Regis. If they wanted a quick result it would have to be Quest, but she was demanding extended leave. Christ!

The lift lurched to a stop and the doors opened. He strode over oil-stained concrete to a black Volvo estate, tossed his attaché case into the back, then climbed inside. Old Merryweather would have understood his problems and held the politicians off with some convincing tale, but it was a waste of time trying to say no to Fallon.

★   ★   ★

Samantha worked her way through the suits and dresses on the rail. Everything was so last year. She had to get away, spend a few days in London and Paris, maybe go on to Milan, and choose herself another wardrobe. If Marcus refused her application for extended leave, she'd resign.

She paused at a filmy white summer dress.

Broad blue stripes around the hem of its full skirt made it look rather nautical: Crispin had had it cleaned, and it looked fit to wear. She glanced through the window. The spring sunshine was strong and she'd be cocooned in the car. She'd risk it, and maybe take the little white jacket to cover her arms when she was making calls.

The encrypted phone began its insistent bleeping. Deciding to ignore it, she headed for the bathroom. When she was halfway across the landing, she muttered, 'Sod you, Marcus,' then returned and snatched it up from the bedside table.

A cultured male voice said, 'That you, Sam . . . Sam?'

Samantha made the sigh audible. 'It's me, Marcus.'

'You said you wanted extended leave. How extended?'

Samantha brightened. 'Five weeks, maybe six. And I want to go to ground. I don't want calling in after a couple of days because some lunatic's filled his pants with Semtex and blown a tube train apart. I'm burnt out, Marcus.'

'It's OK, Sam, I'm going to authorize it.' His tone was placatory, apprehensive almost.

Samantha pressed her lips into a hard line and braced herself.

'If you could just check something out before you — '

'Bugger off, Marcus. It's rough out here, and the killing eats into you. I need some leave.'

'It's something the PM and the Home Secretary have raised with the chief. It's — '

Samantha let out a bitter laugh. 'They've poked their sticks into the wasps' nest, Marcus. Give the PM a gun and tell him to go out and shoot the crazy buggers. And tell the chief to shove her job up her tight little arse. I'm resigning.'

'Sam . . . Sam? Don't hang up. It's not terrorism; it's missing persons. Just something that needs checking out. Only take a day or two and then you can fade away for a while.'

'You're not listening to me, Marcus. Tell Fallon to shove her job up — '

'It's not Fallon's job to shove, Sam.' Marcus retorted angrily. 'Queen and country: we all serve Queen and country.'

'Don't give me that shit, Marcus. And don't you dare start blathering on about your royal connections. I couldn't even joke about it right now.'

'A couple of days, Sam.' His voice was coaxing again. 'That's all it'll take. Just a couple of days in Oxford checking out a missing woman.'

'Oxford's not my patch.'

'The agent who covers that area's in a transit camp, under cover, checking out immigrants before they're deported. He can't be assigned to the job.'

Samantha chewed her lip. Oxford was where she was heading. She closed her eyes and tried to think. Her body had started to shake. The bastard shouldn't do this to her. She was back where she was a year ago. And operating in this exhausted state was dangerous. One slip and she'd be dead.

'Two days, Sam.' The voice was coaxing. 'You might even clear it up in one. Sam . . . Sam? You still there, Sam?'

'I'm still here, Marcus. What's the background?'

'Woman's called Prentice: Ling Prentice. Chinese woman married to some professor of biochemistry. Chief was called to Number Ten late yesterday and told she had to be traced quickly.'

Samantha calmed herself with a few deep breaths. Alice Hadley's concerns weren't misplaced, after all. But why only her brother's wife? What about her brother and his child?

'Have you any details for me?'

'We've got a file on the woman.' There was relief in his voice now. 'I'm driving up to

Edinburgh. Could we meet in an hour? Service area on the M1 at junction twenty-one near Leicester.'

'Sounds OK.'

'You still driving that silver Ferrari Modena?'

Samantha said she was.

'I'll find you in the south-bound car-park. And thanks, Sam. I'm grateful.'

'This one's for you, Marcus; for getting me to Russia so I could deal with the assassin. It's not for Fallon, not for the Queen, and not for the sodding country.'

* * *

The door of the Ferrari opened. Marcus slid a long leg into the passenger footwell, and the interior was suddenly filled by broad shoulders in a double-breasted blue pinstripe suit. The suit needed pressing, but his white shirt was crisp and clean, and the Guards officer's tie looked brand-new.

'Ravishing dress, Sam. Absolutely breath-taking.'

Scarlet lips moved into a reluctant smile. 'You're very kind, Marcus, but saying sweet things won't make me feel any better about this. I desperately need some leave.'

'Just give it a couple of days, Sam. Locate

the woman and then you can vanish.' He lifted the lid of his attaché case, took out a manila folder and flicked it open.

Samantha noticed the *Keep Under Continuous Review* stamp, and said, 'She's been under surveillance, then?'

'For about three years. Started when she married Prentice, but we more or less wound it up after the first Al-Quaeda strikes. Had to reallocate resources after that.'

Marcus began to leaf through photographs of Ling Prentice, her child, and her bearded and then clean-shaven husband.

'What about her husband and child? Presumably they're not missing?' Samantha didn't mention her visit to Alice Hadley. Her extra-mural activities were her own business.

'Politicians only mentioned the woman when they called the chief to Number Ten. Prime Minister had a rant about how urgent it was, and then they started a cabinet meeting and she had to leave. She didn't get a chance to ask questions.'

Reaching amongst the papers, she picked out a copy of a birth certificate for a girl called Ling Haifong. 'This her maiden name?'

'That's a dead girl, born in Liverpool. Someone fixed up Mrs Prentice with her identity. Ling Prentice is an illegal immigrant. Her real name's Ma Weihma. Born in Peking.

28

Worked as a waitress in Leeds when she first arrived; went to evening classes and learned to read and write English. Then she must have met Prentice. We don't have a very complete picture of her before the marriage. It's what she was doing afterwards that concerned us. Beautiful young Chinese marries British academic who's a world authority on biological toxins: we suspected espionage.'

'And was she a cute little Mata Hari?'

'We didn't find a thing. If it had been espionage they'd have got her into the country legally. She was just an economic migrant who worked hard and got lucky.'

Samantha gazed down at a photograph of Ling Prentice in an embroidered silk gown holding on to the arm of a much older man in a tuxedo. 'Maybe it was Professor Prentice who got lucky,' she said.

Marcus chuckled. 'She is a lovely little thing, isn't she?'

'And nothing was done about the fact that she's an illegal immigrant?'

'Ignored it while we kept her under surveillance. Anyway, country's full of illegals. You can multiply the government's figures by at least a factor of three. One more's not going to make any difference, and she is a professor's wife.'

'Why should the Prime Minister and the Home Secretary be so bothered about this? Terrorists more or less bombing at will, race riots; I'd have thought they had more pressing things to worry about.'

Marcus shrugged. 'Prentice is a world authority in his field, involved in government research, gives advice to ministers; perhaps they're worried about him or his wife having been snatched. You'd want a man like that on your side if you were developing biological toxins.'

Samantha closed the folder. 'Can I keep this?'

'Sure. When will you start?'

'I'll book into a hotel in Oxford, read through the file over lunch, and maybe start visiting their friends and relatives this afternoon.'

'There's one or two names in there.' Marcus opened the door and swung a leg out. 'There's not much, but it should get you started on the trail.' He heaved himself out of the low-slung car, then turned and said, 'Give me a ring tomorrow and let me know how you've got on. Promises have been made to our political masters.'

'Your masters, Marcus, not mine.'

He laughed. 'Don't tell me our rabid little republican's descending into anarchy now.

Get me a result as soon as you can, Sam.' He slammed the door and strolled off between the cars, heading for the pedestrian bridge to the north-bound side of the motorway.

Samantha wound a window down to clear the pungent smell of shaving soap and cologne, then keyed the ignition. Three white vans pulled into spaces on the far side of the access lane and Asian families began to tumble out. They'd taken to travelling in convoys of three or four vans, sometimes with hired minders. The terror was having a profound effect on their lives, too. When they'd drifted off, she swung out of the line of cars and cruised towards the slip road.

3

Tucked away down a narrow lane, some distance from its neighbours, the Prentice House hadn't been easy to find. Samantha slowed as she approached it. The local police had said they'd looked through windows when they'd checked the place, so she was surprised to see them boarded over with rough plywood. Nail heads were bright and the boarding was new; perhaps it had been fixed during the space of the past few days.

She drove on for another fifty yards, then reversed the Ferrari through a field gateway. Walking back down the lane, she glanced over her shoulder; felt reassured when she saw the low hedges concealing her car.

Meanly built and devoid of ornament, the boarding over the windows made the house seem almost derelict. What little paint remained on the garage doors was cracked and peeling. Weeds were beginning to encroach into flower beds that bordered the short concrete drive, and the front lawn badly needed cutting. No longer a home, everything about the lonely, isolated dwelling seemed desolate and sad.

There were no gates, just an opening in a low wall. Samantha glanced up and down the lane, saw it was still deserted, then wandered around the back. A small vegetable garden had been planted close to the house. Beyond it, on an area of rough grass, a child's swing and climbing frame cast hard shadows in the sunlight. A faint breeze was rustling the filmy material of her dress: it was the only sound she could hear.

Someone had trampled a path across the vegetable patch. Samantha picked her way along it. When she rounded the back of the garage, she saw a new-looking incinerator and piles of paper ash that had been broken into tiny fragments. Lifting the incinerator lid, she found someone had reduced the mound of ash inside almost to dust.

The back door had mortice and cylinder locks. When Samantha pressed it with her knee, the lower half gave a little. Only the Yale cylinder secured it.

Taking a pack of surgical gloves from her bag, she drew them on, then flicked out a square of springy plastic. Forcing it into the rebate above the Yale, she dragged it down. The sneck clicked. When she turned the knob, the door opened.

She stepped inside. A tiny lobby gave access to a toilet on her left, a utility room on her right, and the kitchen straight ahead. The windows had been carefully boarded. Beyond the spill of light from the open door, the house was in total darkness. She worked a switch and a fluorescent tube flickered on.

There were no dishes in the sink, but evidence of a last meal remained on the pine table: a dish and mug decorated with teddy bears; a blue and white china cup neatly stacked on a matching china plate. One child, one adult. Samantha tugged open the fridge door; found it well stocked with food and drink.

She moved through the house, switching lights on and off as she went. There were signs everywhere of a new bride having done her best to stamp her personality on the home of an academic who'd lived alone. Fresh wallpaper and curtains made old carpets and furniture seem tired and faded. Here and there, new chairs and ornaments struck an oriental and often jarring note. Either Nathaniel Prentice had been too tight-fisted to allow her to really transform the place, or Ling had had the good sense to make modest changes he wouldn't find too disturbing.

A room at the back of the house appeared to be the professor's study. The desk drawers, a couple of metal filing cabinets, and some bookshelves, had been stripped bare. Their contents had probably been reduced to ashes behind the garage.

Samantha climbed stairs into the tomb-like darkness; found an antiquated bathroom, a child's bedroom, and a guest room crammed with discarded ornaments and furniture.

The bedroom Ling had shared with her husband was the one room she'd completely transformed. A substantial white bedroom suite was decorated with deep gilded carvings. Curtains and wallpaper were pale pink, patterned with small white flowers; the plain carpet a deeper, duskier shade of pink. Fluffy white rugs were arranged on either side of the bed. This bed, and the bed in the child's room, were rumpled and unmade. A cotton nightdress had been draped over a chair. There was no sign of a man's nightwear. Either the professor slept in his vest and pants, or he hadn't been with his wife and child when they left the house.

Samantha began to search through the wardrobes, checking the pockets in suits, gazing admiringly at embroidered silk dresses and gowns. Tugging out drawers, she sifted through layers of clothing, then checked the bottoms and backs for items that might have been pinned there. Beneath the lining paper in a dressing-table drawer, she found a crumpled envelope containing a few documents and a birthday card. In an untidy Mandarin script, a friend had written, *To Ling with fondest greetings from Kwan*. There was a photograph inside the card of two smiling girls, arm-in-arm, posing against the knight-on-horseback statue in Leeds city square. Reaching for her bag, Samantha slid documents and card beneath the gun, and clicked it shut.

Returning to the ground floor, she sifted through the contents of a sideboard in the dining-room, and bookcases and cupboards in a living-room, but found nothing. Back in the kitchen, she surveyed the array of cupboards and drawers. She really ought to look through them all, and check cereal packets and food containers. Sighing, she tugged out a drawer and lifted it on to a worktop.

The sudden squeal of brakes was loud and she could hear the muttering of powerful engines in the lane outside.

Snatching her bag from the table, she darted out of the back door and pulled it shut behind her. Van doors were slamming as she ran across the vegetable patch and hid behind the garage. Reaching inside her bag, she slid her hand around the grip of the gun and waited.

Boots began to clump down the side of the

house and she could hear men's voices. Gathering her filmy skirt tightly around her legs, and keeping her head low, she leaned forward and peered around the corner. About half-a-dozen men in black bomber jackets, black jeans and black boots were struggling into protective suits.

'It's all got to go?'

'Everything: carpets, curtains, clothes; the lot.'

'We should have brought another van, Sarge. We won't get a houseful into three vans.'

'We'll do it if we pack it tight,' a cockney said.

'Gloves over cuffs, gloves over cuffs, lads.' The man they'd called Sarge kept his voice low, but it still seemed like a parade-ground bark.

'We could shove some of the stuff in the decontamination van,' a stocky Welshman suggested.

The sergeant pointed to his feet and did a little jig. 'Them's for dancing, Taffy,' he tapped his head, 'and them's for thinking. For Gawd's sake, use 'em. What are we going to do if we contaminate the ruddy decontamination van?'

Taffy grinned sheepishly. The rest of the group laughed.

'Who's got the keys?'

'Here Sarge.' A fresh-faced youth made for the door.

'Wait for it. Wait for it,' the sergeant barked. 'Masks on and hoods up first. And I don't care how sweaty you get, you stay sealed in your suit until the job's done and you've been sluiced down. Gawd only knows what's in that place.'

Goggle-eyed masks with filters and breathing tubes were pulled on; elasticated hoods snapped in place. The sergeant gestured at the one with the keys, then pointed towards the door. The man moved forward and unlocked it, shoved it open with his foot, and they all tramped inside.

Samantha waited a few thudding heartbeats, then stepped out of her shoes and snatched them up. Skirt swirling around her legs, she dashed for the road. One of the trucks had been backed up to the garage; two others and what looked like a military ambulance were parked on the grass verge. All painted dull black, they carried no markings to identify the owning authority.

Out of earshot now, she stepped into her shoes and ran for the car. She climbed inside, released the brake, and let it roll back until she could see the house and the trucks through a gap in the hedge.

Within minutes, the white-suited figures had loaded the truck parked in front of the garage, driven it back on to the road, and replaced it with another. Little care was being taken: everything seemed to be destined for disposal. In less than an hour, the dusky-pink bedroom carpet had appeared and been packed into the last of the vans.

One by one, the men climbed into the smaller truck and reappeared, minutes later, minus their masks and protective suits. Doors slammed, engines coughed into life, and the trucks moved off.

Samantha lurched out on to the highway and followed, hidden by the high banks that bordered the winding lane. Rounding a bend, she saw the rearmost truck turn right on to the main road and head south, away from Oxford. She settled back into the leather and kept them in view, fearful now of the contamination in the house, furious at the casual way Marcus and Fallon had allocated the job to her.

★ ★ ★

'Those vans, Marcus. Up ahead. What are they? There seems to be quite a convoy.'

'Can't tell from here, ma'am. I'll overtake so we can have a closer look.' Accelerating,

Marcus moved over to the outer lane and slowly cruised past the line of black vans. 'Decontamination wagons,' Marcus said. 'About twenty of the things.'

'Are you sure? We've had no intelligence about chemical or biological attacks.'

'The vents, ma'am, along the side, one per cubicle. And the fluid tanks on the cab and between the wheel arches. They're definitely decontamination wagons.'

'But why are twenty or more heading south?'

'Impossible to say, ma'am. They're military trucks; tell by the cab structure. Regimental insignia have been blacked-out.'

'Just like the water-cannon trucks the police are using on riot control,' Loretta Fallon muttered.

'Army are manning the water cannons,' Marcus said. 'A couple of regiments have been drafted in and put in police uniforms.'

'Some of these developments worry me, Marcus.'

'Developments?'

'That meeting with the PM yesterday. The Home Secretary was there, and the new Minister for Internal Security. What do we need a Ministry for Internal Security for?'

'Jobs for the party faithful?' Marcus suggested.

Loretta frowned. 'I hope it's only that, but I'm wondering if they intend to transfer duties and responsibilities.'

'Diminish us?'

'That, or worse. Governments don't trust us, Marcus. Think about it. Our business is intelligence gathering and national security. We know a lot of secrets. They only get told what we want them to know. The only control they have over us is by fixing the budget and making the most senior appointment. They can't get in amongst the detail. And since the emergency powers legislation, we've got agents out there acting as judge, jury and executioner; for serious crime as well as terrorism.'

'Maybe they're still smarting over that business with the party supporters and child prostitutes?'

Loretta laughed. 'Don't think so. Nine-day wonder. And politicians ditch discredited colleagues and camp followers faster than monkeys picking off fleas. No, it's something I can't quite put my finger on. A feeling they've started moving other people on to our turf; people they're not telling us about.'

Marcus returned to the inside lane and risked a glance at the tall slender figure sitting beside him. Away from headquarters, she'd abandoned the trademark blue suit and was wearing a rather low-cut black dress. Her hair was loose around her shoulders, not tied back. Fragrantly attractive, Marcus mused. And he was finding the aura of authority quite a turn-on.

'That convoy,' Loretta said thoughtfully, 'Get someone to find out why decontamination trucks are being taken out of the holding depots and driven south. And while they're at it, they can find out which agency's holding unmarked vehicles and having them painted black.'

'I could have a word with Mulholland at the Ministry of Defence and Rogers at Serious Crime, ma'am.'

'Don't use the old-boy network, Marcus. Send a couple of agents in and do it covertly. We don't want them to suspect we're concerned about fragmentation.'

'That could be a problem, ma'am. I don't think I could spare a couple of agents to — '

'You're stone-walling me, Marcus.' Loretta was using her nanny-in-the-nursery voice now; acting the stern governess. She found that usually worked with the public-school types. 'Nothing could be more important than other organizations moving in on us.'

Send in a couple of agents! She didn't realize what she was asking. Everyone was run ragged. He was pushing Quest and a couple of others to breaking point. Somehow managing to sound enthusiastic, he said, 'Leave it with me, ma'am. We'll do our best.'

Loretta peered into the darkness, towards a frosting of lights on a distant hillside. 'Where are we now?'

'Moving through South Yorkshire. That's Barfield on the rise over there.'

'Where Quest lives?'

'That's right. Nondescript little three-storey town house,' Marcus said.

'You've paid her a visit, then?'

'God, no! She's not the kind of woman I'd care to call on. We had a security system fitted before she moved in: camera surveillance of all rooms accessed from a terminal in the garage. She can look the house over before she goes inside.'

'I hear she does a little moonlighting; has a private investigation business on the side.' Loretta's tone was icy.

'You're very well informed, ma'am.'

'And have you had a word with her about it?'

'It's good cover, ma'am. And she developed the business a couple of years ago when she was given gardening leave.'

'Gardening leave?' Loretta sounded out-raged.

'Al-Qaeda was having her stalked by two

assassins: retribution for killing an entire clan and then exposing their Moscow cell to the Russians. It wasn't safe for her to operate until they'd been eliminated.'

'I'm aware of the background, Marcus. I'm asking if you've had a word with her about the moonlighting. There could be a conflict of interest.'

'Like I said, ma'am, it's good cover and there's no evidence of it compromising performance. She handed us the London tube bombers on a plate, worked down the kill lists, took the blighters out by the cellarful.'

Loretta sniffed reprovingly. He was digging his heels in on this one. Would he do it for a man? Would he do it if the woman wasn't so incredibly attractive? She didn't like it. For the salary she'd authorized, Quest belonged to the department body and soul.

'She can't serve two masters, Marcus.'

'With respect, ma'am, I don't think it's quite like that. Quest gives her all to the job. She'd march right up to the cannon's mouth for us.'

He wasn't going to budge. Loretta decided to let it ride until she had him in her office, on her own ground.

Marcus turned up a slip road, began to circle a round-about, heading for the M1.

'Has Alex made any progress with the search for that professor's widow?' Loretta asked. 'What's her name?'

'Ling Prentice,' Marcus prompted. 'I put Sam Quest on the job.'

Loretta glanced at him. 'It's in Oxford. That's Alex's patch.'

'You said you needed a quick result, ma'am, so I put the best agent I've got on it.'

'Does Alex know?'

'He knows. And he's relieved. He's gone into that internment camp near Bognor Regis, as a Turkish repatriate, now we've sorted out the paperwork. We need to resolve outstanding issues with some of the people in there.'

Loretta laughed. '*Resolve outstanding issues*! That's a rather charming evasion, Marcus. I hope they don't start to riot when the bodies are dragged away. It's not long since the inmates burnt a new camp down.'

'He'll be discreet, ma'am. And if the camp does burn down you can rest assured they won't be able to pin it on us.'

Loretta laughed. 'You like her, don't you, Marcus?' she probed, going off at a tangent.

'Like her, ma'am?'

'Samantha Quest. You like her a lot?'

'I admire her immensely. She's the best agent I've ever had.'

'You're being evasive again, Marcus. I'm asking you if you're attracted to her. I mean, she must be the ultimate male sexual fantasy: her face and figure, that husky voice.'

Marcus laughed. 'Not mine, ma'am. Hard as diamonds, cold as ice: that's how your predecessor used to describe her. Admiring her professionalism, admitting she's beautiful, doesn't mean I'm attracted to her.'

'Rubbish, Marcus. I don't believe you,' Loretta chided.

'You'd be surprised, ma'am. If you'll forgive me for saying it, I've always found you infinitely more attractive.'

'Marcus! You're utterly outrageous! Why, I'm . . . ' She was going to say, 'almost twenty years older than Quest', but checked herself, and said, ' . . . I'm shocked at you.'

'I've embarrassed you, ma'am. I'm sorry.'

'You've flattered me outrageously, and I don't believe a word of it.'

Loretta let out a shocked little laugh. She'd never marked down old related-to-royalty Marcus as a sycophant, but he was ambitious. Maybe he was trying to ingratiate himself, manoeuvring for the number-two slot. Whatever it was, she didn't find it unpleasant. And he did have big hairy forearms and those powerful footballer's thighs; things she'd always found quite compelling.

46

She gave him a sideways glance. He looked uncomfortable. She'd embarrassed him by laughing, but what the hell did he expect? She flicked back a fall of greying hair, uncrossed and crossed her legs, and didn't bother to tug the hem of her dress back over her knees.

'Has Quest made any progress?'

'She's only had the job a few hours. I'll contact her tomorrow and give you a report.' He overtook a car transporter. 'Must say, I'm a bit puzzled about the urgency. What's the problem with the Chinese widow of a professor of biochemistry? Is it espionage?'

'I wasn't told,' Loretta said. 'The new Minister for Internal Security seemed a bit sheepish and the PM looked flushed and wild-eyed. I think he'd had a good rant before they called me in to the cabinet room. It's more than espionage.'

They rode on in silence for a couple of miles, then Loretta said, 'I really am worried, Marcus. Something's happening. Rival factions could be setting up their own covert organizations. They must have an eye to things going into total melt-down. The situation's coming close to civil war.'

'Where would they be recruiting from? Army?' Marcus asked.

'Army's my guess. Trained, disciplined, got

the resources. And if things do tip over the edge, it's the military that'll take control.'

'Trouble is,' Marcus muttered, 'when things start to descend into chaos, all the political wierdos crawl out of the woodwork. It won't just be pimply youths in bother-boots. There're plenty of establishment figures who'd like to remodel society on less democratic lines.'

'Who can we trust, Marcus? How many of your operatives would you instinctively trust?'

'About half.'

'What about Quest?'

'She's a loose cannon, ma'am. She'd always act as she thought fit. Loner, very anti-establishment, strong republican tendencies.'

'She must rib you about your royal connections.'

Marcus laughed. 'Endlessly, ma'am.'

'How much longer 'till we reach London?'

'Couple of hours.'

'Do you need a break?'

'I'm OK, ma'am. I enjoy driving.'

'When we get to my place, you must come in and have a rest. I'll do you coffee and bacon and eggs,' Loretta insisted, in her no-nonsense voice.

'That's very thoughtful of you.'

'And Marcus?'

'Ma'am?'

'When we're away from headquarters and alone together, don't keep calling me ma'am. You sound like one of the sheep your wife breeds. How is the bishop's daughter, by the way?'

4

Uncomfortable in damp tangled sheets, Loretta was surfacing from sleep and trying to work out why her bed was in such a mess. She heard a man's voice, deep and urgent, then turned and saw Marcus's broad naked back. He was sitting on the edge of the bed, holding a mobile phone to his ear.

She'd spent the night with Marcus! Suddenly aware of her own nakedness, her mind began to race. She couldn't let him see her like this. Twenty years ago she could have flaunted herself; aroused the man with a reminder of the delights he'd enjoyed the night before. Almost fifty, she had to be discreet with her body now. Silk and lace and soft lights; allowing its nakedness to be explored by the hand rather than the eye.

She tugged at the duvet. It wouldn't move. She tugged harder, felt it slide towards her when Marcus obligingly rose to his feet and turned to face her, nonchalant in his nakedness.

Loretta's eyes were drawn to the flaccid organ sprouting from the explosion of hair at the top of those powerful footballer's thighs.

Its uncircumcised flesh was wrinkled and dark. Definitely not a pretty sight, she decided.

Holding the duvet over her, she slid from the bed, then wrapped it around her back before darting across the landing and into the bathroom. She locked the door. Calmer now, she allowed herself the pleasure of recollection. It hadn't been quite what she'd expected. Her smile broadened. He'd been tenderly deferential, almost like an inexperienced boy, until he'd unbuttoned her dress and slid his hand inside. He'd become quite passionate then. Two or three times.

Loretta squatted on the toilet. God, it was like peeing red-hot needles. And her back ached. The morning-after was always like this. She didn't make love often enough, and when she did the men she chose were usually too vigorous and went on for too long.

Twenty minutes later he'd joined her in her white and terracotta kitchen. She nibbled daintily at a triangle of toast while he attacked the bacon and eggs she'd promised him the night before.

He ate hungrily, with a brisk efficiency she found rather off-putting. She couldn't fault his table manners: they were impeccable; it was just the masculine vigour. Sleeping with Marcus had been more than pleasant, but she wouldn't want to look across the table at this spectacle every morning. And she couldn't cope with her private space being invaded on a permanent basis.

' . . . It rather supports what you were suggesting last night,' she heard him saying.

Loretta had been gazing at him but not listening, his words barely touching her consciousness. 'I'm sorry, Marcus. I didn't quite catch the point you were making.'

He swallowed coffee and began to spread butter on a slice of toast. 'Quest,' he repeated. 'That call, this morning, from Sam Quest. She was peeved to say the least. Asked me what other agencies were involved in the Prentice search.'

Loretta frowned. 'Other agencies? When the PM briefed me he made it clear he was passing the job to us. What does she mean, other agencies?'

'She went to the Prentice house yesterday; found it boarded up. While she was doing a search, men arrived in black trucks and emptied the place. She hid and watched. Thing is, they put on protective suits and brought a decontamination wagon along. Quest tailed them to Porton Down.' Marcus paused, toast halfway to his mouth, while they gazed at one another over the breakfast-table clutter.

'Contamination,' Loretta muttered. 'The PM and the others said nothing about infection or contamination.'

'And it does bear out what you were saying, ma'am . . . '

Loretta was relieved he'd begun to address her formally again: the discretion of the perfect gentleman. She'd been shrewd in taking him as a lover. She raised an eyebrow, inviting him to go on.

' . . . about our no longer being the only players in the game. And Quest's got a hunch that Professor Prentice didn't leave the house with his wife and child.'

'Hunch?'

'Small things she noticed when she did the search. She didn't elaborate.'

'The PM and the Home Secretary only mentioned the Chinese woman when they briefed me,' Loretta said. 'Could have been an oversight, or perhaps they were being economical with the truth.'

Marcus frowned at her for a moment, then began to eat the slice of toast.

'We've no intelligence about a biological attack or any contamination,' Loretta said. 'And we've been particularly vigilant in that area.'

'Like I said, ma'am, it does seem to confirm your suspicions. Quest asked for guidance. I told her we had sole authority and if she encountered interference to use her discretion.'

Loretta nodded. 'What about the trucks she followed?'

'She had a check run on the plates and all four were from vehicles burnt out in the riots about a year ago.' Marcus reached for another slice of toast, tore it in half and began to wipe the remains of egg and fat from his plate.

Public school, Loretta mused. Meal-time parsimony and adolescent hunger; habits formed and never forgotten. She dabbed her mouth with a paper napkin, careful not to smudge her lipstick.

'Quest says she might need to get into Porton,' Marcus went on.

'Make the arrangements,' Loretta said, grimly. 'Get her whatever she asks for.'

'What about contamination? What if it's something serious?'

'I presume she's had all her shots?'

Marcus nodded. 'Everything. She was returning to MI6 and they were assigning her to the Middle East, but I held her back. I thought she was needed more at home. She didn't object.'

'In that case, she's had all the protection we can provide.'

'What if it's something the programme doesn't cover?'

'We all take risks, Marcus. It comes with the territory. And she's smart enough to know what she's tangling with.'

'It's just that she's the one agent I really wouldn't want to lose.'

Loretta gave him a knowing smile. 'You really do have a soft spot for the gorgeous little Samantha, don't you, Marcus?'

He laughed. 'I told you last night, ma'am. I find you much more attractive.'

Loretta tossed the paper napkin down and pushed her chair back; felt a stab of pain in her back as she rose to her feet. 'Don't say flirtatious things you can't possibly mean, Marcus.'

'But last night . . . you must have realized?'

'Realized what?' she demanded brusquely.

He began to blush. 'That I . . . I hope you didn't find it unpleasant?'

'No, Marcus, I certainly didn't find it unpleasant.'

'Perhaps we can — '

'*I'll* let you know when,' Loretta interrupted, in her nanny-knows-best voice. 'Now, I think you should drive me to headquarters. That half-wit of a Home Secretary is going to explain to me about men in protective suits.'

★ ★ ★

Samantha checked her face in the mirror, then fumbled in her bag for her lipstick and made good the damage caused by eating the apology of a breakfast. She turned and looked over the items laid out on the bed: attaché case, laptop, overnight bag, her dress in its nylon cover. Everything was there.

She lifted her grey spring coat from the arm of a chair and drew it on. As she was reaching for her gloves and keys, her mobile began to bleep. She took it from her bag.

'Miss Quest?'

Samantha sat on the bed. 'Speaking, Mrs Hadley.'

'Have you any news for me?'

'It's early days yet, but you were right to be concerned.'

'Some men called yesterday. Said they were from the police. I didn't much like the look of them so I asked for identification. *Serious Crime Unit Yorkshire Region* was printed on the cards they showed me. They asked me if Nat's wife had been, or if I knew where she was.'

'And what did you tell them?'

'That I'd not seen Nat or his family since Christmas. I don't think they believed me. I thought they were going to search the house.'

'You didn't mention that you'd engaged me?'

'Of course not. We agreed: mum's the word.'

'And you've not told your husband?'

'No, Miss Quest. I did as you asked. Anyway, I didn't want him laughing at me and making smart remarks about the cost.'

'It's even more important that we keep this to ourselves now,' Samantha said. 'Did the men say why they're only searching for your brother's wife?'

'They said Nat's visiting the States. It seems he kept phoning the house and when no one answered he contacted the police. They've been to see Lilith, but she couldn't tell them anything.'

'Serious Crime are involved now, Mrs Hadley. They've confirmed your brother's in the States; they're searching for his wife and presumably his child. Do you want me to stop looking?'

Samantha heard a nervous little laugh. 'I feel more worried than ever now, Miss Quest. Bruce had a word with Peter, the Home Secretary, but he said the Serious Crime people answer to Tim Saunders, the Minister for Internal Security, so he couldn't help.'

'Didn't you tell me your daughter's a researcher for Saunders?

'Jessica? Yes. Bruce thought it best not to involve her. He asked Peter to talk to Tim

Saunders and see if he could find out something.'

'What would you like me to do, Mrs Hadley?'

'I'm more than a little frightened. That awful dream I told you about, and now these rather unpleasant Serious Crime people are involved. Why aren't the ordinary police dealing with it? And if Nat was worried about not being able to contact Ling, why didn't he phone here? Bruce and I could have driven down in a couple of hours.'

Samantha glanced at her watch. She was running late. 'Tell me what you want me to do, Mrs Hadley.'

'I'm worried sick about Ling and the little girl. I'd like you to stay involved. The cost isn't a problem.'

'I'll be charging the time to some other business I have in Oxford,' Samantha said evasively. 'You can forget the cost. But it's more important than ever that we keep this arrangement to ourselves. We've got to be absolutely clear about that. And if you get any information from Peter Clayton or Tim Saunders, let me have the details.'

'Of course. Is there anything else I can do?'

'Just keep lighting the candles, Mrs Hadley. And whatever you do, don't let anyone know you've engaged me.'

Samantha switched off the phone. Having Mrs Hadley involved in this way had its dangers, but they were probably outweighed by information she might get via the family's political connections.

★ ★ ★

Boars Hill was an exclusive and reclusive place where detached homes seemed to have been built in small forest clearings. Samantha slowed almost to a stop, eased the Ferrari over a traffic calmer, then began to cruise down the narrow private road, peering through trees, searching for the house Alice Hadley had described.

The road forked. When she turned left she saw it: a big place, built in the Arts and Crafts style, with a moss-covered tile roof, wide overhanging eaves, and pebble-dashing above a brick plinth. A sagging oak gate was pegged back and half-buried under a drift of rotting leaves. Weeds were growing through the gravel driveway. She drove down it slowly, trying to prevent stones peppering the underside of the car.

An oak door was flanked by tiny leaded windows and protected by a deep canopy. Samantha swung her legs out of the car, felt the gravel through the delicate soles of her shoes, then climbed a couple of steps and pressed the bell. She heard nothing, waited a few seconds, then gave the oak a pounding with a big iron knocker and listened to the sound booming through the house.

The door opened a few inches and a young girl peered through the gap.

'Miss Weaver?'

The girl nodded.

'I understand your mother and father were friends of Professor Prentice and his wife?'

'That's right.' The refined voice was wary.

'I'm from Baxter, Allot and Jones, solicitors. We're trying to trace Mrs Prentice. It's in connection with a legacy. Could I come in and talk to your mother?'

'She's not well.'

'Is she too ill to talk to me for a few moments?' Samantha made her voice coaxing. 'Quite a large sum of money's involved.'

'Can you wait there?'

'Of course,' Samantha said.

The girl was about to shut the front door, realized how offensive that would seem, and left it ajar. Samantha touched it with her foot, eased it open a little, and saw oak panelling and red wall-to-wall carpet that needed hoovering. She could hear voices: the girl apologetic, the mother irritated.

A door opened and the girl returned across

the hall. 'She'll see you,' she said, then lowered her voice as she added, 'the place is in a bit of a mess. My father died a few weeks ago and Mummy's been very depressed since the funeral.' Having done her best to excuse the housekeeping, she stood aside and Samantha stepped into the hall.

'It's OK,' Samantha said. 'I understand. And I won't keep your mother long.'

The girl led her across the hall and through a door into a room where the curtains had been drawn, shutting out what sunlight managed to penetrate the trees surrounding the house. A plump woman eased herself up from a reclining position on a sofa and lowered her legs to the floor. Her hand groped up the stem of a table lamp, a switch clicked, and subdued light revealed a dishevelled figure in a crumpled dress. The roots of her auburn hair were grey.

'This is . . . ' The girl looked at Samantha.

'Quest,' Samantha said. 'Samantha Quest. Baxter, Allot and Jones.'

An ammonia-like odour, faint but unmistakable, permeated the humid atmosphere in the room. The woman nodded towards an armchair facing the sofa. Samantha sat on the edge of the seat, reluctant to sink back into it.

'Thanks for seeing me, Mrs Weaver. I understand you and your husband were friends of Professor Prentice and his wife. I'm trying to locate her, but I'm having no success. Have you any idea where she might be, or do you know of any other friends I might contact?'

The woman was looking her over, very deliberately and without bothering to hide her hostility and envy. The hem of the woman's dress had ridden up, her knees were parted, and the darker material at the top of her tights was clearly visible.

'Can you help me, Mrs Weaver?' Samantha repeated.

'That's a beautiful dress and coat,' the woman said bitterly, ignoring her question.

'Thank you,' Samantha murmured, thinking it best not to reveal it was an Ungaro.

'And the grey shoes: they're snakeskin, aren't they? Snakeskin and suede?'

Samantha nodded.

'Match the coat perfectly.' The woman sniffed and continued her scrutiny. She seemed to be becoming more hostile by the minute. 'I could have understood it if she looked like you.'

'I beg your pardon?' Samantha murmured.

'The dirty little bitch my husband was having an affair with. A bit younger than you. One of his students. Doing her doctorate. Mousy little thing with straggly hair and spectacles. No shape.'

'I'm sorry,' Samantha said softly.

'Sorry? What have you got to be sorry about? Job, looks, clothes. You're not married, are you?'

Samantha shook her head.

'Exactly! What have you got to be sorry about?'

'I'm sorry you're so upset,' Samantha said gently. 'But could we talk about Ling Prentice. I have to find her.'

'Ling Prentice is beautiful,' Mrs Weaver reflected. 'In an oriental way, of course. Black hair, like yours, but hers is long, not cut in that shortish Cleopatra style.'

'Do you know where she might be?' Samantha asked again.

'Her husband doted on her.' The woman sniffed noisily, still ignoring her questions. 'When your looks have gone, you're finished. There's no such thing as eternal love, Miss . . . Miss?'

'Quest,' Samantha prompted.

'No 'until death do you part'. If Martin had been bedding you or Ling Prentice, I could have understood it. I might even have forgiven him. But that drab little thing? It had to be a meeting of minds. She was his soul mate. He loved the pathetic little bitch.' The bitter voice was becoming tearful. She groped amongst the cushions, tugged out a grimy handkerchief, and blew her nose into it.

'He died in her bed, you know. Massive heart attack. She managed to get his shirt and pants on before the ambulance arrived, but the inquest was humiliating. I wasn't going to attend, but the police told me I had to. Trouble was, I went to school with the coroner, and that made it even more embarrassing. The little bitch was mumbling her evidence into her flat little chest and he had to tell her to speak up. How would you feel, Miss Quest, listening to some drab little tart saying your husband groaned, with pain not passion, then withdrew and rolled off her; sat gasping on the edge of the bed for a few seconds, then collapsed on to the floor? How would you feel?'

'I'd be pretty cut up about it,' Samantha said. 'But glad the anger was driving away the grief.'

'Anger!' Mrs Weaver snorted. 'You don't know the meaning of the word. I lost control at the funeral, in front of Martin's colleagues from the university, relatives, the vicar, the undertakers. I disgraced myself, Miss Quest. Women in my position are supposed to comport themselves.' She buried her face in her hands and gave way to tears. 'Dear God, I feel so ashamed.'

Samantha crossed over to the sofa, sat on the arm and touched the woman's shoulder. 'They'd understand,' she said softly. 'The provocation was extreme.'

Mrs Weaver shook her head. 'I just can't believe what I said and did. I must have been insane. And my brother's a clergyman: a rural dean. He was so embarrassed and disgusted he walked off.'

Samantha picked up the soggy handkerchief between finger and thumb and handed it to her. The woman blew her nose and dabbed her eyes, then snuffled into it as she said, 'And as if that wasn't enough, Rachel and I had to go for tests the day after.'

'Tests?' Samantha became more attentive.

'Sent some sort of ambulance for us that had shower cubicles in the back. We were taken to an isolation ward at the hospital and they took blood samples. Had to wait there all day while they did tests.'

'Did they say why?'

'Said it was a precautionary measure because of the work Martin had been involved in.'

'I understand your husband was a mathematician, Mrs Weaver. What work could he have been doing to warrant blood tests on his family?'

'He was working with Professor Prentice.

He was doing some sort of analysis for him. It was supposed to be important. He worked all hours. At least, he said he was working. That drab little bitch was his research assistant. She was his confidant. She'd know.'

'And Ling Prentice?' Samantha reminded her.

Mrs Weaver sank back into the sofa and looked up at Samantha. Her eyes were blank and uncomprehending.

'Ling Prentice,' Samantha repeated. 'Have you any idea where she or her husband might be?'

The woman shook her head. 'I've not been out of the house since the funeral. Only person I've spoken to is Rachel. I'm trying to come to terms with it all, but I don't think I ever will.'

There was a knock at the door and her daughter came in. She glanced at Samantha and said, 'Sorry,' then turned to her mother and went on, 'I've got to go to the shops, Mummy. To get something for lunch. What would you — ?'

Mrs Weaver interrupted her daughter with a dismissive wave. 'Anything. Just get anything.'

Rising to her feet, Samantha said, 'I'm leaving now. If you like, I'll drive you to the shops.'

As she was about to step into the hall, Samantha looked back and saw the woman swinging her legs up on to the sofa. 'Thanks for talking to me, Mrs Weaver.'

The woman was settling herself into the cushions. 'It was no trouble,' she muttered absently. 'No trouble at all.'

Rachel, shopping bag on her knees, guided her down lanes that led to the ring road.

'Shall I take you to a supermarket? Would that be OK?' Samantha asked.

'It's a long way: further than the shops.'

'I don't mind,' Samantha said. 'I'll bring you back.'

'Would you? Thanks. It's a great car.' Rachel settled herself into the leather upholstery, a rather unkempt figure in a short skirt and brown anorak. There were holes in her black tights and her ankle-length boots were down-at-heel and scuffed.

'You used to baby-sit for Ling Prentice.' Samantha began to direct the conversation; to try and salvage something from her meeting with the traumatized mother and her neglected daughter.

'Mum told you that? She must be feeling brighter today. Mrs Prentice was nice. I liked her. And she was gorgeous when she wore those long embroidered dresses and piled her hair up. Daddy used to call her the Empress of China. Turn right here. Sorry: should have told you sooner.'

Tyres squealed, a horn blared, and Samantha cheekily swung the Ferrari Modena into the stream of traffic on the ring road.

'I don't suppose you've any idea where she might have gone? Did she have any friends or relatives?'

'I don't think she had relatives in England. She used to visit Mummy and Daddy with her husband, and I think they socialized with other people at the university.'

'No one really close?'

'Not that I know of. I've not really thought about her since she went away. Things haven't been good at home for a while, and then Daddy died suddenly and Mummy's been in a pit of despair ever since. And there was that dreadful scene at the funeral. Unbelievable! Mummy's kept the curtains drawn in that room since they brought her home. I can't wait to go to university and get away from it all. All my friends know about it. God, I feel so embarrassed and ashamed.'

'Your friends will have forgotten all about it,' Samantha said. 'You should try to forget it, too.'

'I suppose so,' Rachel sighed. 'Anyway, it's Mrs Prentice I've got to thank for my going to university.'

'Why do you say that?'

'I had this boyfriend. Well, he was a man really. I was sixteen and he was twenty-six. He was a farmworker on the Cosgrove estate. I'd let him in sometimes when I was babysitting. He was with me one night when they came back early. Another ten minutes and it would have been really embarrassing. Mrs Prentice had one of her Empress of China dresses on. She just glared at Roger and said, 'I think you should leave, young man. Miss Weaver's going to have supper with me now, and we're going to have a talk'. Turn off here, after the post office. You'll see the supermarket then.'

Samantha followed the girl's directions. 'You had a talk . . . ' she prompted.

'She told me not to cast my pearls before a particularly unpleasant swine.' Rachel laughed at the recollection. 'She didn't mince words. She said I'd end up in a dreadful mess if I didn't get rid of him. Pregnancies, poverty and drudgery. Said I should work hard, go to university and be an independent woman. She said if I promised to stop seeing Roger, she wouldn't tell my mother.'

Samantha turned into the supermarket car-park and began to cruise down rows of cars, searching for a vacant slot.

'Mrs Prentice asked me if I wanted to go

on holiday with them not long after. I think she was trying to get me away from him.'

'And did you go?' Samantha asked, alert to the possibility that she might be hearing something useful at last.

'I was all set to go, but Mummy and Daddy had one of their flare-ups. Mummy had found out about his friend and she was in a dreadful state. I thought I'd better stay at home. Anyway, Mrs Prentice needn't have worried. I was going off him. He was really good-looking, but he was arrogant and stupid and he was pretty mean to me.'

'Were the Prentices going abroad on holiday that time they invited you to go with them?'

Rachel shook her head. 'Don't think so. They had a holiday home somewhere. They started going when Wei was about two. Not very often: no more than twice a year. Professor Prentice liked to do some of his writing there. It must have been remote because they always filled the car boot with food and stuff. And they told me to bring warm clothes.'

'Do you know where it was, this holiday home? Did they rent it?'

'Rented it, owned it: I don't really know. And I can't remember where it was. They sent me a postcard with a picture of the house. I might still have it.'

'Could you find it for me, when I take you home?'

'I'll try.'

'Do you know where your father's colleague lives, the young lady who was his research assistant?'

'You mean Ella Remick? She's got a flat near the Ashmolean. In St Cuthbert's Road. I'm pretty sure it's number fifteen, on the first floor. I used to deliver and collect documents for Daddy. Mummy will have told you they were having an affair. God, she keeps banging on and on about it. I know it sounds disloyal, but I thought Ella was quite nice. Bit disappointed in Daddy, though. I mean, he was sleeping with her and she wasn't that much older than me.'

Samantha parked the car close to the supermarket entrance. When she reached down to unfasten her seat belt she saw tears trickling down Rachel's cheeks.

'I'm sorry,' the girl said. 'I'm just chattering on and on about nothing, but since the funeral I've hardly seen anyone except Mummy, and she just moans non-stop about Daddy and Ella.' Her head sagged forward and she began to sob. 'I do miss Daddy. I really do miss him.'

Samantha reached over and squeezed her

hand. 'Of course you miss him,' she murmured huskily. 'And I think you need some help with the house and with your mother. What about relatives?'

Rachel shook her head. 'Daddy has a sister, but she's in South Africa. She didn't even come to the funeral. Mummy has a brother, Uncle James, who's a vicar. Mummy's lapsed, Daddy was an atheist, and I'm a bit New Age, so Uncle James isn't that friendly. He never came back to the house after the funeral. I think he was bit stunned by Mummy's tantrum.'

'All the same, would he come and see your mother? Being able to talk to someone her own age, someone — '

'God, no!' Rachel interrupted. 'You don't know him. He's a sanctimonious old prat: always nagging at Mummy about going to church. I'd leave home if he came to stay.'

Samantha laughed and squeezed her hand again. Rachel managed to smile. 'Come on,' Samantha said. 'Let's go and have a meal in the restaurant, then we'll find your mother something tempting for lunch.'

* * *

Samantha drummed her fingers on the steering wheel. Rachel Weaver couldn't find

72

the postcard showing the Prentice's holiday home, and Ella Remick, Dr Weaver's mistress, hadn't been in when she'd called. So far, the time she'd spent in Oxford had been completely wasted. She looked down the long access lane towards a cluster of buildings that were mere specks beneath a vast cloudless sky. She sighed. She was probably about to waste some more.

She let out the clutch and began to close on a plain, red-brick farmhouse. A tiny garden and a hedge separated the front of the house from endless fields. At the rear, brick barns and outbuildings were arranged around a yard, their high walls forming a sheltered private space. One of a pair of massive close-boarded gates was open. Samantha eased the Ferrari through and parked on stone pavings.

The empty yard had been swept clean. Ornate brackets, fixed to the enclosing walls, carried bronze bowls. Samantha saw they were stained with oil and soot; realized they were torches, not elaborate containers for plants.

She climbed out of the car. The hiss and chatter of a pneumatic tool hammering on metal was loud now. A low pedestrian door was set in the middle of a sliding door to a huge barn. Crossing the pavings, she pushed at it, then lowered her head and passed through.

It was like stepping into a dream. Shocked, she gazed at the larger-than-life figures ranged around the walls of the high, gloomy space: dancing hares, nymphs in flowing robes, lustful satyrs. Some were made from what looked like plaster, some were formed in wax, a few were cast in bronze. Under bright lights, in the centre of the makeshift studio, a woman was passing a vibrating tool across the shoulders of a massive minotaur.

Ears ringing with the noise, Samantha began to walk between polystyrene and plaster blocks, discarded armatures, stacks of metal bars: all the clutter of a sculptor doing things on a grand scale. The woman wielding the pneumatic chisel was standing on a platform that raised her up to the chest of the bronze figure. Not as tall as her sister, Alice, voluptuous rather than plump, her red hair was pinned up beneath a canvas hat. A leather apron covered her green cotton dress; goggles, earmuffs and a mask protected her eyes, ears and throat.

The woman saw her, switched off the tool, then removed the coverings from her face and ears. Samantha gazed up at her, smiled, and said, 'He's very impressive.'

'Thanks. Sorry about the noise. I'm

chasing and fettling: getting rid of the casting marks. What can I do for you?' She gathered up the hem of her dress, sat on the edge of the platform, then dropped down on to the concrete floor.

'Baxter, Allot and Jones, solicitors,' Samantha said. 'We're trying to locate Mrs Ling Prentice. I understand she's your sister-in-law. I wondered if you might know where she is?'

'Police yesterday, lawyers today: what's the lovely little Ling been up to?'

'We're acting as executors for an estate. She's mentioned in the will. A substantial sum.'

'Didn't think she had any relatives.' Lilith tugged off her gloves, revealing plump hands with delicate, tapered fingers. Her skin was smooth and milky-white; her small eyes black. 'Couldn't help the police; can't help you. I've not seen brother Nat and his family since' — she gazed up at the rafters while she did a calculation — 'Lammas eve, two years ago.'

'You've no idea where she might be?'

'None. Wouldn't be surprised if she's taken the kid and cleared off. Old Nat leaves her on her own too much. All he was ever interested in was Petri dishes and microscopes.'

'Do they have a holiday home, some place

she might have gone to stay for a while?'

Lilith's shoulders shook with silent laughter. 'My brother doesn't know what a holiday is, Miss . . . ?'

'Quest,' Samantha said.

'The last thing he'd go to is a holiday home.'

'I've heard he's quite indulgent where Ling's concerned. Could she have persuaded him to buy or rent a place somewhere?'

'You've been talking to Alice,' Lilith snorted. 'Don't take any notice of her. Catholic church has made her soft in the head, always babbling on about how charming Ling is and what a lovely little family Nat has. Ling's changed him, though, I'll give her that; made him more affable. But a holiday home?' Lilith gave her a disbelieving look.

'You don't think she might have persuaded him? If not for her, then for their little girl?'

'Anything's possible, but I'd be amazed. Nat never took a holiday in his life, unless you count his lecture tours in the States as holidays.'

'I understand he's in the States now?' Samantha said.

'Wouldn't surprise me.'

'Could he have taken Ling and their little girl?'

Lilith shook her head. 'She'd never leave

76

the country. Says she's terrified of flying. He always goes on his own. Like I said, he leaves her by herself too much.'

'Thanks,' Samantha said. 'Thanks for talking to me.' She gazed up at the minotaur. Its posture was slightly hunched and its arms outstretched, as if trying to grab something. 'That really is very impressive, Mrs Elliot. It emanates sexual menace.'

'Supposed to,' Lilith said. 'It's the centrepiece of a group composition. He's surrounded by four dancing hares. Birmingham City commissioned it. I wanted to give him a lot more sexual menace, but the Arts and Entertainments Committee objected when they saw the maquette. Mostly men on the committee, of course. Probably made them feel inadequate.'

'Inadequate?'

'Penis size. They made me reduce it.'

Samantha held back a smile. 'He's still amazingly well endowed.'

'He's ten feet tall, Miss Quest.' Lilith made her way through the clutter to the wall of the barn, tugged at a sheet, and exposed a huge prancing hare. 'This is one of the bunnies. Got to have the casting marks fettled, then she'll be ready to go.'

Samantha studied the sinister creature, then her gaze shifted and focused on a shadowy form in a dark corner. Drawing her coat tightly around her legs, she stepped between tubs of hard wax and sacks of plaster to get a closer look at a life-sized figure enthroned on a dais.

She heard Lilith's voice, soft and low, say, 'The horned god,' then stood, chilled, in front of a seated man with the head of a goat.

She glanced round, saw Lilith smiling at her, then asked, 'Who commissioned this?'

Lilith laughed. 'It's not a commission. That's one I made for the group.'

'Group?'

'Our coven. We practise Wicca. I'll bet little Alice was too embarrassed to mention that.' She moved past Samantha and rested her hand on the god's thigh. 'He's cast in resin tinted to look like bronze.' She pointed to metal rings bolted through the sides of the throne. 'It's got to be reasonably light. Poles are slid through these and four men carry it in procession when we celebrate the Great Rite.'

'The Great Rite?' Samantha studied the pentacles and other symbols carved into the throne and around the sides of the dais.

'Ritual sex,' Lilith said. 'It can be performed in true or in token. Our group performs it in true. It symbolizes the horned god uniting with the spirit of the earth.'

Samantha backed away from the too-realistic goat's head on the muscular, broad shouldered body. 'Are there many in the group?'

'Should be twelve: six men and six women, but one of the women's moved out of the area, so we're looking for an initiate.' Lilith laughed softly, then asked, 'Does it appeal to you?'

'Not really. In fact, not at all.'

'It's not all ritual sex. That's only a tiny part. It's about opening out the psyche, penetrating one's inner being, then harnessing the new found strength and freedom. And the men in the group are rich or powerful or both. Physically attractive, too.' She paused for a moment, then her tone became persuasive. 'They can be a great help to an ambitious woman, quite apart from all the pleasure they give. The women members choose them, and we're very discerning: there's always plenty of men wanting to join.' Lilith gazed at Samantha, contemptuous of the distaste that shaped her beautiful features. 'I've shocked you, haven't I?' she said softly.

'Nothing shocks me, Mrs Elliot.' She flashed the woman a frosty smile. 'But if you can't help me locate Ling Prentice, I may as well head back to Oxford.'

Lilith watched Samantha weave her way

between sacks of plaster, bars, blocks of stone and discarded armatures, towards the tiny door. Pity, she mused: stripped of all the expensive clothes, a body like that would have given the Great Rite real meaning.

5

It was a male voice, a very upper-class male voice, that combined authority and refinement. 'Is that you, Sam?'

'I'm here, Marcus.'

'I need to meet you. Are you still in Oxford?' Encryption was making the sound metallic and there were fleeting gaps in the speech.

'I was hoping to leave tonight, but there's someone I have to see and they've not turned up. I might have to book into a hotel again.' Samantha kept her eyes on the entrance to the house in St Cuthbert's Road.

'How about dinner?'

'It's tempting, Marcus, but I'm waiting and watching and if I don't make contact tonight, I'll waste another day.'

'I've got information for you, Sam. And I'd appreciate a progress report.'

'I haven't made any progress. And can't we talk over the phone? Isn't that what it's encrypted for?'

'There are things I have to hand over, and an item you need to see. Have dinner with me. There's a place just south of Oxford.

81

Faxton Hall. It's a decent hotel. We could dine and you could book in for the night.'

Samantha was tempted. She'd been waiting for Ella Remick to return home for almost two hours. 'Where is this place?'

'Out of Oxford on the London Road. Faxton's the first village you drive through. The hotel's down a lane on the far side. You turn right.'

'I'll give this another half-hour, Marcus. If I make contact I'll do the interview, so if I'm not there by eight, you go ahead and dine and I'll join you later, OK?'

'Try not to be any later than nine,' Marcus pleaded. 'I must get home tonight. I've been away for days.'

★ ★ ★

Faxton Hall was half-timbered and medieval; much enlarged to form a hotel. A youth with a bad case of adolescent acne and a red waistcoat had carried her bags up to the honeymoon suite, the only accommodation they could offer. The black-beamed ceiling, big oriel window, sloping floor and twisted walls gave the room character. Turquoise-blue silk draped around the four-poster bed and the softness of a deep pile carpet made it luxurious.

Samantha washed her hands and re-did her make-up, put her coat and suit on hangers in the built-in wardrobe, then headed for the stairs.

She entered a quiet, almost sleepy, dining-room where a few affluent-looking and mostly grey-haired diners were being served by young waiters. Marcus had a table next to an inglenook fireplace with a basket grate that held the glowing remains of big logs. When he saw her approaching, he rose to his feet.

'Glad you got here in time for a meal, Sam.' They sat down. 'Gorgeous blue dress, by the way. I suppose you're going to tell me it's a Dior or something.'

'It's an Ungaro, Marcus, and it's grey, not blue. But it's very sweet of you to notice. How are your wife and beautiful daughters?'

'Fine. As far as I know, they're fine.'

Samantha gave him a searching look. Tall, powerfully built, his dark hair streaked with grey, he seemed distant and preoccupied. He was usually effusive when she enquired about his wife. This almost dismissive response was unusual. She put it down to tiredness.

They ordered, and while the meal progressed she gave him a no-progress report on her search for Ling Prentice. She didn't mention the envelope she'd found under the lining paper in Ling's dressing-table drawer, or Rachel Weaver's talk of a holiday home.

'Was your steak OK?'

'Perfect,' Samantha said. 'The whole meal was perfect.' She plucked a loose thread from the black piping around the lapels on her dress.

'How about dessert?'

'Not for me, Marcus, but a brandy and coffee would be pleasant.'

He beckoned a waiter over, ordered coffee and a large brandy, then reached beneath the table and lifted a battered attaché case on to his lap. He clicked it open. 'You said you wanted to get into Porton Down? You're going as an instrument technician to check over equipment in the microbiological centre; that's where Professor Prentice does most of his research.' He handed her an envelope. 'This is your pass and there's an ID badge in there. You're called Georgina Grey. When you get through the security gate, you'll see the Centre for Applied Microbiological Research signposted. A Dr Conrad Franklin's in charge, but their chief technician, someone called Kevin Sorby, will deal with you and tell you if anything's wrong with the gear. And this' — he reached down and slid bulging brown paper packages to her side of the table — 'is your lab coat and a Bio Med tool kit. Might be a good idea to be wearing the lab coat when you arrive: they're used to a bald-headed bloke who needs a shave. I don't think they could cope with something shapely drenched in Chanel Number Five.'

'I don't, Marcus.'

'Don't what?'

'Drench myself in Chanel Number Five.' Samantha gazed down at the envelopes and packages. 'How will I know how to service the equipment?'

'The maintenance manuals for the Bio Med gear are in there somewhere, and there's half-a-dozen replacement circuit boards. They've marked the things you've got to adjust in the manuals, and there's a memory stick you plug in to the machine to simulate a DNA test.'

Samantha sighed and piled everything up alongside her chair. 'This could put biological research back ten years, Marcus. how long is this checking supposed to take?'

'Usually takes two or three days.'

'Would they let me stay on into the night?'

'Not a chance. Security's very tight. You'll have to find out what you can while the place is occupied.'

White-jacketed waiters began to bustle around the table. One set out green and gold cups while another poured coffee from a matching pot. A third brought her a brandy from the bar.

Samantha gave them a radiant smile.

'Service is always good when we dine together, Sam. Drop your neckline another inch and we'll have all the damn waiters around the table.'

Samantha laughed. 'Don't be peevish, Marcus. It's a good hotel and they're doing their job, that's all.' She took a sip at her brandy. 'When you phoned this afternoon you said you'd something to show me?'

He reached inside the attaché case. 'Two things, actually.' He drew out a swatch of papers. 'Transcripts of phone conversations between Prentice and his wife, extending over a month or more.' He passed the sheets over. 'Most of it's husband and wife stuff, but the final conversation's interesting. Prentice is saying it's all gone dreadfully wrong, and Ling must take that holiday they'd talked about; find someone to care for the little girl. Ling asks why the child can't go away with her, and he says it would be too dangerous. She asks if Wei can stay with her aunt Alice, and Prentice says no, she's got to leave her with a friend.'

Samantha leafed through to the last sheet. 'It says here: *Prentice's voice weak and indistinct. Wife in tears.*' She looked up at Marcus. 'How did you get this? And where's the original recording?'

'After you'd searched the house the chief realized we'd been short-changed with the facts. We've got someone in Serious Crime. He copied this from their files. No disk or tape, just this transcript. Didn't find anything else, but their system's still being searched.'

Glancing through the sheets, Samantha smiled and said, 'They certainly didn't know the line was tapped.'

Marcus laughed. 'Or they didn't care. Felt quite envious. Charlotte's never whispered things like that to me. Don't think she'd understand half the things they're talking about.'

'His wife's patient,' Samantha mused. 'She's saying how much she's missing him, but she's not giving him grief about working all-hours.' She frowned thoughtfully, folded the sheets and slid them into her bag. 'And that last conversation: I don't think she's in tears because he's been away for so long. Something had happened that they'd fore-seen and he was urging her to do something they'd pre-arranged.' She looked up at Marcus. 'You said there were two things?'

Marcus nodded, drew a yellow envelope from beneath the papers in his case, and shook a large colour photograph from it. He passed it over the table.

She gazed at an image of herself, lips

puckered for a kiss, arms around the neck of an extravagantly handsome man, her fingers combed into bronze-coloured curls at the nape of his neck.

'Where did you get this?'

'One of our people was being followed. He killed the tail then searched his car; took the memory chip from a camera he found in the glove compartment. When we put the chip in a printer we got this shot of you and about half-a-dozen pictures of the agent who made the kill.'

'Someone was trying to identify us?'

'Presumably.'

'And what do I have in common with the other agent?'

'He covers this area. He'd normally have been assigned to locate the Prentice family, but he's gone into one of the transit camps, so I called you in to handle the job. Apart from working for the same organization, that's the only link.'

'The professor's involved in biological warfare, isn't he?' she asked.

'What's made you say that?'

Samantha shrugged and turned the corners of her mouth down. 'Just instinct.'

'As far as we know, only indirectly,' Marcus said. 'About six months ago immigration control picked up an Algerian who'd disembarked from a cargo carrier that docked in Hull. He was carrying a sample case full of expensive fountain pens. The guy in charge of the immigration unit had the sense to have the pens checked. The people at Porton Down found that half the ink cartridges were filled with toxin. It wasn't anthrax or smallpox or anything they could identify, so they called Prentice in. When he studied the DNA scan he said it had been engineered.'

'Engineered?'

'Assembled, chromosome by chromosome. Man-made in a laboratory somewhere. According to the intelligence we have, and it's not very reliable, Prentice thought it might have been racially targeted, but that was suppressed. We know he was booked on to a flight to the States about three weeks ago. Perhaps he left in a huff because he thought he wasn't being listened to.'

'A mathematician called Weaver was helping him,' Samantha said. 'Why a mathematician?'

'They were looking for patterns; searching for DNA markers that would confirm the stuff in the pens had been racially targeted. You could say they were code breakers, and mathematicians make good code breakers.'

'You sent me chasing after people who've been in contact with some virus and you didn't even warn me?'

'Only Prentice handled the virus, Sam. Anyway, everything we had was in the file, I swear it. The chief had to threaten to resign today before she could get more details. Until you saw the men in protective suits, we'd no idea there might be a contamination risk.'

'And who laid on the removal men?'

'Home Secretary and the Internal Security Minister denied all knowledge of it; said they'd check with other ministers.'

'They're lying.'

Marcus laughed. 'The chief didn't believe them, either.'

'Did immigration control seize all of the virus?'

'How can we tell? Since this started to unfold we've been calling in data from the Ministry of Health. Seems there's been outbreaks of some flu-like illness in Leeds and Birmingham.'

'How serious are these outbreaks?' she asked.

'At the last count more than a hundred dead in Leeds and about sixty in Birmingham, and it's rising. They're holding big stocks of conventional flu vaccine, but it doesn't give much protection. If you're very young or very old or weakened by other illness, it tends to be fatal.' Marcus picked up a spoon and began to toy with large crystals of brown sugar in a silver bowl. 'First symptoms are a bit like influenza,' he went on, 'then body temperature soars. Actual cause of death is usually pneumonia, three or four days after the first symptoms show.'

'They've really kept that quiet,' Samantha breathed. 'And is this plague targeted?'

Marcus winced. 'Don't call it that, for heaven's sake.'

'What is it if it's not a plague?' Samantha demanded.

'Let's call it a spread of infection, shall we?' He sighed out his irritation, then muttered tetchily, 'More than ninety per cent of the victims are white north Europeans, even where the pockets of infection adjoin large immigrant areas.'

'You suddenly know a lot about it, Marcus.'

'Chief demanded to be told. They invited her to sit in on a briefing given by some scientist at the Ministry of Health. Saunders, the new internal security minister, objected, but he was overruled. Prime Minister kept going on about the compelling need to find Prentice's widow. Saunders looked a bit sheepish, and the chief got the impression his people had tried to find her and failed.'

Samantha finished her brandy. 'His people? Who are *his people*?'

Marcus shrugged. 'Don't know, Sam. Serious Crime Unit answers to Saunders' ministry now. Chief thinks we scared the politicians when the troubles started: the way we moved in on the terrorists made them see us as a potential threat. Perhaps they've begun to use other agencies in a covert way.'

'It's getting crowded out there, Marcus.'

'The chief's been assured we're on our own with this, Sam. You can assume any interference is hostile and act accordingly.'

She gave him a thoughtful look. 'Do *you* believe it?'

'Believe what?'

'That business about the man with the fountain pens? It's as fanciful as a Vivienne Westwood frock.'

'The chief got it at the cabinet briefing, Sam.'

'Has the department tried to locate Professor Prentice?' she asked. 'It wouldn't take long to phone round the Ivy League universities.'

'We've sent a man over to the States. Problem is, Prentice had contacts throughout the wider scientific community. He could be anywhere.'

'Why do you think they want to find his wife so badly?'

'Containment. They're probably worried

about what she knows. They'll want to have her in and recite the Official Secrets Act; frighten her about leaks.'

'Could she be infected?'

Marcus shrugged. 'The outbreaks in Leeds and Bradford are either naturally occurring or they've been seeded by another terrorist who got through. We've no intelligence that there's been an escape of material Prentice was handling.'

Samantha folded her napkin and laid it on the table, smiled sweetly at Marcus, and said, 'Then why did the removal men wear protective suits. I think the PM and the Home Secretary are lying bastards. It was a Government project. Prentice was experimenting with racially targeted toxins and it went wrong.'

Marcus stifled a yawn. 'It's all conjecture, Sam,' he said wearily. 'Whatever it is, we've got to find the woman. And let me know when you've located her. I'll have her picked up by our own team.' He rose to his feet. 'Got to get home, Sam, it's been almost a week.'

As they strolled out of the dining room he said, 'Who was the man in the photo?'

'Mmm . . . I suppose you'd call him my valet.'

Marcus gave her a shocked look. 'He dresses you?'

Samantha laughed. 'Of course not. He cleans the house, does my washing and ironing, sometimes cooks me a meal, takes things to the cleaners. He's my hairdresser's partner. Professionally he's a male model, but the work's not regular.'

'Doesn't she mind?' Marcus asked.

'She?'

'Your hairdresser.'

'It's a he. They're a gay couple.'

Marcus was looking puzzled now. 'Then why the fond embrace?'

'Just affection. He's kind and sensitive, and he does a great job, so I sometimes give him a hug and a kiss.'

'And he washes your underwear? Bit purvey, a bloke washing and ironing your smalls.'

'Hand washes,' she said, revelling in his distaste. 'The kind of things I wear need to be hand washed. And it's less strange than your wife washing and ironing your boxers. He's gay, for heaven's sake. He's not interested.'

They rounded a bend in the corridor. Marcus pushed at a swing door, stood aside while she passed into the foyer, then said, 'It could be dangerous, Sam. Does he know what you do?'

'He thinks I'm a high-class tart.' She glanced up at Marcus and laughed. 'The

94

underwear, the fashionable clothes; I come and go at all hours in an expensive car, and I'm often away overnight and weekends.'

Stepping out into the darkness, they began to stroll across the car-park. Away from the sodium glow of the city, stars could be seen, and the clear sky was making the night cold.

'Be careful, Sam.'

'There's no danger. He's no idea what I do.'

'I don't mean that, Sam. I mean be careful with this Prentice business.'

They reached his car, a big Volvo estate.

Samantha peered through the rear window at the boxes and packages crammed inside. 'You couldn't get much more in there, Marcus.'

'Provisions. The girls aren't going back to college after half-term. They're going to stay on the farm with their mother.' He lowered his voice. 'I've got four assault rifles and a thousand rounds; had them delivered from the armoury, just in case.'

'Just in case?'

'Just in case things suddenly go very wrong, Sam. the rioting; all the political weirdos coming out of the woodwork. If they don't control the spread of this infection, if the terrorists have a few more big successes . . . '

He squeezed into the car. Even the front passenger space had been filled with crates and boxes. He wound the window down and started the engine. Samantha stood with her arms folded beneath her breasts, hugging herself to keep out the chill.

Reaching through the window, he took her hand and held it. The uncharacteristic tenderness of the gesture surprised her. Since she'd last seen him he seemed to have aged ten years, and there was a strange sadness, a detachment, in his manner.

'Find the Prentice woman, Sam. And for Christ's sake, be careful. Things are starting to unravel. It's soon going to be every man for himself.'

He released her hand, drew his arm into the car and let out the clutch. He didn't wave or look back; just drove through the gates and turned into the cold blackness of the lane that led to the village.

Samantha watched tail lights fade to red dots, then headed back to the deserted dining room and gathered up her packages.

6

Samantha glanced around the cluttered flat, at the books and papers arranged in neat piles on an old gate-leg table, at the keyboard and computer screen on a desk beside a window that looked down into the sunlit street.

Ella Remick snatched a blouse and a pair of tights from an armchair. 'Sorry about the mess. Sit here. I'll turn the heating up. These old buildings: the ceilings are so high it's difficult to keep the rooms warm.'

'Don't worry, I'm not cold,' Samantha said, then sat back in the chair and unbuttoned her coat. She watched the slim fair-haired young woman gather up dirty plates and cups, then disappear into a tiny kitchen.

'Coffee?'

'That would be pleasant. I'm not delaying you, am I?'

'I'm not going into college this morning,' came a voice from the kitchen. 'There are one or two things I've got to catch up with here. And I was expecting you.'

'Expecting me?'

Ella Remick appeared in the kitchen

doorway. 'You are from the hospital, aren't you?'

For a few seconds Samantha toyed with the idea of going along with the misunderstanding, then decided it wouldn't get her anywhere, and said, 'I don't think you can have heard me over the intercom. I'm from Baxter Allot and Jones, solicitors. I'm trying to trace Professor Prentice's wife.'

The young woman pushed up her tiny wire-rimmed spectacles and laughed. 'The door intercom's needed fixing for ages. You can hardly hear what callers are saying.'

'You mentioned the hospital. I hope you've not been ill,' Samantha said.

'Not that I know of. I had to go in for some blood tests. They said I was OK, but they promised to send someone to talk to me about an immunization programme. When you came in with the attaché case, I just thought . . . Kettle's boiling. 'Scuse me a minute.'

Samantha listened to the clatter of crockery, then Ella Remick came through with a tray, limping slightly as she crossed the room.

Ella levelled piles of books on a coffee table, then settled the tray on top. 'Sugar?' She pressed the filter down in the cafetiere.

'Just a little milk.'

She handed Samantha a cup, dragged the

swivel chair away from the desk and sat facing her. 'I hardly know Mrs Prentice,' she said. 'I met her husband a few times, but that was in connection with research I'm doing. What made you think I know her?'

Samantha decided to probe a nerve on the off-chance it would provoke a useful response. 'Mrs Weaver told me you worked very closely with her husband and Professor Prentice. I know it's a long shot, but I thought there was just a chance you might have overheard where the Prentices had gone.'

The colour began to drain from Ella Remick's face. Shoulders hunched beneath her white cotton blouse, black-trousered legs pressed together, her voice was reproachful as she said, 'You've talked to Mrs Weaver?'

'The Weavers used to socialize with Professor Prentice and his wife. I thought she might know where they are, but she couldn't tell me.'

Ella Remick gave Samantha a bleak look. The skin around her mouth was white and her chin was trembling. 'Did she tell you she almost killed me?' she asked.

'Mrs Weaver seemed too distressed about her husband's death to tell me anything, Miss Remick.'

The young woman met Samantha's gaze for a few moments, then seemed to come to a decision. 'We were lovers,' she said simply. 'Mrs Weaver's husband and I were lovers. I know it was wrong, but it just happened.'

'Happened?'

'Mrs Weaver was right, we did work very closely together. We were in one another's company for most of the time. One evening he took hold of my hands, pulled me towards him, and kissed me, very tenderly. That was it. It just happened. We'd drifted together. His wife found out about a year before he died. Made his life hell. She kept phoning me and writing me vicious little notes. Martin was going to leave her when Rachel went to university, but ... ' Ella pressed her lips together and sniffed back tears. 'I know it was very wrong of me, but she didn't have to be such a bitch. And if she'd behaved at the funeral, we'd both have kept our dignity.'

Samantha gazed at her steadily and remained silent.

After a few tearful sniffs, Ella took a sip at her coffee, then went on. 'The funeral was beyond belief: utterly surreal. I still have nightmares. It was almost over. We were standing around the grave and the vicar was going through the rites. I wasn't even looking at her. I was looking down at the coffin and thinking about Martin, when she lunged at me and started screaming bitch and whore.

She was slapping me and pulling me around by the hair, and then she pushed me into the grave. I fell on top of the coffin and she was screaming, 'You killed him, you bitch, you fucked him to death'. And she was kicking earth and those sheets of plastic grass down on top of me. There was hardly any space around the sides of the coffin, and I ended up sitting astride it with all this earth and stuff showering down on me and she was yelling, 'Go on, shove your fanny in his face, bitch. That's all you've been doing for months, isn't it? Shoving your fanny in his face'.'

'One of the undertakers climbed down into the grave and lifted me out, then they put me in a car and took me to hospital. I must have gashed my leg on one of the coffin handles, because there was blood everywhere. It needed six stitches.'

'How have you been since?' Samantha asked.

'Shaky.' Ella gave a tearful little laugh. She looked up and watery-blue eyes gazed at Samantha through the wire-rimmed spectacles. 'That was three weeks ago and I haven't spoken a word about it until now.' She took another sip at her coffee. 'I hope I've not shocked you. I . . . I feel better for having talked to someone about it.'

'You've not shocked me,' Samantha said.

'And it takes two to tango. I don't suppose you'd have got involved if Dr Weaver hadn't kissed you.'

Ella shrugged. 'I wanted it,' she said. 'I loved him. I was as much to blame as he was, and I knew it was wrong to get involved with another woman's husband. That's why I didn't do anything when the people at the hospital said I should report it to the police. Anyway, it would only have got into the papers, and we'd have been an even bigger laughing stock.'

They gazed at one another in silence for a while, then Samantha said, 'The injections you thought I'd called about: were they because of the injury to your leg?'

Ella shook her head. 'It was because of the project. Before he left for the States, Professor Prentice was working on some virus. They were just making sure there'd been no escape. We were all tested, whether we'd had much contact with Professor Prentice or not. They said they'd come and talk to me about precautionary immunization, but that was three weeks ago and they haven't been yet so it can't have been very important.'

'How do you know he's gone to the States?'

'I thought it was common knowledge. He's taken his part of the research as far as he can, but our team's carrying on.'

'Catching up?'

Ella Remick laughed. 'Not quite. It's related but different research.'

'Has the project been abandoned?' Samantha asked.

'Abandoned?'

'Dr Weaver's dead . . . '

'Heavens, no. Dr Kilgannon's stepped up to lead the mathematicians doing the analysis.'

'And what are you analysing?'

'Human DNA. We're searching for the racial markers.'

'And why would you do that?' Samantha asked.

'Diseases,' Ella said. 'Some races are more susceptible to particular types of cancer and there are other conditions that have a racial bias. The Americans have done a lot of work, but we're trying to refine it and take it further.'

'How would you do a search like that?'

Ella Remick had brightened and colour had returned to her cheeks. Talking about her work had allowed her to forget the trauma of her lover's death. 'We examine thousands of DNA profiles. They're scanned by a machine and the data is processed by a computer. The programme we've been using is based on

Werner's formula. That's how I became involved: Werner's formula's the subject of my doctoral thesis. It's on the frontiers, as they say. Werner only published his paper a couple of years ago. I've developed a computer programme that applies it to raw data so recurring patterns can be identified, even when they're deeply hidden.'

'Sounds fascinating,' Samantha said, without irony.

'It is!' Ella beamed at Samantha, then her smile suddenly faded and she looked down at her cup and muttered, 'It's certainly helped me to cope since Martin died.'

'The DNA profiles?' Samantha asked. 'Where do they come from?'

'Mostly from a new police lab they've set up in Yorkshire. And quite a few come from labs in Leicester and Lancashire.'

'Why would that be?'

'Stable, immigrant communities with places of origin that can be verified.'

Samantha raised an eyebrow. 'Fascinating, Miss Remick. Absolutely fascinating.' She finished her coffee. 'But you can't help me with Mrs Prentice's whereabouts?'

'I'm sorry. Like I said, I didn't really know her and I've been so preoccupied with my own affairs I hadn't even realized she'd left Oxford.'

Samantha slid her cup on to the tray and rose to her feet. 'Thanks for the coffee, Miss Remick. I'm sorry I've troubled you.' She picked up her attaché case and headed for the door. The young woman limped after her and stood on the landing while she descended the stairs.

Drawing her coat around her to keep it away from the bicycles in the hallway, Samantha glanced back. Ella Remick waved, then Samantha moved out into the morning sunlight.

Their conversation had made her even more convinced that Prentice was involved in racially targeting biological toxins. Perhaps he'd done all the work he could on the virus immigration had seized, and it was up to the team searching and analysing human DNA to find the things that made one group more susceptible to it than another. And was it weapons development, or was it counter terrorism?

A parking ticket had been tucked under a windscreen wiper. She tugged it out, slid inside the Ferrari, then tore it up. The plates weren't listed and the car couldn't be traced.

Having followed all the leads, however unpromising, there was nothing left for her to do in Oxford. She keyed the ignition, drove out of the narrow street, swept past the

Ashmolean, then turned left and headed for the ring road.

★ ★ ★

Tim Saunders frowned at the file of unanswered correspondence from his constituents. It was getting thicker. He flicked it open and saw it wasn't only letters: there was a bundle of query forms from his constituency office in there, too. He ought to hold a surgery, make an appearance in that God-forsaken hole of a place they called Barfield.

He flicked through the letters and forms: what the local council had done, what it hadn't done; unemployment benefits denied, disability payments withdrawn; wives refused entry, husbands deported. Complaining bastards! Country was shattered by riots and terrorism, and all the useless buggers could do was whine, whine, bloody whine.

He heard a faint tapping on the door and called out, 'Come in.'

His mood suddenly lifted. God, the girl could fill a sweater, and she looked enticingly virginal when she pinned her hair up that way. 'Jessica! How are we this morning?'

'Very well, thank you, Minister.' She handed him a large manila envelope. 'This came in with your post, marked strictly

106

personal, so it's not been opened. It's been through X-ray and the thing that checks for chemicals. They've not detected anything untoward.'

He stared at the Manchester postmark. It was the same as last time. 'Thanks, Jessica. Thank you very much.'

'The PM's office phoned, Minister; said the PM wanted a quick meeting with you and the Home Secretary at eleven.'

'In his office here?'

Jessica shook her head. 'Cabinet room at Number Ten.'

Tim Saunders began to draw a paper knife across the flap. He glanced up. 'Thanks, Jessica.'

She flashed him a nervous smile, then turned and headed for the door.

He paused in mid-cut, his eyes fixed on the retreating figure. What a fabulous arse. He had to cultivate a more intimate relationship with the girl.

'Jessica?'

She paused, halfway through the door, and looked back.

'No more of this minister business. Call me Tim. I want the office to be friendly, not formal.'

She flashed him one of her timid little smiles, then closed the door behind her.

Tim Saunders slit open the envelope and peered inside, saw a note and some eight-by-six glossy photographs. The bastard was persistent. Ignoring the last one hadn't made him go away. Saunders got up, crossed over to the door and locked it, then returned to his seat. Emptying the envelope on to the blotter, he began to flick through the images. The birthmark in the small of his back was the only thing that identified him. His face was hidden by the mask. It was difficult to use your mouth with the damn thing on, and he'd wanted to rip it off. Thank God he'd had the presence of mind not to.

He unfolded the note and read:

I donated £200,000 to 'party funds' and you didn't even put me on the short list to tender for the hospital contracts. I'm facing bankruptcy if I don't get at least one. You owe me. Do something. The next set of photographs goes to the press and there won't be any doubt about who you are (you took your mask off when you had Bernice and Megan). You've got ten days.

He looked through the photographs again. They were clear, despite the flickering torchlight, and he hadn't noticed any camera flash. His thin lips shaped into a smile. Camera flash? He wouldn't have noticed if the farmhouse had caught fire. That first time had been earth-shaking: truly transcendental. The other times had been good, too, but never quite like his initiation. Away from the place, he knew the torchlight rituals, the chanting, the invocations to the horned god, were a load of nonsense. But when he'd stood there, stark naked, fired up with the stuff they'd made him drink from the golden cup, he'd felt released, free, wonderfully alive.

Tim Saunders relaxed back in his chair, closed his eyes, abandoned himself to vivid memories. What an experience! He didn't regret it. Even if he'd known this little shit was going to blackmail him, he'd still have joined the group.

He recalled the cool touch of hands on his arms as the women led him to Lilith, lying on sheepskins heaped in front of that statue of the horned god. He held his breath. He could almost hear the chanting, the rhythmic drumming, urging him on while he'd performed the rite. And then it had been a free-for-all. Six women in a night! Viagra and brandy. He could have gone on for ever. And they were eager. God, they were eager. These weren't passive bodies performing a duty, or legs being reluctantly spread to pay back a favour. It was frenzied. It was the Grand Rite.

He opened his eyes. His breath was coming in short gasps and his mouth was dry. No, he couldn't say he was sorry, no matter what the cost. He reached for the phone. He'd bloody-well make sure it didn't cost him anything.

Almost immediately, a refined female voice said, 'Yes, Minister.'

'Get me Major Trantham. He's based at Catterick, on secondment to the Serious Crime Unit.' He crashed the phone down. No use having power if you were afraid to use it. Home Secretary with his MI5 wasn't the only player in the game any more. And the emergency powers legislation had been a good cover for his manoeuvring. He'd spent the past two years building up his own —

The phone cheeped. He snatched it up. 'Major Trantham?'

'Minister.'

'We've found the bugger who's been supply-ing explosives to those radical groups in the Midlands. Traced it back from the last round of tube bombings. White building contractor, would you believe? Does demolition and tunnelling work, so he's a licensed user.'

Tim Saunders heard a sigh. 'Why?' the major said. 'Why would a prosperous white British national supply explosives to terror-ists?'

'God knows. Money, his own agenda; perhaps he's a convert to radical Islam. Thing is, this is too sensitive for arrest and trial. Terrorists learn too much from the media just by following police press briefings. Things come out that threaten security. And it's vital they don't discover how we traced the explosives back to the contractor.'

'You want it dealt with, Minister?'

'Exactly.'

'And the action we're taking is covered by powers conferred on you under the emergency legislation?'

'Precisely so,' Tim Saunders said glibly.

'Give me the details, Minister.'

'Man's called Daniel Langdon, building contractor, currently doing the Northern and General office tower in Manchester. There's been a lot of problems with progress and building defects, and he's on site himself most days.'

'I presume this office block's quite tall?'

'Tallest in the city when it's topped out.'

'And is it well advanced?' the major asked.

'I understand the steel frame's up, and they've started the cladding.'

'Would you leave it with me, Minister?'

'I'd be pleased to. When will you . . . ?'

'Twenty-four hours, Minister.'

'One final thing,' Tim Saunders said. 'The

people who've handled surveillance have reported he maintains his own office on the site. I'd like the team to clear it out: not plans and things to do with the building; just his laptop and any personal papers in the desk. And I'd like the stuff boxed up and delivered here. I'll see you're issued with a pass to get the box through security. And, Major?'

'Yes, Minister?'

'I want you to know that what you're doing is appreciated here. Your name's pencilled in on next year's list.'

★ ★ ★

Tim Saunders rapped at the door, shoved it open, then strode over thick carpet towards the two men seated beside the window.

The Prime Minister glanced up. 'Tim! Peter and I are just going over the Prentice business. Did your people get the house cleared?'

Tim Saunders pulled out a chair, tossed his papers on to the table, and flopped down. 'Cleared twenty-four hours ago, Charles. It's all been carted to Porton Down. Took the lot, carpets, curtains, clothes: everything.'

'Presumably they've burnt it?'

'Stored it. Very low risk of any contamination now, and we may need to sift through it.'

Peter Clayton, the Home Secretary, chuck-led. 'There's more than a chance Mrs Prentice might start asking questions about it when we find her.'

'We'll cross that bridge when we come to it,' the Prime Minister said. 'How's the search going?'

'Not had any feedback.' Peter Clayton took his spectacles off and began to polish the tiny lenses. 'Perhaps we should call Fallon in and give her a grilling. Four or five days since Tim handed the job over. She should have some news for us.'

'Don't suppose we know who's been assigned to the search,' the Prime Minister muttered. 'They always keep that to them-selves.'

'It's Quest,' Peter Clayton said. 'Had a drink with Marcus at the club yesterday evening. When Fallon said the job was top priority, he gave it to his finest.'

'Finest?' The Prime Minister's voice was bitter. 'Never forget what that bitch did to some of our people in Tim's constituency.'

'They were very unwise, Charles,' Peter Clayton said. 'Men in their position getting involved with under-age immigrant girls: what did they expect?'

'They were prostitutes,' Tim Saunders sneered. 'Dirty little whores. They may have been under-age, but they'd had more men than we've had hot dinners. Ridiculous for the police to charge community leaders with sexual offences.'

The Prime Minister gave a tired sigh. 'We'd got it all under control until Quest supplied that videotape to the DPP. Couldn't intervene after that. Had to let it take its course. Trouble with people like Quest, they don't understand the rules of the game. Loners, outsiders with no loyalties; they can't be influenced.' He glanced at Tim Saunders. 'I know you've passed the job over, Tim, but if Quest's involved, I think it would be wise if your people remained vigilant.'

'Vigilant, Charles?'

'Kept Quest under surveillance. The smart little bitch can do the legwork, then your people can close in on the Prentice woman when she's been located.'

'That's not cricket,' Peter Clayton protested. 'Old Marcus gave me the information in confidence. If we act on it in this way, we could compromise him with Fallon. We should let them get on with it. They've served us well in the past. They're still serving us well.'

The Prime Minister gave him a steady look. 'I don't think you've really come to terms with the seriousness of all this, Peter. If the widow has her husband's tapes and papers, she's got us by the short hairs.'

'She cleared out his study,' Peter Clayton protested. 'She's probably burnt the lot.'

'Probably isn't good enough. We don't know what she's burnt. And we're talking far more than political survival here, so let's forget the Queensberry Rules. We find out what we can, any way we can, and we use the information to protect our backs.'

The Prime Minister glanced from Saunders to Clayton, then rested his hands on the table. 'Tarts and political survival pretty well sums up what I really wanted to talk to you both about. I've told the whips to have a word with all the backbenchers; tell 'em to keep their peckers zipped up.'

Peter Clayton's rosebud mouth puckered into a smile. 'Peckers, Prime Minister?' He began to laugh softly.

'Our majority's small; only eleven seats; ten if old Fletcher goes into hospital again. And there's a groundswell for a coalition to govern through the emergency. Any whiff of a sexual scandal, *any* scandal, and we'll fall. We'll not ride it out in this climate.'

'What about women members?' Saunders chuckled. 'What should they zip up?'

'You're not taking this seriously,' the Prime Minister snapped. 'The women seem to keep themselves out of trouble.'

'They might not find that too difficult,' Peter Clayton said.

'I don't know,' Saunders laughed. 'That member for Portsmouth South. I wouldn't mind a — '

'For heaven's sake,' the Prime Minister fumed. 'We're on the bloody ropes. Take it to heart, you two, and spread the word amongst the troops: not a whiff of scandal, OK?'

They nodded their assent.

'Now,' the Prime Minister said, 'I understand you've some news for me about the Manchester and Liverpool bombings, Peter.'

'Fallon contacted me this morning. They've got the organizers: four men, all living in Bradford, all British nationals.'

'This hasn't been leaked?'

Clayton shook his head. 'She phoned me in the early hours. The leader of the opposition doesn't know a thing about it.'

The Prime Minister smiled for the first time. 'Should be able to cut Armstrong down to size at Question Time. He's been dogging me for weeks about the organizers going free.' He frowned. 'I thought Fallon said she was searching for nine or ten suspects?'

'Quest was assigned to it. She killed five.'

The Prime Minister sighed. 'This is what

worries me, Peter, the woman knows no restraint.' He turned to his Minister for Internal Security. 'Start the surveillance today, Tim. Have her watched around the clock.'

7

Samantha parked in front of a flat-roofed, single-storey structure that sprawled across a twenty-acre compound. Enclosed by mature trees, built from prefabricated concrete panels, it was one of those temporary buildings that linger on for years.

She dragged a leather hold-all and her attaché case from the passenger seat and made her way to the reception desk. Four women were tapping on keyboards and staring into screens. A light began to flash on a switchboard, and a mini-skirted blonde rose and answered the incoming call. She flicked it through to an extension, then came over to the counter.

'Can I help you?' *Jesus Saves* was printed across her white cotton T-shirt. A spectacular bust was emphasizing and separating the words.

'Georgina Grey; Bio Med Instrumentation. I think your chief technician, Mr Sorby, is expecting me.'

The woman picked up a phone, keyed in a number and muttered something to a man called Kevin. She smiled at Samantha. 'He'll be out in a moment, Miss Grey.'

Samantha sat on a plastic chair, drew her lab coat over her black skirt, and glanced around. White vinyl floors, pearl-grey walls and illuminated ceilings made the Government's Centre for Applied Microbiological Research look cleaner and more pristine than most hospitals. She didn't have to wait long. After less than a minute, a tall gangling figure, with dark hair that needed cutting, pushed through double doors and loped over.

'Miss Grey? Kevin Sorby.' He held out a big hand that felt clammy when she shook it.

'It's Georgina, isn't it?'

Samantha nodded and discreetly wiped her palm on the lab coat.

'Can we call you Georgina?'

'Why not?' She watched him operate a digital lock to release the door from which he'd just emerged, then followed him through.

'Glad you've come. We've lost two of the DNA analysers, and the others don't give consistent results.'

'Lost?'

'They've been sealed up in an area that's being decontaminated.'

They were heading down a long corridor. Windows looked out on to small paved courtyards enclosed by more of the drab concrete buildings.

'The machines you have; I presume they're not producing identical scans from the same sample?' Samantha was doing her best to act the part.

'You've got it.' He pushed at swing doors and they passed into another corridor.

'You turn the sensitivity up too high, that's the problem,' Samantha said glibly. She'd spent half the night poring over the maintenance manuals and some notes the technician had written.

Kevin Sorby laughed. 'Ned always says that. I say the plots should be consistent at all sensitivity settings. The machines cost enough.'

'Ned?'

'Ned Baxter. The man who usually calls. How is he, by the way?'

Samantha shrugged. 'I've been sent from the northern office. Perhaps he's sick.'

'Hope not. Old Ned usually has a pint with me in the Frog and Parrot in Charlton. Nice little pub. You fancy having a drink this evening?' Big brown eyes were imploring her.

'I'd like to get the job done and head back. Would they let me work on?'

He laughed. 'Don't think so. Dr Franklin insists on everyone except the cleaners and the security staff being out of the place before he leaves.' He turned into another corridor, identical to the one they'd left. 'Down here, not much further.'

'Would Dr Franklin be the man to ask?'

'You could ask, but you're wasting your time. Talk to Wendy at reception. She'll take you in to him.'

Up ahead, a red light was flashing above some double doors and a signboard was resting against the wall. As they strode past, Samantha read: *Decontamination in Progress. Do not Proceed Beyond the Air Lock.*

'What's happening in there?'

'Lab's been shut down,' Kevin Sorby said. 'They were working on viruses. Sealed it up three or four weeks ago so it could be cleaned and decontaminated. Specialists come in every week, check it over, then lock and reseal it.'

'Specialists?'

'Men in protective suits. They clean accessible areas, release a gas to sterilize concealed spaces, then take swabs and do tests. The other two analysers are in there. I'm hoping to get them back next week.'

'I'm surprised you bring specialists in. I'd have thought you'd deal with that in-house,' Samantha said.

'Usually do. Don't know why, but old Franklin called outsiders in to deal with this one. Look like Ministry of Defence types:

121

come in a black army truck and the protective suits they wear are heavy-duty battlefield things.'

Samantha glanced back at the flashing light. 'Do all the labs have air-locks?'

He shook his head. 'Just the three they use for critical research. They call it an air-lock, but it's no more than a lobby area with lockers and a couple of spray cubicles for decontaminating the suits before they disrobe.'

Kevin Sorby walked with long, loping strides. He hadn't offered to carry the hold-all stuffed with maintenance manuals, or the case full of tools. Samantha's long tight skirt and high-heeled shoes were restricting, and she had to keep breaking into a trot to keep up. She was relieved when he led her into a brightly lit workroom.

'I had the analysers brought in here for you. There's a 'scope if you need it, and a current-limited power supply.'

''Scope?'

'Oscilloscope.' He nodded towards an instrument with a small screen and a lot of controls.

'Oh, a 'scope,' she said, laughing. 'Thanks.'

'I'll be in room three-six-three if you need anything. Just go back to the main corridor, turn left, and keep going for about fifty yards.'

He paused in the doorway, his big brown eyes giving her another beseeching look. 'Sure you won't have that drink with me later? Ned usually makes the visit last three days.'

Samantha smiled. A conversation with the chief technician could be revealing. 'If Dr Franklin says I can't stay on, I'll have a drink with you.'

His long face brightened. 'Better go and tell him to kick you out then. Give me a shout if you want anything.' He flashed her a smile, then slipped out of the door.

Samantha listened to his footsteps retreating down the corridor. When she heard the distant thud of the swing door, she left the workshop and made her way back to the doors beneath the flashing red light.

Air was hissing through tiny gaps around the frame; she guessed they'd lowered the pressure inside to prevent the escape of dangerous things. Moving on a few paces, she paused by a window and looked into one of the courtyards. An extractor fan and filter unit, about the size of a small car, was attached to the outer wall of the contaminated laboratory. It was humming faintly. Above the extractor, a single pane of glass was held in a metal frame. The glass was obscured internally by some translucent material; the frame was bedded in rubber and screwed to the concrete panel.

A short passage off the main corridor led to male and female toilets. Moving down it, she found a fire door that opened into the courtyard. She'd discovered an alternative way in to the laboratory. She wouldn't have to break the seals on the door beyond the air-lock.

On her way back to the workroom she peeped around doors, into laboratories where white-coated men and women moved behind walls of chemical glassware. The corridors might be deserted at this hour, but workers were busy in the endless honeycomb of rooms.

Alone in the workshop, Samantha unrolled her Bio Med tool kit, opened the maintenance manuals, and began to explore the workings of the machines that charted the genetic codes of living things.

Less than an hour later, Kevin Sorby poked his head through the door. 'Brought you a coffee.' He ambled towards her with a couple of plastic cups, passed her one, then hitched up his pants and perched on the bench. When he noticed the tangle of wires and circuit boards spewing from a machine, he laughed and said, 'You've got stuck in. Ned never goes to this much trouble.'

Samantha took the offered cup, sat on a

laboratory stool, and smiled across at him. 'Power supply regulators,' she said airily. 'They're outside limits. I think that's why you're getting the inconsistent results.' She crossed her legs, allowed her lab coat to fall open. The hem of her skirt had ridden a few inches above the knee, and a strappy shoe was dangling from her toes. He wasn't looking at the disembowelled machine now.

'Did Professor Prentice ever work here?' she asked.

'You know Prentice?'

'I've met his wife and little girl,' she lied.

'Didn't realize Prentice was married. His wife and kid can't see him much. He almost lived here until about a month ago. In fact, they brought a bed in for him when he was nursing the mutations through the final stages.'

'Mutations?'

'He was trying to mutate some virus. I could tell that from the equipment he asked us for, but that's really all I know. My degree's in engineering, not biology.'

'And they brought a bed in for him?'

Kevin Sorby dragged his eyes from the swaying leg and gulped noisily at the coffee. 'Old iron-framed hospital thing. The maintenance men were told to leave it in the lab's air lock, and a couple of Prentice's assistants took it in. Things were at a critical stage and he didn't want to risk the cultures being disturbed.' He drained the cup. 'What's she like?'

Samantha gave him a questioning look.

'His wife: Mrs Prentice. What's she like?'

'Thirties, Chinese woman, more than pretty.'

'And he had a little girl?'

Samantha nodded; tried hard not to grimace when she sipped at the lukewarm coffee.

'I'm surprised,' he said. 'Pretty wife and a little kid: I'd have thought he'd have tried to spend at least some time at home.' He shrugged. 'They abandoned the project when he left for his annual lecture tour in the States. That's when they sealed the place off and began the decontamination protocol.' He stood up. 'Seen Dr Franklin yet?'

Samantha shook her head and nodded towards the work bench. 'I really do need to stay.'

'You'll be lucky. How about a meal after we've had that drink? I know a nice — '

'Come back at four,' she said. 'I'll have seen Dr Franklin by then.'

★   ★   ★

Smiling to herself, Samantha closed the door of the toilet cubicle and slid the bolt. The older men got the more hopeless they became. Dr Franklin hadn't been very impressed with her high-level security clearance. It was only when she'd given him the big smile, leaned over his desk and pushed perfumed cleavage under his nose while he studied her identity badge, that he'd capitulated, phoned the man on the gatehouse, and told him she'd be staying on until ten.

Peeling off the lab coat, she stepped out of her shoes and gathered up the protective suit she'd purloined from the locker in the laboratory air-lock. She grimaced with distaste. Some man must have spent hours sweating into it. Hitching up her skirt, she slid a foot inside and began to draw it on.

A door thudded open. She heard the clatter of metal buckets and women's voices.

' . . . She found another pair. In the glove compartment this time.'

'Another pair?'

'Knickers. He'd been up to his tricks again. And they weren't small. Doris said they'd fit a very big woman. Lace trimmed satin things with an open crotch.'

'Open crotch! Filthy trollop.'

'When she tackled him about it he denied all knowledge; said one of his mates was trying to fit him up.'

A bucket scraped across the floor, a tap creaked and water began to pour into it.

'Fit him up?'

'Don't repeat everything I say, Maud. It gets very wearing.'

'Sorry, May. Hearing's a bit bad. She ought to leave him. I wouldn't put up with it. And I don't know what all the women see in him. Ugly little devil, I always thought.'

'She says it's his technique.'

'Technique?'

'Maud, do you have to — '

'Sorry, May.'

'The way he does it. I mean, he's her third, so she should know. She said no one can — '

'May! Bucket's running over!'

'Do you think we need to do in here?'

'No. Let's leave it. Women's is always good for three days. It's the men's, dirty beggars; pee all over the floors, splatter marks all round the pans. If I had my way . . . '

Maud's words were lost beneath the sound of water being emptied from the bucket. The door opened and thudded shut, and Samantha was alone again.

Gun, lock picks and tools distributed amongst the pockets in the suit, mask strapped on, hood zipped up, tiny feet lost in man-sized rubber boots; Samantha left the cubicle, emerged into the passageway, pushed at the panic bar, and stepped down into the courtyard. Air, pouring from the extraction unit, rippled the fabric of the suit as she padded over and clambered on to the ducting.

She got to work on the screws securing the window, managed to remove all but one, then used the screwdriver to prise the frame from the wall. Rubber seals yielded, and it swung down.

Samantha peered in. With her head and shoulders through the opening, she could see jars, a tray of pipettes and some Petri dishes. She reached down, cleared a space, then lowered herself on to a work surface. Swinging her legs over the edge, she stepped down on to the floor of a small store room.

The door, like all the other doors in the contaminated wing, was open. She stepped through it, in to a laboratory. Translucent film over the windows plunged the interior into a watery twilight; made forms and shapes indistinct. Isolated in the protective suit, peering out through goggles, she felt like a diver, wading through the compartments of a sunken ship. She gazed around. Half-a-dozen benches were arranged, back-to-back, and separated by rows of instruments, much like the ones she'd been pretending to service. All work surfaces had been cleaned, and all glassware tidied away.

Between the rows of benches, bright-yellow gas cylinders rested in metal trolleys. The chemical formula for the gas was stencilled in red above the words, *Decontaminant. Extremely Toxic. Use only in evacuated areas.* Wheel valves at the top of the cylinders were open. Pointers on pressure gauges had settled at zero. Presumably the gas had been released slowly, and doors opened to ensure circulation through the network of rooms.

A small office was separated from the laboratory by a glass screen. Samantha stepped inside and checked the desk drawers and a filing cabinet. They were empty.

Moving down the line of benches, she passed through a doorway at the far end of the laboratory. Fewer windows and the failing evening light made the room almost dark. She could hear the drone of a compressor. A relay clicked, and the room fell silent. She patted the pockets of her protective suit, pulled out a torch, switched it on and swept the beam around.

Benches and other furniture had been pushed against the walls, and six metal chests arranged in a neat row in the cleared central area. Stepping close, she played the torch over the top and sides of the nearest container. About eight feet long, three wide and three high, it was painted a drab camouflage green. She brought the torch close to the scratched and dinted surface, saw the crown and lion emblem, read the words, *Ministry of Defence. Refrigerated Storage Unit. Return to Catterick.*

A narrow gap around the chest marked the line of the lid. After trying to force her fingers into the crack, she used the screwdriver as a lever, heard a film of ice tear apart, then heaved it open.

The black woman was naked. Eyes, clouded with frost, stared up out of a purplish-brown face. Broad hips and fleshy thighs were squeezed between the frost-covered sides of the casket. Plump arms were folded beneath huge breasts. There was a wrist tag. Samantha brought the torch closer, wiped her sleeve over the goggles in her mask, and read, *Winifred Olulu.*

A compressor behind a grille at the end of the casket began to throb. Opening the lid had allowed the temperature to rise and triggered the refrigeration unit. She let the lid drop back, then moved on to the next; found a slimmer, Latin-American-looking woman. The third casket held the body of a young white man; the fourth, a middle-aged white male whose name tag was inscribed *Martin*

Weaver. She recognized the body in the fifth: a tag said it had belonged to *Nathaniel Prentice*. The sixth casket was empty.

Moving through a doorway, she entered a small room containing a metal-framed hospital bed, a bedside cabinet, a drip stand, oxygen cylinders and a vital signs monitor. The bed had been stripped, and its plastic mattress covering gleamed in the torchlight.

Two cheap single beds were arranged in an adjoining room. Beyond, a short corridor gave access to toilets and a small kitchen. The kitchen seemed to have been improvised in what had been a room for washing laboratory glassware. All of the rooms were clean and bare, uncluttered by clothing or possessions, or any trace of human occupation.

Hot in the protective suit, Samantha returned to the room where the dead were concealed. Five compressors were humming now, trying to lower the temperature in the caskets she'd disturbed. She stepped over power cables and headed back to the window in the store room.

There was no more to see. Desperate to escape from the gloom and get out of the protective suit, she clambered on to the bench, heaved herself over the window cill, and crawled out on to the ducting. She turned, reached inside, slid the jars and tray

132

into their original positions on the bench, then refixed the window, taking care not to disturb the rust on the heads of the screws.

Re-entering the building through the fire door, Samantha crept to the end of the passageway then glanced up and down the brightly lit corridor. It was deserted. She ran to the laboratory air-lock, stepped into a tiled cubicle, and turned on the sprays. The powerful jets of decontaminating fluid felt cold through the fabric of the suit.

Minutes later, she was back in the toilets, trying to smooth the creases from her skirt and tidy her hair.

She heard footsteps moving along the main corridor and a voice she now recognized as Dr Franklin's, calling, 'Miss Grey? Miss Grey? Georgina, are you there?'

Shit! She didn't want to be trapped in this deserted warren of a place with some amorous old geriatric. Cramming her lab coat into the hold-all, she stepped into her shoes, then breezed out and began to trot down the corridor, heading for the entrance. She heard swing doors thudding behind her, quick footsteps, and Dr Franklin saying, 'There you are, Miss Grey. Thought I'd just stop by and make sure you're OK.'

Samantha slowed, glanced over her shoulder, gave him a dazzling smile, and said,

'That was sweet of you, Dr Franklin.'

'Conrad,' he panted. 'Please, call me Conrad.' Catching up with her had left him out of breath. He began to walk with her to the entrance, pushing open doors and stepping aside so she could trot through.

'May I carry your bag and that attaché case? They look rather heavy.'

She flashed him another smile. 'Sweet of you, Conrad, but I'm used to it.'

Dr Franklin pushed at a final door and they swept into the reception area. Breathless with the effort to keep up, he panted, 'I thought you might care to have a drink with me.' His voice was coaxing. 'Dinner if you'd prefer. We could drive into Salisbury or Andover.'

Samantha paused beside the entrance doors, smiling sweetly while she waited for him to operate the lock. His gaze was wandering over her diaphanous blouse. Cut and styled to flatter, he was obviously finding its misty concealment rather tantalizing. Leaving the lab coat off had been a big mistake. She didn't want to have to kill the drooling old bastard. She had to get through the door.

'Your car, Conrad, is it outside?'

'Hmm?' He hadn't heard. Lecherous old eyes were busy caressing the shapes beneath the ruffled layers of ivory silk.

'Your car, is it outside?'

He dragged his gaze up to her face. 'Car? Yes, of course it's outside.'

'Dinner would be pleasant, and I think Salisbury would be best,' Samantha said. She nodded towards the door, saw his fingers trembling as they punched numbers into the digital lock. 'Why don't you lead the way in yours, and I'll follow in mine?'

She felt a surge of relief when she stepped out into the cool twilight of the car-park.

'Why don't we both go in mine, Georgina? I could bring you back in the morning.'

In the morning! The doddering old goat clearly had more than dinner in mind. She gave him another sweet smile. 'I've finished the job here, Conrad. I've got to head back north in the morning. And what would the man on the security gate think? Best if we take both cars.'

Samantha was standing beside her Ferrari now. She opened the door, tossed the hold-all and attaché case on to the passenger seat, and slid inside.

'This yours, Georgina?' He patted the roof of the car.

'All mine.'

'It's a bit of a beast.'

'Conrad, I've been shut up in that place all

135

day. I need dinner and a few drinks. We can talk all you want later. You lead and I'll follow.'

'Of course. Salisbury it is.' He scampered off towards a red Peugeot.

'And don't dawdle, Conrad. I'm hungry.'

Samantha followed him through the security gate and across the science park. When he turned right off the dual carriageway, heading for Salisbury, Samantha drove straight on, accelerating hard down the deserted road towards Andover.

One of the machines she'd serviced was probably damaged beyond repair; the others wouldn't generate a display when she'd inserted the memory chip Marcus had given her. And she'd brought the Government's Director of Applied Microbiological Research to a state of coronary-threatening arousal, only to leave him racing off into the night. The staff at Porton Down would have plenty to gossip about in the canteen tomorrow.

Five dead bodies, one of which was supposed to be interred in an Oxford churchyard, were a lot for her to think about tonight.

* * *

Daniel Langdon slid the drawings back into the plan chest, gathered up his laptop and an

136

old briefcase, and stepped out of the site hut. He'd have to put in a couple of days at head office this week, discuss that shopping mall tender with his chief estimator. He'd been neglecting the big picture, spending too much time here, trying to get the contract out of the red and back on schedule. And sifting endlessly through the drawings and progress charts hadn't made any better of it. Even if they encountered no more problems, there'd be hardly any profit in the job. He needed another major contract, preferably two, something that would keep the firm going over the next year.

He looked beyond the excavators, dump trucks and piling machines, corralled in the secure compound. The Northern and General tower was taking shape. Eight-hundred-and-thirty-two feet of bolted and welded steel: an up-yours finger challenging the Manchester sky line. He felt a rush of satisfaction that made all the hassle worth while. He was erecting the city's tallest building; creating another landmark. Mr High-Rise they called him at Rotary and the Lodge. The cheating bastards who'd had his cash then forgotten their promises couldn't take that away from him.

Tim Saunders was a smarmy sod. Two-hundred thousand donated to party funds on a firm promise he'd be awarded at least two of the new hospital contracts. When they'd cashed his cheque, Saunders soon watered that down to an assurance he'd be on the short-list to tender. Now the lying bastard was saying the list had been finalized, but he was sure to be allocated a contract in the next phase. Next bloody phase! He dropped the briefcase in the boot of his Mercedes, then laid the laptop beside it. Next phase was no use to him. The firm wouldn't survive another year if he didn't get some big projects.

'Mr Langdon?'

He glanced round, saw a stocky figure in a red hard-hat. The man was holding a clipboard and carrying some plans under his arm.

'O'Donnell: Brendan O'Donnell. Arnold and Rankin, steelwork fabricators.' The man held out a hand.

'You're keen,' Daniel Langdon said. 'Still on site at' — he glanced at his watch — 'almost seven.'

'We've got concerns. We think the structural engineers have under-designed the stanchion connections on floors twenty-five and twenty-six.'

Langdon slammed down the boot of the car. 'What's made you think that?' He braced himself. More bloody trouble.

'Hair cracks radiating from the bolt holes. Looks as if the flanges are failing in shear.' O'Donnell nodded towards the site office. 'Shall we talk inside?'

'How bad are these hair cracks?'

'You can get your fingernail into them close to the bolts,' O'Donnell said.

'I'd like you to climb back up and show me,' Langdon said grimly. 'The brackets for the cladding are being fixed tomorrow. If remedial work's required, I need to know now.'

They began to trudge up rough concrete stairways. 'The ruptured flanges,' Daniel Langdon asked, 'are they on the inner or outer faces of the columns?'

'Outer. Not a sign of distress on the inner flanges. I think it's because they're welded to the floor beams.'

'We should have brought a couple of safety harnesses,' Langdon said. 'Keen as mustard on safety regulations in Manchester. Have you been using one for the inspection?'

O'Donnell shook his head. 'Just knelt at the edge of the floor slab and leaned forward; got my head round the stanchion base. If you wear a harness, you spend more time hooking it and unhooking it as you move round the building than you do doing the job.'

Daniel Langdon watched the man climb the stairs a couple of steps ahead of him. There was a spring in his step, despite the lateness of the hour. Broad shouldered, lean, hard-looking; he radiated briskness and efficiency. 'You been in the services?' he asked.

The man turned. 'Royal Engineers. Finished my last term a year ago. Decided to call it a day and find a job in civvy street before I'm too old to get something decent.'

'I'm always on the look-out for good site managers. You ever thought about that?' Langdon asked.

The man grinned. 'Consider anything if the pay's OK.'

'Come to the site office tomorrow and we'll have a chat. Just won a contract for the Roebuck hotel in Leicester. Probably start on site in about a month. I need a no-nonsense organizer who can drive the job along.'

They climbed in silence for a while, then Daniel Langdon began to check the numbers daubed on the steel columns. 'Twenty-fourth. One more to go,' he grunted, breathless after the brisk ascent.

As they climbed the final flight, O'Donnell glanced back at Langdon and said, 'It's most pronounced where the wall of the main block over-sails the entrance atrium.'

They reached the twenty-fifth floor and headed across the expanse of rough concrete to the fenced outer edge.

Daniel Langdon's spirits were sinking. The cost, the delay: this could drive the job irredeemably into the red. He should have had at least one of those hospital jobs. Two-hundred thousand and not a penny of it tax deductible. And he'd welcomed Tim Saunders into his home as a friend; warmly recommended him when he'd asked to join Lilith's group. Sod it! He'd copy those images to a disk tonight and post them to a national daily tomorrow; wipe the smile off the arrogant bastard's smug face.

O'Donnell stood back when they reached the high mesh barrier; watched while Daniel Langdon released fastenings and swung a section open. He glanced at the number on the column, then flicked through sheets on his clipboard. 'This isn't the worst, but it's pretty bad.'

Moving through the opening, O'Donnell knelt at the edge of the floor slab. When he removed his hard-hat, the cold breeze began to ruffle his blond hair. Leaning forward over the drop, he slid his hand down the massive plate that linked the columns.

'Yes, you can feel it. You can get your fingernails into the cracks, even on the top row of bolts.' He leaned further over the edge. 'And if you get your head a bit below slab level, you can see the cracks, clear as day.'

He rose to his feet, stepped back, and with a wave of the hand invited Daniel Langdon to take a look for himself.

Langdon tossed his hard hat against the safety fence, dropped to his knees, then got his head and shoulders below the level of the floor slab. It all seemed OK. Clean neat job. Couldn't see any cracks across the area of bright metal where they'd ground the drilling burrs off. He straightened up and looked over his shoulder. 'Where did you say the cracking was?'

'Tends to be worse on the lower rows of bolts. Reach down as far as you can and drag your fingernails around the holes. You'll feel it then.'

Daniel Langdon did as he was asked. 'I still can't — '

He felt powerful hands grab his ankles, then lift and shove. In an instant he was off the slab, spinning head-over-heels, dropping through the cold clear air.

His lurching heart turned a scream into a whimper. Concrete and girders were rushing past in a blur. Mind amazingly lucid, he realized he wasn't going to survive this. It was his time. Why? The photographs: it had to be the photographs. Tim Saunders had moved in on him.

The wind was roaring in his ears, tearing at his jacket. Knowing it would be his last, he dragged in an enormous breath, then screamed, '*Bastards. Bloody bastar . . .*'

8

Samantha sipped tea heavily laced with whisky while she sifted through the papers in the envelope she'd found beneath the lining paper in Ling Prentice's dressing-table drawer. They were very personal.

She unfolded copies of birth and death certificates for a Ling Haifong; father a doctor, mother a radiologist, both of Liverpool. Cause of death, at age four, multiple injuries sustained in a road accident. A certificate of marriage between Ling Haifong and Nathaniel Prentice, and a birth certificate for Wei Prentice, were clipped to a photograph of a baby in what looked to be Christening robes.

Samantha glanced again at the birthday card inscribed, in Mandarin, *To Ling, with fondest greetings from Kwan*, then gave the tattered envelope another shake. Some dog-eared papers covered in Mandarin text fell on to her lap: a Chinese birth certificate and employment documents issued by the Shing Peng clothing factory in Peking to a woman called Ma Weihma. There had been a copy of the Chinese birth certificate in the file Marcus had given her; presumably the British embassy had obtained it.

Hidden amongst the papers was a small advertising card for the *Blissful Moments Sensual Sauna and Massage*, an establishment that offered a very discreet and professional service. She turned the card over. On the reverse was a telephone number and a simple map showing the location of the place on an industrial estate close to a motorway junction near Leeds.

There was no passport, no identity card, and no social security papers.

Samantha gathered up the documents and slid them back into the envelope. Did Professor Prentice know his wife was an illegal immigrant who'd stolen the identity of a dead British girl? Did he know she'd probably worked in the sex trade?

She sipped her tea, enjoying the reviving glow from the whisky. It was comforting to be back in this nondescript little town and in her own modest home. The developers had called it a town house: garage and utility room on the ground floor, kitchen and sitting-room on the first, and two bedrooms and a bathroom on the second.

Rising to her feet, Samantha crossed over to the window and held the lapels of her white silk dressing-gown together while she looked down into the cul-de-sac. There was a black van parked across the road. It had been there when she returned from her trip to Oxford. And someone had taken a photograph of her embracing Crispin. The photographer was dead, but she still felt uneasy about it all; felt that the anonymity she'd enjoyed for so long was being stripped away.

Perhaps the watchers were waiting for her to lead them to Ling Prentice? If the widow and her child had avoided being found for this long, they were either dead or comparatively safe. Best to let well alone for a while, she decided. If the politicians became more agitated they might reveal more, and she'd be better placed to decide how to act.

She began the climb up to the second floor. The weather was unusually warm. She could wear that snazzy little Alberta Ferretti dress, or perhaps the Rocha . . . The faint bleeping of her mobile followed her up the stairs. She returned to the sitting-room, groped between the cushions on the sofa and tugged it free.

'Sam . . . that you, Sam?'

'I'm here, Marcus. Signal's poor. I'm losing — '

'It's the encryption system. Problem's at our end. They're working on it now. How's progress with the Prentice search?'

'There isn't any.' She took a vengeful pleasure in saying that. He'd dumped the lousy job on her, persuaded her it would only take a couple of days when he must have known it could tie her up for a month. He could fume and fret.

'Christ, Sam. Things are desperate. The chief was called to Number Ten again yesterday. Home Secretary and the PM are getting manic about it. They want the Prentices found.'

Samantha laughed huskily. 'What's new, Marcus? I thought the useless bastards were always manic.'

'It's not a laughing matter, Sam. This is as serious as it gets. They've got to be found. The chief took a real battering yesterday.'

'We're not miracle workers, Marcus. It's only a matter of days since they passed the job over.'

'Give it your best, Sam. Do any bloody thing, but find them.'

'I'm working on it,' Samantha lied. 'Night and day. Giving it all I've got. OK?'

'Don't ring off, Sam. There's one more thing . . . '

'I'm still listening.'

'The spread of infection we talked about. Health Ministry are getting daily returns from the regional authorities and the

147

situation's deteriorating. We've made arrangements for all key personnel to be inoculated. You're booked in with Dr Merrill in Leeds at three this afternoon and you're name's still Georgina Grey.'

'Which hospital?'

'At his home. Senior police and army people are being dealt with at the hospital, but that's too exposed for us.' Marcus gave her the address.

'Where's the vaccine coming from, Marcus?'

'It's Swiss, and you wouldn't believe what it's costing. Americans are producing it, too, but they won't release any.'

'There are outbreaks in Europe?' Samantha asked.

'Holland, Belgium and Germany: same rate of spread, same racial distribution, same mortality rates.'

'That crazy tale about fountain pens could be true.'

'Looks like it, Sam. It's the same engineered virus that's spreading across Europe.'

'What's the proportion of whites affected?'

'The returns we've had in so far indicate it's pressing ninety per cent, even in areas that are heavily settled by non-Europeans'

'Sounds bleak,' Samantha muttered.

'I'll call you for a progress report same

time tomorrow. You call me if there are any developments, day or night. And Sam . . . '

'I'm still here, Marcus.'

'Did you manage to get inside Porton Down?'

'I'm not hearing you Marcus,' she lied. 'System's blanking out most of what you say. I'm going to close, OK?'

Samantha tossed the encrypted phone amongst the cushions. Marcus could wait. She'd use the visit to Porton Down for her next report, eke out what little material she had, string him along while she waited for the widow and child situation to develop.

★　★　★

A slim smartly dressed woman, probably the doctor's wife, gave her a reserved little smile. 'Miss Grey?'

Samantha nodded.

The woman stood aside, Samantha stepped into the hallway of the big Edwardian house, heard the door shut behind her, then followed her across gleaming parquet into a surgery in what had once been a dining-room. The air was heavy with the smell of wax polish.

The woman announced her, then left her with a tall, distinguished-looking man who was wearing a dark-blue suit and a pink shirt and tie. 'Please . . . ' He nodded towards a chair.

Samantha sat down.

'Miss Grey . . . Miss Grey.' He was running his pen down a list of names. 'Ah!' Bright eyes looked up at her over half-moon spectacles. 'Georgina, is it?'

Samantha nodded, and he made a tick on the list.

'You don't have a cough or a cold, do you? No history of respiratory or heart problems?' His manner was brisk and business-like. She wouldn't dare have any problems.

'Not that I know of.'

'Could you expose your upper arm for me?'

Samantha put her bag and gloves on his desk, unfastened buttons, then drew the collar of her yellow dress over her shoulder and down her arm.

He tugged at the door of a small refrigerator. It opened to reveal tiny vials of serum arranged in rows on polystyrene trays.

'Does it have to be refrigerated?' Samantha asked.

'If you're storing it long-term, yes; but it remains viable for a week or more so long as you keep it cool.'

He plucked out one of the tiny glass containers, closed the fridge door, then bustled back to the desk and laid it on the blotter. Taking a plastic pack from a pile on a tray, he tore it open and shook out a hypodermic.

There was a discreet knocking on the door and the slim woman looked in. She flashed Samantha one of her reserved little smiles, said, 'Forgive me, Miss Grey,' then glanced at the doctor and went on, 'I've got Mrs Kovaks on the line. It's her husband. She's very distressed.'

He sighed. 'Would you excuse me, Miss Grey? I'm sorry, but . . . '

'Don't worry about it,' Samantha murmured. She heard the heavy door slam shut behind her.

Samantha lifted her dress back over her shoulder, stepped around the desk and opened the refrigerator door. Up close she could see the glass ampoules nestling in holes in polystyrene strips, about ten to a strip, with ten strips loosely bonded together to form a tray. She slid out the bottom tray, broke off the rearmost strip then slid it back. She closed the fridge door, grabbed a handful of the syringes, returned to her seat and buried it all beneath the clutter of cosmetics in her bag.

Two minutes later, the doctor bustled back into the room. 'Sorry about that, Miss Grey.'

He got behind the desk, peeled open an antiseptic wipe, beamed at Samantha and said, 'Your arm?'

She slid the collar of her dress over her shoulder again and he rubbed at her skin with the alcohol soaked pad. She watched him snap the top off the tiny vial of serum and plunge the hypodermic into it.

'And what ministry do you work for, Miss Grey?'

'I don't,' Samantha said, huskily. 'I'm the Prime Minister's mistress.'

Bushy eyebrows jerked up, then his lips parted in a smile, exposing gold incisors. 'Really!' He chuckled. 'I can only congratulate him on his very good taste. If he could use the same judgement when he conducts the nation's business, we'd all be a lot happier.'

She felt the needle prick her skin, heard the doctor's noisy breathing, then he pressed the antiseptic wipe against her arm.

'Could you hold that for a moment, Miss Grey, while I get a dressing. We don't want your sleeve marked.' He bustled around the desk, tore open another pack, and came back with a plaster. 'Beautiful dress. Did the Prime Minister choose it for you?' He was laughing; enjoying their little joke.

'Would you trust him to pick you a suit?'

The doctor's shoulders were shaking. 'I don't think so, Miss Grey.' He suddenly became brisk and business-like again. 'You may have some pain and swelling in your arm tonight, but you shouldn't have any other symptoms. If you do, phone me.' He scribbled a number on a pad, tore off the sheet and passed it across.

Samantha took the paper and dropped it into her bag, then buttoned up her dress. 'Thanks, Doctor. Thank you very much.'

'You're welcome, Miss Grey. Do give the Prime Minister my regards.'

★ ★ ★

Two cardboard boxes, each the size of a small suitcase, were stacked behind his desk. Tim Saunders reached for the paper-knife. They'd be safe to open, he could be sure of that. Jessica would have sent them to security, had them put through X-ray and checked for toxic things.

He slit the adhesive tape and folded back the flaps. Beneath a couple of layers of bubble-wrap was an expensive laptop. In an envelope embossed with a lion and crown was a plastic wallet containing five compact disks. He lifted out some more bubble-wrap. There was nothing else.

Moving the box aside, he applied the knife to the tape on the one beneath. Inside, he found an old leather briefcase and a couple of files. One contained business correspondence of a personal nature; the other minutes of Rotary Club meetings. Lifting out the briefcase, he clicked it open. A stainless steel flask was half-full of coffee, and a polythene box held the mouldering remains of an egg and cress sandwich. The draft of a rather abrasive letter to a firm of quantity surveyors was scribbled on a pad, and a small notebook contained basic details of about a dozen contracts.

That was it. As far as he was concerned, it was all that remained of the tall, rather handsome man who used to lead the bearers of the horned god into Lilith's torch-lit yard. He smiled. He might not have kept his pecker zipped up, but he'd dealt with the man who'd been stupid enough to photograph him while he'd had it out.

The knocking on the door was so timid he hardly heard it. He called out, 'Come on in,' and a dark-haired girl entered, looking apprehensive.

Utterly gorgeous, Tim Saunders mused. Nothing was more enticing than firm young female flesh. Out loud, he said, 'You really are looking very lovely today, Jessica.'

The girl blushed crimson and averted her eyes. Did he have to stare at her breasts like that? It was so demeaning. And most men did it. She'd even caught Father Malone taking furtive little looks when he came to say mass in her mother's chapel. But Saunders was different. The way he looked scared her; made her flesh creep. She held out the folder. 'Press cuttings, Minister. The coverage of Daniel Langdon's death.'

He reached over the desk and took the file. The girl's face was still crimson, her eyes still averted. He said, 'You've not been listening to me, have you, Jessica?'

'Listening, Minister? I don't understand.'

'All this formality. How long have you been a member of the team?'

'Almost three months now.'

'Then you've got to stop this 'minister' business. I don't know what they do in the other members' offices, but it's strictly Christian names here. So call me Tim.'

Jessica gave him a nervous little smile. God, she wished she was in another office. If only Peter Clayton could have found her a place. He was one of the few men who didn't stare; who treated her like a person. She swallowed hard. 'Would you like me to continue searching for reports of the death?'

'It could be useful, Jessica. Langdon was a

major contributor to the party, and he made no secret of his political leanings. We ought to be on the look-out for critical comment. What have the press been saying?'

'On Tuesday they reported he'd fallen to his death on a building site. Today they're saying it could have been suicide. It seems he had financial worries.'

'Could you keep looking until the end of the week? And could you ask Maureen to do me a condolence letter to the widow? She's called Bernice. There are three teenage daughters, too, but I can't recall their names. Ask Maureen to mention them in the letter.'

Jessica nodded. 'Maureen asked me to remind you about the meeting with the head of the Serious Crime Unit at four.'

Tim Saunders frowned. He wanted to take a closer look at the contents of the boxes; see whether or not the images the bastard had been threatening him with were on one of the disks. 'Could you ask Maureen to give Sir Nigel a ring, tell him I've been called to an emergency meeting at Number Ten, and ask him to reschedule the appointment.'

'The meeting with Sir Nigel *is* at Number Ten, Min — Tim.' Jessica tried to conceal her loathing. If he could keep his mind off her breasts and on his job, he'd remember appointments.

'Is it? Of course it is.' Tim Saunders glanced down at the files and battered briefcase. 'What time is it now, Jessica?'

'Almost twenty to four.'

He sighed. 'In that case I'd better start making my way to Number Ten.'

9

Samantha parked the Ferrari in the garage, plugged the lead from a palm-top computer into a socket on the wall, then began to view the rooms in the house.

Crispin had been. He'd collected her things from the cleaners and laid out a dress and a couple of suits on the bed in the spare room. When she flicked down to the first floor she saw he was still here, dusters and cloths tucked into the belt of his jeans, his tray of cleaning things with the long carrying handle at his feet. He was in the kitchen, scouring stains off the cooker hob.

She used the remote to close the garage doors, tugged the lead from the wall socket, then headed up the stairs.

'Home early for once.' He didn't turn as she entered, and his voice had a brittle cheerfulness.

'What's wrong, Crispin?' Samantha laid her bag and the tiny personal computer on a worktop, and went close to him.

'Don't talk to me, Sam, or I'll start to blub.' Gaze averted, he went on rubbing frantically at the hob while he gabbled, 'I just had to get out of the flat, so I thought I'd come over and give you a good clean through. I got your things from the dry cleaners. Well, everything except the red Prada suit. There were some marks on the cuffs. All the money you spend there! I told them they'd got to try harder.'

Probably stains from the gun, she mused. The cleaners wouldn't get them out. She slid her arm around Crispin's waist and laid her cheek on the tanned flesh of his upper arm. Physically, he was the most beautiful man she'd ever known. Under the white cotton singlet, his hard depilated body was hot, almost feverish. She squeezed him, then said gently, 'Why did you have to get out of the flat?'

He began to polish the taps. 'Don't, Sam. I can't . . . ' He suddenly turned and buried his face in her hair. She slid her arms around him, held him tight, felt his chest and shoulders heaving with silent sobs.

'Jeremy's dead,' he gasped out eventually.

'God, no!' Samantha held him more tightly. 'How?'

'He went to see his mother in Richmond. She was ill with this flu thing. He phoned me last Monday night to tell me she'd died before he got there, and he'd be coming back the next morning. He didn't arrive and I didn't hear a thing and I was getting really worried, so on Friday I phoned and spoke to his sister. Nasty little cow. She just said, 'Jeremy died yesterday, so you won't be able to corrupt him with your filthy perversions any more, will you?' His family didn't approve: of me and Jeremy, I mean. Deeply religious. Bloody born-agains.'

'I'm sorry,' Samantha whispered huskily. 'I'm so sorry.' She stood on tiptoe, pressed her cheek against his, then kissed him.

He drew away, turned back to the sink, a little embarrassed, and began to polish the taps again. 'It scares you, Sam. I mean, I was kissing him goodbye on Monday morning, and he was dead by Thursday night.'

'How did he die?'

'That flu, love. Going down like flies with it. The salon's shut. One of the girls has been taken into Barfield General and one's died at home. Jeremy said custom was falling off a couple of weeks ago. I'm scared shitless.'

'Go into the sitting-room.' Samantha insisted. 'I'll be with you in a second.'

Crispin draped his polishing cloth over the taps, and did as she asked.

Samantha took the strip of tiny glass ampoules from her bag, plucked one out, then hid the rest at the back of the fridge.

Crispin's news had suddenly made this plague thing real to her; made her fearful for Prentice's widow and child. One or both of them could be dead. Peeling the wrappings from a syringe, she followed Crispin into the sitting-room.

'What's that?' He sounded alarmed.

'Flu vaccine. I got it from a doctor this afternoon. Just sit on the sofa.'

He sat down. 'Was he a client?'

'Client?' Samantha gave him a puzzled look. She was concentrating on drawing the vaccine into the syringe.

'The doctor: had he hired you for sex?'

Suddenly understanding, Samantha gave Crispin a knowing smile.

'Bet he liked the dress.'

Samantha laughed. 'He asked me if the Prime Minister had chosen it.'

'The Prime Minister's screwing you?' Crispin sounded amazed.

'Just don't go there, Crispin. There are things a girl draws the line at.' She poured brandy on to a wad of kitchen towel and reached for his arm.

'Don't mark me!' He recoiled from her.

'It won't mark. It's only . . . '

'I can't be marked,' he protested. 'I'd lose work. I've got to look perfect on a shoot.'

'Push your jeans down then.'

Obedient, he unbuckled his jeans, tugged at the zip, then drew the skin-tight fabric down to his ankles.

'Spread your legs for me.' Samantha slapped his knees and muscular thighs parted. She knelt down and ran her fingers over tanned hairless skin, searching for some softness. Then she stuck the needle in and drove the plunger down.

'Bloody hell, Sam! Do you know what you're doing?'

'Don't moan. This stuff's as scarce as hens' teeth. And I'm probably saving your life.' She withdrew the hypodermic and pressed the wad of brandy-soaked tissue against his thigh. 'Hold this over it until the bleeding stops. I don't have a plaster.'

She rose, went over to the drinks table, poured the remainder of the brandy into a glass, and handed it to him. 'Drink that.'

'I don't really care for — '

'Drink it,' she insisted. 'While I shower and change. Then we'll go over to your flat and you can put that Armani suit on. I'm taking you out to dinner.'

'Sounds good.' He took a tentative sip at the brandy. The tears had stopped and he looked a little less desolate.

'I'll hang on to your arm,' Samantha went on. 'And you can look as if you adore me.'

'But I do adore you! Shit, Sam, you're the cat's meow.'

Samantha laughed, rested her hands on his shoulders, then bent down and kissed him. 'And you're the dog's bollocks, Crispin. You're the sweetest man I know.' She ran her fingers through the mane of bronze-coloured hair. 'And quite the most beautiful.'

He smiled up at her gratefully, then took another sip at the brandy. He seemed to be developing a liking for it.

Samantha smiled back. Beautiful he might be, but sitting there in the snowy-white singlet and Calvin Kleins, with his jeans pulled down to his trainers, he looked rather comic.

'There's something I might want you to do for me, Crispin,' she murmured huskily.

The smile faded and big blue eyes began to look wary. He took another sip at the brandy to fortify himself.

'I might want you to help me look after a child.'

Crispin coughed out the spirit. 'You're pregnant!'

Samantha laughed and gave him another kiss. 'No, Crispin, I'm not pregnant. This is a little girl I might have to care for until I can make some permanent arrangement. I'd need you to look after her while I'm away on business.'

163

'But you're always away. And you want *me* to look after a little girl? I'm a single man. The gossips would have a field day. People say such vicious things, and I should know.'

'She's five, going on six. She could manage to deal with intimate things herself. She just needs an adult to protect her, feed her, order her life, be a companion. No one could do that better than you, Crispin,' Samantha coaxed.

'I'd look after her here?' he asked.

Samantha shook her head. 'It could be dangerous. I'd rent a house or a bungalow for you. Scarborough, Bridlington, somewhere like that.'

'What about getting her to school?'

'Forget school. She needs to be hidden and protected until I can find her mother.'

'You're in some sort of trouble, aren't you, Sam?'

'Nothing I can't handle.'

'And what if my agent calls? He's trying to get me on a Gucci photo shoot in Rome.'

Samantha took the brandy-soaked pad from his fingers, dropped it in the bin under the document shredder, then sat on his bare knees. She wrapped her arms around his neck, and kissed him on the cheek.

He flashed her a rueful little smile. 'Sorry, Sam. It doesn't do it for me.'

Ignoring him, she went on, 'It would be

good for you, Crispin. You need a diversion, and it would get you away from the flat and all the memories. And how often has your agent been going to send you to Rome on a photo shoot?'

He sighed and shrugged, took another sip at the brandy, then asked, 'When will she arrive?'

'Not sure. In two or three days maybe. Would that conflict with the funeral?'

'Funeral?'

'Jeremy's funeral.'

He looked crushed. 'His sister said she'd no idea when it would be. This flu thing's causing so many deaths, funerals are being delayed by a month or more. Of course, she may have been lying. They wouldn't want me there. I'd be an embarrassment.'

'That's not going to be a problem, then.' She rose from his knees, took hold of his hand and drew him to his feet. 'Pull your pants up and come upstairs. You can pick what you want me to wear and talk to me while you finish your drink.'

When she reached the landing she heard Crispin calling after her, 'Your mobile, Sam. I can hear it ringing in your bag. Shall I bring it up?'

'Please, Crispin.'

He took the stairs three at a time and handed it to her. She turned it on.

'Miss Quest?'

'I'm here, Mrs Hadley.' Samantha glanced down into the street. The black van was still there.

'Those men have been to the house again; you know, the Serious Crime people. They kept going on and on about Nat's wife and child, asking me if I'd had any contact, or if I'd had them to stay. They didn't seem to believe me when I said I'd not, and had the cheek to ask me if they could take a look round the house and grounds.'

'Did you let them?' Samantha stared down at the roof of the van, wondering how much she could tell Alice Hadley.

'Bruce came in, thank God. When he warned them he was going to talk to Peter about them harassing us, they left.'

'Peter?'

'Peter Clayton, the Home Secretary. I think I told you, Bruce is his agent; manages his constituency office. Bruce tried to contact him this morning, but I don't know whether he got through. Have you any news for me?'

'None, Mrs Hadley, but I'm working on it. And the fact that these people are searching for Ling and her little girl is reassuring in a way.'

'I'm not sure what you mean,' Alice Hadley faltered.

166

'It means they're probably still alive.'

'You seriously thought they might have been killed?'

'Or had an accident or become ill,' Samantha said.

'But if they'd become ill, Ling would have contacted me.'

Samantha said nothing; just listened to the faint sound of panicky breathing coming down the line. Alice Hadley seemed to be unaware of the epidemic. But then, the Government was doing more to prevent the spread of information than it was to prevent the spread of infection.

'And why hasn't Nat phoned me from America?' Alice demanded. 'Surely, if he was worried about Ling and his little girl he'd have done that? He'd have done it before he contacted the police.'

Samantha frowned. It wouldn't be wise to reveal things Bruce Hadley might raise with the Home Secretary. 'Perhaps your brother didn't want to worry you,' she said. Then, trying to end the conversation, she asked, 'Could you let me know how Peter Clayton responds when your husband tackles him about the Serious Crime people?'

'Of course.'

'And it's important that no one knows you've engaged me.'

167

'I understand,' Alice Hadley said, then her voice became bleak as she asked, 'What shall I do, Miss Quest?'

'Just keep lighting the candles. And make sure you light one for me.'

Leaving the door open so she could talk to Crispin, Samantha stepped into the bathroom and began to unbutton her dress.

★ ★ ★

Loretta Fallon looked at the tense angry faces of the three men seated at the far side of the table in the cabinet room.

'I'm at a loss to understand why you gave the Quest woman the job,' the Prime Minister said. 'I mean, we want someone who can be controlled, someone we can rely on to always do the correct thing.' His voice was tired and he was eying her bleakly.

'Who told you Quest had been assigned to locate the Prentice family?' Loretta demanded.

'You did,' Tim Saunders, the Internal Security Minister, said. 'At yesterday's briefing, or perhaps the briefing the day before.'

Loretta held his gaze. Liar, she thought. You unprincipled bloody liar. I'd never reveal agents' names, and I'd never reveal their assignments.

The Prime Minister sniffed, leaned forward

on his papers and stared at her. He was waiting for an answer.

'You made it clear finding the Prentice family was an absolute priority, so I assigned my best agent to the job,' Loretta said.

'But there's been no progress. I mean, we're no further on than we were a week ago, Miss Fallon. And I can't understand what possessed you to give a sensitive job of this kind to a woman no one seems to be able to control; a woman with such strong republican and anti-establishment sentiments. If we can't trust the people who serve us . . . '

'I thought I'd explained that, Prime Minister. It's because she's the best; because she'll do whatever needs to be done to find Prentice and his family.'

'It's what she'll do if and when she finds them that concerns us,' Peter Clayton, the Home Secretary, said.

'I'm not sure what you mean, Minister.'

'They need to be taken into protective custody,' Peter Clayton went on. 'And all documents and personal possessions seized. Quest might have an agenda of her own.'

'And why would Miss Quest have an agenda of her own?' Loretta demanded icily. 'She'll do whatever's necessary.'

'What she thinks is necessary, and what we require, may not be the same thing,' the

Prime Minister retorted.

Loretta looked from Prime Minister to Home Secretary, then let her cold grey eyes come to rest on the Minister for Internal Security. 'I don't think you've been completely open with me, gentlemen. You've assured me twice that I've sole responsibility for locating Professor Prentice and his family, but I'm getting constant feedback that other agencies are involved.'

Saunders met her gaze for a few moments, then stared down at his papers and began to doodle in the margins with an expensive-looking pen.

'We've been over this, Miss Fallon, and I've given you my absolute assurance that you have sole responsibility for the search,' the Prime Minister said irritably.

'And am I permitted to know why these people are wanted so badly?'

Saunders looked up. 'Knowing why won't help you to find them.'

'It could,' Loretta retorted. 'And knowing why might colour the way we approach the task. More particularly, it could influence the way we act when we locate them.'

'We want them dead or alive, Miss Fallon. That's all you need to know.' The Prime Minister's voice held no emotion.

'And without more information, your

170

instruction could be unacceptable to me,' Loretta snapped.

The Home Secretary gave the Prime Minister a shocked glance.

'Do I have to remind you that you're a servant of the Crown, Miss Fallon?'

'Need I remind you that you and the Home Secretary are lawyers, Prime Minister? You both know the actions of ministers are regulated by the law. Servants of the Crown aren't obliged to accept instructions blindly. I'll ask you again, why do you want to locate Professor Prentice and his wife and child so desperately?'

'And I'm saying you have all the information and assurances you require. You do as we ask, or you give me your resignation.'

Loretta smiled at the Prime Minister over the gleaming top of the huge table. On an ornate mantelpiece, a black pedimented clock with a silver chapter ring was measuring out the hours. Loretta listened to a few sonorous tick-tocks, then said, 'That's something I'm not offering, Prime Minister. If you want rid of me, dismiss me, and give your reasons to Parliament.'

She rose to her feet and replaced the heavy mahogany chair under the table. 'I'll take the assignment away from Quest. I couldn't really spare her from counter-terrorism anyway.'

She looked from the Prime Minister to Saunders. 'And in view of your assurances, we'll regard all other involvement in the search for the widow as hostile, and act accordingly.'

She turned and headed for the door.

'I haven't said the meeting's over, Miss Fallon.' The Prime Minister's nasal voice was shaking.

Loretta pulled the door open and glanced back. 'And I don't think there's any more we can usefully say to one another. Good-day, gentlemen.'

She headed down the corridor that led to the front of the house, all the time expecting some lackey to come running with a message demanding her return. She crossed the blue and gold carpet in the hallway, an attendant opened the door, and she stepped out into Downing Street. A policeman touched his helmet and murmured, 'Ma'am.'

She gave him a tired smile and strode off, wondering if she'd ever set foot inside the place again.

* * *

'The brazen arrogance of the woman!' the Home Secretary muttered.

The Prime Minister sniffed and nodded.

'We'll deal with her, but not now. We're badly exposed to the opposition on so many fronts. I don't want the dismissal of the head of MI5 thrown at me at Question Time.'

'At least she's taken that bloody Quest woman off the job.' Tim Saunders had doodled down one margin and was beginning to extend his intertwined initials across the bottom of the sheet. 'We'll all sleep a little easier now.'

'Invasion of Iraq did it,' the Prime Minister reflected. 'Civil servants and advisers all got wary after that. They can't seem to grasp how important presentation is. Now they want to endlessly clarify the questions you're asking, and some of their written responses . . . ' He rolled his eyes heavenwards, then studied the bleak faces of his colleagues. Drawing no encouragement, he rambled on, 'Prentice seemed more easygoing. I'd no idea he was recording the meetings. They were off-the-record brainstorming sessions, that's all. We were just exchanging ideas and exploring possibilities.'

'He was close to old what's-his-name . . . ' The Home Secretary frowned and clicked his fingers. 'Hmm . . . The biological weapons expert: the one who committed suicide . . . '

'Jardine,' Saunders offered. 'Dr Howard Jardine.'

'He's the one: Jardine. Prentice must have learned something from that experience.'

'I don't remember our ever making a direct request to Prentice for help with racial targeting.' Saunders gazed admiringly at the doodle across the bottom of the sheet, then got to work on the other margin.

'But that's what the meetings were about,' the Prime Minister said. 'And when we seized that virus and old Prentice found it was engineered, he was ecstatic. We definitely raised the possibility of modifying it so it could be retargeted on other racial groups.'

Saunders stopped doodling and looked up. 'If that ever gets out . . . '

'It's not going to get out.' The Prime Minister's voice was tired but confident. 'Talk to Marcus, Peter. Ask him to quietly keep us in the picture about the investigation. Stress the importance of this for the security of the state. You can throw in the safety of the royal family, if you like. That should keep him on our side. Make it absolutely clear that your people must go in when the Prentice woman's been located. And it's vital that Prentice's tapes and documents are sealed into boxes and delivered here.'

'Can we trust Marcus?' Saunders asked.

'Rock solid,' Peter Clayton insisted. 'Public school, Guards regiment, related to the royal family, married well: wife's a bishop's daughter. Our sort. Knows the rules. He'll play a straight bat.'

'Should have got the job instead of Fallon,' Saunders muttered. The doodle was nearing the top of the sheet.

'He didn't have the intellectual rigour,' the Prime Minister said.

Peter Clayton cleared his throat. 'I think I told you that Prentice is related to Bruce Hadley, the chap who manages my constituency office. He's his brother-in-law.'

Tim Saunders looked up from his doodling. The Prime Minister began to frown at Clayton.

'Bruce phoned me this morning. Complained about men from Serious Crime harassing him and his wife. It seems they've called at their home twice, asking about Ling Prentice and the child.'

'So?' Tim Saunders demanded truculently. 'We agreed my people should keep Quest under surveillance and maintain an involvement.'

'I think visiting Prentice's sister is more of an involvement than we had in mind,' Peter Clayton said icily. 'The job's been passed over to my people, and they should be left to get on with it.'

'Trouble is, Peter,' Tim Saunders smirked,

175

'we don't have much control over your people, do we? It's like a bloody black hole. We can't even find out what progress they're making.'

'At least we can be sure of a result,' Peter Clayton snapped.

'Gentlemen, gentlemen,' the Prime Minister said. 'Let's not argue amongst ourselves. Far more than our political survival's hanging on this. Let's stay focused or we'll lose control of the situation.'

'I've no problem with staying focused, Charles,' Peter Clayton said. 'But Bruce Hadley's more than my agent, he's a friend. A very dear friend. It's bad enough having to hide what I know from him. I want this harassment to stop.'

The Prime Minister looked at Saunders. 'That's reasonable, Tim. Your people should stay at arm's length and let Fallon and MI5 get on with it now.'

'We should at least keep Quest under surveillance; make sure she really has been taken off the job,' Tim Saunders muttered.

'I think we'd all go along with that,' the Prime Minister said. Then he stiffened himself and took a deep breath, as if determined to dismiss a nightmare from his mind. 'Now,' he snapped, 'the agenda for Friday's cabinet meeting. Have you got anything?'

'Refrigerated lorries,' the Home Secretary said. 'We've allocated some to hospitals, but we need more: enough to store a six or seven-week backlog of bodies. We might have to requisition them from haulage contractors. If that fails, we've got to consider mass burials.'

'We ought to be closing schools and places of public assembly,' Saunders offered. 'Has any progress been made with mass immunization?'

'Forget mass immunization,' the Prime Minister said. 'We can't even manage ring-fence immunization to contain the outbreaks.'

'It's been almost eight weeks. We got that Swiss serum for key personnel, surely — '

'We can't get the stuff in quantity. They need it for themselves. We might have to go through the motions, though. Administer whatever flu vaccine we've got.'

'Doctors wouldn't go along with that,' the Home Secretary muttered.

'We hold all vaccine stocks,' the Prime Minister said tetchily. 'We announce a matching strain of avian flu, and they'll administer the inoculations. That's what they're contracted to do, isn't it?'

'You're sticking to the avian flu story, then?' The Home Secretary sounded dubious.

The Prime Minister shrugged wearily. 'Don't see what else we can do. If we reveal it's bio-terrorism using an engineered virus, the rioting we've had so far will seem like a tussle at a choir boys' outing. We've used emergency powers to get a firm grip on the media. We'll just have to ride it out.'

The Home Secretary forwned. 'If we're sticking to that story, we ought to get a written scientific opinion to support it. Someone who's had no involvement so far.'

'Only Prentice knew it was engineered; only we know where it came from, and they're calling it avian flu on the Continent. It shouldn't be too difficult,' Saunders said.

'Why not have a word with Norden at the Ministry of Health?' the Prime Minister suggested. 'He'll give us a few names. And if they all turn out to be reluctant, we can hint at the possibility of a knighthood. That usually brings the buggers round.'

★   ★   ★

Loretta Fallon crossed Birdcage Walk, passed through the gates of St James's Park and headed out over the grass. It was cold now, and there was a hint of rain in the wind.

When she was well clear of strolling lovers, dog walkers and pram pushers, she took out her mobile, called Quest's number on to the screen and keyed it in.

The bleeping stopped, but there was no answering voice.

'Miss Quest?'

'Speaking.' The voice was husky and low. Distorted by the encryption, it could have been a man she was talking to.

'Loretta Fallon. We have to meet. Urgently.'

'Just say where.'

Loretta smiled. There was almost a note of boredom in Quest's voice. She was probably painting her nails. When she phoned some of the male agents she could hear them springing to attention.

'How about halfway: Peterborough? Grantham?'

'Fine. You choose.'

'Grantham. I'll come by train. Meet me outside what passes for a booking office in Grantham station in about two hours. Don't mention this to anyone. And I really do mean anyone.'

'I'll be there, and I won't.'

The connection went dead. Laconic little thing, Loretta mused. She closed the phone, began to slide it into the pocket of her coat, then paused. Her Judas kiss. When would Marcus collect his thirty pieces of silver? She flicked the phone open again and keyed in his number.

'Marcus?'

'Ma'am?'

'I've driven north. I'm somewhere between Peterborough and Grantham.'

'There's trouble?'

'House hunting. The terror's brought prices down. I thought I'd look for a retreat outside the city.'

'I think you're wise, ma'am. If things get much worse . . . '

'I'm going to try to find a hotel later. I wondered if you'd care to join me?'

'Marvellous! Would that be for dinner?'

Loretta smiled. He seemed genuinely keen. 'Just for the night. I've another property to see, then I'll book in somewhere. If you can get something to eat and head north, I'll call you about nine and let you know where I've landed.'

She clicked the phone shut, slid it into her pocket and began to walk back to the pathway.

10

The room was surprisingly large, the decorations a little faded, but the hotel seemed clean and well managed. Loretta stepped over to the window and drew red velvet curtains to shut out the night. 'Grantham!' she said, then laughed.

Samantha yawned. 'Thatcher country. The corner-shop shrine to profit and public service.'

Loretta turned. 'Can you remember Thatcher?'

'Not really. Family did a runner to Israel on election night.'

Loretta tugged open the mini bar. 'How about a drink?' She looked over the bed at Samantha and saw she'd settled into the only chair.

'Whisky would be fine.'

'Anything with it?'

'Neat.'

Loretta brought over the glass, then mixed a gin and tonic, kicked off her shoes and curled up on the bed. 'Sorry to bring you all this way, but we had to meet somewhere remote. You weren't followed, were you?'

'I could almost guarantee I wasn't. I'm

being watched closer to home, though.'

'That's probably going to stop. I've told the Prime Minister you're being taken off the search for the Prentices.'

'May I ask why?'

'They don't know how you'll respond when you find them.'

Samantha shrugged and raised her eyebrows.

'They want them dead or alive.'

'You mean they want them dead,' Samantha retorted.

'Probably.' Loretta looked down at her glass and shook it to make the ice tinkle.

'Why do they want them dead?'

Loretta gazed at the elegant young woman perched in the little Regency chair. 'Steady; we're only surmising they want them dead.' She sipped at her drink. 'When I demanded to know why they had to be found, they asked for my resignation.'

'Someone knows too much about something, or they're holding incriminating material. Who put the finger on me? Was it Marcus?'

Shrewd, Loretta thought. Out loud, she said, 'I think it's just the nature of the assignment and your reputation.'

'My reputation?'

'Perhaps they feel you're not compliant and

you'll refuse to act blindly.'

'It is Marcus!' Samantha laughed. 'The old related-to-royalty arsehole. They've been chattering over brandy and cigars at some club for smug bastards.'

'You're not, of course,' Loretta said.

'Not what?'

'Being taken off the assignment. But I'm going to instruct Marcus to move you back to counter-terrorism. I'll tell him I've asked another section head to find an agent to continue the search. How's progress, by the way?'

'Not made any,' Samantha said. 'Marcus got me into Porton Down and I looked over Prentice's laboratory. It's been sealed because of contamination. Found five bodies in those big refrigerated caskets the army sometimes uses to bring dead personnel back home. Prentice, a mathematician called Weaver, plus two women and another man. One casket empty.'

Loretta Fallon looked surprised. 'They weren't there yesterday.'

Samantha raised an eyebrow.

'Franklin, the director, phoned Bio Med Instrumentation and played merry hell about the woman they'd sent to do the servicing. They had to send a real maintenance man in and Marcus put an agent in with him. He reported a contaminated lab had been opened up. They serviced two instruments that had been sealed inside, and he helped carry the things back in. Everything seemed normal. He certainly didn't report bodies in freezer caskets.'

'What about beds?' Samantha asked. 'Did he see any beds in rooms off the laboratory?'

Loretta shook her head. 'You found beds?'

'Hospital bed with a drip stand and a vital signs monitor in one room. Ordinary beds in another. I surmised the two women were nurses brought in to care for Prentice. Perhaps the man was a doctor. I've no idea what Weaver was doing in there. He's supposed to be buried in a churchyard in Oxford.'

'Have you got the names of the women and the man?' Loretta asked.

Samantha reached for her bag, found a pad, and read out the names she'd taken from the wrist bands.

Loretta noted them down. 'What you say about nurses and doctors makes sense, but I'll have it checked out.'

'Wonder where they've taken the bodies?' Samantha said.

'God knows. Could still be in storage somewhere.' Loretta slid her glass on to a bedside table. 'Has the search for Ling

Prentice gone completely cold?'

'Not quite. She could be parted from her child. Marcus got a transcript of a phone tap: Prentice telling her to take a holiday and leave the child with a friend. I might be able to locate the friend. And Dr Weaver's daughter said she'd try and find a postcard of a holiday place she half-remembered Ling Prentice having sent her a couple of years ago. Sounds pretty tenuous, but perhaps I could go back to Oxford and check it out.'

Loretta shook her head. 'Don't go back to Oxford now you're officially off the search. I'll send someone to follow that up. How did you go in?'

'Solicitors trying to locate Ling Prentice in connection with a bequest: Baxter Allot and Jones. It's all in the report I submitted to Marcus.' Samantha watched Loretta Fallon making notes in a tiny leather-bound diary. 'The whole thing stinks,' Samantha went on. 'I'm pretty sure I'm under surveillance, they probably know I've checked out the lab at Porton Down, and Ling Prentice's sister-in-law's been visited twice by Serious Crime. We're not alone out there. I think we should let it ride; wait for the politicians to get impatient and show their hand.'

Loretta studied the black-haired woman sitting in the chair. Her long legs were crossed, and one of her strappy red and black shoes was dangling from her toes. The black suit with its broad red pinstripe looked fabulous. She must have had it specially made.

Their eyes met, and Samantha held her gaze. Jesus, Loretta thought, those eyes! It was like falling into an icy green sea and sinking into the darkness. She understood then what Marcus had meant when he'd said she wasn't the kind of woman a man would want to pay a call on. The treacherous old devil hadn't been lying about that. She lowered her gaze to the ice in her glass, shivered, then said, 'We can't let it ride. The PM's on my back about this one. If we don't get a result they'll put someone else in, and it would be better for the woman and her child if you found them first.'

'They're probably hoping I'll lead them to her,' Samantha said. 'Perhaps that's why they're having me watched.' She drained her glass. 'It's a typical politician's muddle. They've been naughty and now they're shitting themselves, trying to cover their tracks in case they get found out.'

Loretta Fallon laughed. 'Men! They never grow up. Where did you get that suit, by the way? Fits like a dream.'

'Little boutique in Knightsbridge. They've

got an angel of a seamstress who does the fitting. Who do I report to?'

'Me, of course. But don't try and contact me. I'll contact you.'

'What if I need instructions or clearance or something?' Samantha asked.

'You've got all the instructions you need. Just take whatever action you consider necessary and find the widow.' Loretta reached across the bed for her purse, clicked it open, and took out a credit card. 'Use this for travel and hotels. Don't include anything to do with the search on the expenses claims you submit to Marcus. And draw whatever you need from Ulrick at the armoury. If she queries something, just say it's for the Eden project.' She scribbled a number on a page at the back of the tiny diary, tore it out and passed it over. 'She'll ask you for digits from that number if you say Eden.'

Rising to her feet, Samantha said, 'Don't come down. I'll get reception to call a taxi to take me back to the car.'

'Find her,' Loretta said softly. 'And when you do, protect her and secure every document she has. I want to know what the widow's got that's bringing the buggers out in such a sweat.'

★ ★ ★

187

Samantha feigned memory lapse and made the driver take her from pub to pub, supposedly searching for her car. She kept checking the rear window, peering down brightly lit town-centre streets, dim urban streets, and night-black country lanes. When she was certain there was no tail, she directed the driver to the Brickmaker's Arms at Skelton.

It was after closing time and the floodlit car-park was empty. She climbed into the Ferrari Modena and roused the engine into life. As she pressed down the clutch, she caught the faint bleeping of her mobile phone. She took it out of her bag.

'Sam?'

'I'm here, Marcus.'

'Where the devil have you been. I've been trying to reach you for hours.' The refined voice betrayed tiredness and irritation.

'Out and about, trying to trace the Prentice family.'

'That's really why I'm phoning. Any progress?'

'None.' She smiled to herself. She could almost feel his agitation.

'Christ, Sam, the chief's taking a daily battering. Can't you come up with something we can tell the politicians?'

'Not a thing, Marcus, but I'm working on it, night and day.'

He let out a bitter laugh. 'You can say that

again. There was a hell of a row about your visit to the biological research centre.'

'Row?' she said sweetly.

'One of the machines you serviced is a total write-off, the other three were barely worth repairing. And they cost more than twenty-thou' apiece. Franklin, the director, went ballistic with Bio Med Instrumentation. I had to agree to meet the cost, plus a sweetener for old Franklin.'

'And what's the sweetener that's put the smile back on Conrad Franklin's face?'

'We've arranged a long weekend in Burgos with a rather fetching young lady we have on the books. Did it covertly through Bio Med, of course.'

'Burgos in northern Spain?'

'That's the place. He wanted somewhere he wasn't likely to be recognized.'

Samantha laughed huskily. She'd done more for old Franklin than he'd ever realize.

'Sent one of our people in with the Bio Med engineer,' Marcus said. 'He didn't notice anything unusual. How about you?'

'Pretty much the same,' Samantha said evasively.

'It's late. I'll leave you. Give it your best, Sam, and let me have a report tomorrow, even if it's no progress.'

She switched off the encrypted mobile,

tossed it on to the passenger seat, then coasted out of the car-park's misty light and roared off into the dark.

★ ★ ★

Liz Clayton relaxed her shoulders against Bruce Hadley's chest, settled her buttocks on to his naked thighs. She felt his hand move from her hip, his fingers spread across her stomach and comb into wiry hair. She gave a contented little sigh. These moments of calm after the passion, the time when he tenderly kissed her neck and shoulders, were always so very sweet.

'Peter's home tomorrow,' she said.

'Tomorrow's Thursday.' Bruce kissed the lobe of her ear. 'He comes home on Friday. His surgery's on Saturday morning.'

Liz laughed. 'You know more about his comings and goings than I do.'

'I had to book the room, put an ad in the paper and get a few letters out to constituents and the party faithful.'

'Do you think Alice suspects?' Liz's voice was distant; hardly more than a whisper.

The gentle kissing stopped. 'Why do you ask that?'

'Mmm . . . No reason. But women have a sixth sense.'

'Don't think so. We've been so careful, and the times we've been together in public we've had good reason to be.'

She turned her head towards him. He was planting kisses on her cheek now, his mouth moving slowly towards hers. 'Would you leave her?' she asked.

'Why on earth are we talking like this, Liz? You certainly pick your times.'

She laughed softly, felt his hand rise up her stomach and begin to fondle her breasts. 'Because,' she said coquettishly, then asked, 'would you?'

'Would I what?'

'Leave Alice?'

'You know I wouldn't. She'd be devastated. And she'd walk away with half a business that's been in the family for five generations.'

'I'd leave Peter,' she said. 'Like a shot. I've come to almost loathe him.'

'Why, Liz? He's a thoroughly decent human-being. He's my best friend. We went to school together; grew up together.'

'You know very well why.' There was a forlorn hopelessness in her voice. 'And what a sad old cliché: having an affair with your best-friend's wife.'

Bruce propped himself up on an elbow, returned his hand to her hip, and looked down at her. 'What's the matter, love? Have I

191

done something wrong?'

Liz Clayton sighed. 'No, Bruce, you've not done anything wrong. That's the trouble, you're so right for me. I just want more of you.' She rolled on to her back so she could look at him. He was frowning down at her. 'Sometimes,' she said, 'when it's over and we're lying like this, I get a weepy feeling because it won't be long before you leave me and go back to Alice, and I know it's never going to be any different.'

'I couldn't hurt Alice, Liz. And I'd be mortified if we hurt Peter.'

She drew a fingertip down the line of his nose, then stroked his lips. 'He hasn't touched me in a sexual way since we lost Matthew. I can see him now, cradling the body in his arms and crying like a baby. Bloody doctors should have known it was meningitis. And the selfish bastard thought the loss was only his; that he was the only one feeling any pain.'

Bruce drew her close, kissed her on the mouth, then hugged her. 'What the devil's got into you tonight, Liz?'

Moist eyes gazed up into his. 'Guilt, grief: God knows.' She began to caress his thigh, and almost immediately felt his flesh hardening against her hip. She choked back a sob, then let out a shaky laugh. 'You're a randy devil, Bruce Hadley.'

He dragged a pillow down the bed, settled it under her buttocks, then slid his body over hers. 'It's you. I just can't get enough of you,' he said, then kissed her on the mouth.

She wrapped her arms around him and closed her eyes; suddenly craving the fleeting release from guilt and sadness he was about to give her.

⋆ ⋆ ⋆

Tim Saunders loaded another disk and clicked the icons on the screen. Daniel Langdon had certainly been systematic; a disk for every year and a separate file for every sabbat. This was the last disk. He'd not found any images of himself without a mask on the previous four. Perhaps on this one?

He scrolled through Imbolc, Beltane and Lammas. When he opened up the file for Samhain, he found them: six clear pictures, his face exposed on every one, coupling with four different women. The horned god, that sinister presence in the torchlight, was in soft-focus on three of the shots. It would be obvious to anyone that the Government's Minister for Internal Security was participating in some kind of occult orgy.

His gaze wandered over the images of the

naked women. He could almost feel the warm willing flesh under his hands, hear the chanting and drumming, smell the aromatic oil burning in the torches. He wouldn't destroy the disks. The pictures they contained would nourish memories; keep them vivid. He'd hide them here, in his desk. They'd be something to relieve the tedium while he waited to vote during the endless all-night sessions they kept having now.

A red phone on his desk began to bleep. He picked up the handset and muttered, 'Saunders.'

'Trantham here, Minister. You're staying on late at the House, tonight?'

'Debating an extension to the emergency powers legislation, Major. Considering internment.'

'Not before time. Did you receive the boxes?'

'I did, and many thanks. Passed them on to the counter-terrorism people. They're sifting through the stuff now.'

'Good. Jolly good,' Major Trantham said. Then, changing the subject: 'We've had to remove the bodies from Porton Down.'

Tim Saunders sat a little straighter in his chair. 'I thought Conrad Franklin agreed to seal up the lab for six months; let the dust settle and give us time to sort out the disposal?'

'Conrad contacted me last night, Minister. A woman visited the place to service instruments and made an absolute mess of it. He wondered if she'd been sent in.'

'What did this woman look like?'

'Black hair, glamorous, expensively dressed. Oh,' — Major Trantham suddenly remembered something — 'and driving a Ferrari sports car.'

Saunders chuckled. 'Bet she made an impression. Doesn't sound like an instrument engineer.'

'That's what Conrad thought, so he contacted me and we did the move during the night. When he played merry hell with the instrument makers, they confirmed she was one of their people. Very apologetic; said she'd just finished training. Sent men in straight away to put things right.'

'Did she get into Prentice's laboratory?'

'Door seals were intact and the windows can't be opened; they're bedded into the lab walls on rubber gaskets. Had them checked for signs of tampering, but they didn't notice any. Conrad examined the laboratory himself and didn't find any signs of disturbance.' The major's voice was unruffled. He was just doing his duty, imparting information to his political master.

'Can we trust old Franklin?' Saunders asked.

'Absolutely, Minister. One of us. Completely on the square. Thing is, we've got to give some thought to the disposal of the bodies now he's turfed them out and claimed his lab back.'

'Remind me again how many, Major?'

'Two women and three men. And we've no death certificates. I had the truck bring them back here, to Catterick. Got them locked in an empty ammunition store.'

Tim Saunders felt uneasy. 'Won't word get round the camp?'

'Told the men who transported the bodies here that they were medical personnel shipped back from Iraq. Said they'd been exposed to contamination so they'd had to be checked at Porton; said we were having difficulty tracing next of kin because of the flu epidemic. Trouble is, without death certificates, disposal by conventional means is out of the question.'

Might not be in another month, Tim Saunders reflected grimly, then said, 'Can't we consider unconventional means? What about the team that went in and switched the third nurse for Weaver's body, just before the burial?'

'Conrad insisted on that, Minister. He had to have Weaver's body for tests to make absolutely sure there'd been no infection spread. And swapping a body at a small independent undertaker's is one thing; disposing of five at one go is quite another.'

'I take your point,' Saunders said, then laughed. 'Good job the widow didn't ask to view the corpse.'

'Did the swap in the early hours, just before the coffin went into the hearse. Anyway, not much chance of the widow wanting a last look. It seems he died in his mistress's bed.'

Saunders chuckled. 'If I provide you with death certificates for three men and two women, could you get some undertaker to arrange disposal at the local crem'?'

'I think that would be best, Minister.'

'Bell's ringing. I'll have to get down to the division lobbies. You'll have the certificates within the next forty-eight hours, Major. Keep me posted.'

11

Samantha glanced down into the cul-de-sac. The black van was parked across the road again today. They still had her under surveillance, and it was likely that her mobile calls, and her land-line calls from the house, were being monitored, too.

She went down to the first floor and entered the sitting-room. More images of wreckage and destruction were flickering across the television screen. Realizing she hadn't caught the news the day before, she turned up the sound.

' . . . and the two Algerians arrested in connection with the derailment of an Edinburgh to London train, just south of Peterborough, early yesterday morning, have been charged with offences under the terrorism acts. The death toll currently exceeds a hundred and fifty, with more than two hundred seriously . . . '

Despite all their efforts, the terrorists were still bombing at will. She sighed. The train derailment would be someone else's problem. After this Prentice business was sorted, she was taking leave, and if Marcus didn't authorize it, she'd resign. As she switched off the set, she suddenly remembered Loretta Fallon had been in Peterborough. Loretta could have been a passenger on the train. If the chief was amongst the dead, there would be changes. She had to consider what that might mean for her. On a purely practical level, she had to contact Ulrick, the armourer, before any successor changed the rules of engagement.

Her mobile began to bleep. Tossing aside the copies of *Vogue* and *Harper's* strewn over the sofa, she uncovered it and keyed it on.

'Got some bad news for you, Sam.' The male voice sounded apprehensive.

Samantha took a deep breath. It could be about Fallon. 'What might that be, Marcus?'

'I've got to take you off the Prentice search.'

She laughed. He'd had his instructions. 'That's good news, Marcus. I can take the extended leave you promised.'

'Well, Sam, it's not quite that simple.' His voice was wheedling.

'Seems simple to me, Marcus. You don't want me on the Prentice search; you promised I could take leave when it was over: what could be more simple than that?'

'The derailment, yesterday. Blighters mined a hundred yards of track, watched the train pass over, then triggered the detonators. We've got the people who laid the mines: immigrant agricultural workers. Farmer housed them in caravans in a field overlooking the line. Counter-terrorism people found mines and detonators in one of the vans.'

'Russian stuff?'

'American. They probably picked it up in Iraq. Powerful enough to turn a tank over. Crowded train, not many survivors: it's a wipe-out. I've got to ask you to join the hunt for the organizers.'

Samantha smiled. He'd removed her from the Prentice assignment very deftly. On reflection, she had to say yes to the job. It would be some kind of cover while she went on searching for the mother and child. 'You said I could take leave, Marcus.' Her voice was accusing.

'Sam, I'm sorry, but the situation's dire. Move in on this one and do what you can. I'll try and slide someone else over within a couple of days, a week at the most.'

'And I'm off the Prentice search?'

'Finished with it,' Marcus said.

'I want that leave, Marcus. I can't go on like this for ever. I'm burnt out, a danger to myself and the department. I'll give it a week, and then we must have a serious talk.'

'Thanks, Sam.' He sounded relieved she'd

not protested more. 'Just give it your best and I promise . . . '

Samantha switched off the encrypted mobile. The old related-to-royalty arsehole with all his empty promises was becoming too much of a bore.

She couldn't procrastinate any longer. She had to begin the search for Ling Prentice and her child. Alice Hadley had placed her trust in her, and Loretta Fallon's instructions had been simple and clear.

Samantha buttoned up the jacket of her suit and linked the hooks that fastened the astrakhan collar around her throat. Balenciaga in military mood. The bold hound's-tooth check made it rather fetching in a business-like kind of way. After making a hurried choice of shoes, she took a blank envelope, went down to the street, and headed for the post box at the junction with the main road.

The walk back gave her an opportunity to study the van. There was no one in the cab, but a partition had been installed to screen off the back. She gazed at her reflection in rear windows that had the impenetrable glitter of insects' eyes. Were her watchers staring back at her? She stuck out her tongue, smiled brazenly, then let her hips sway as she strutted back to the house. If they were intercepting calls, she hoped they'd logged the one from Marcus that morning and heard him taking her off the Prentice search. And if they were decoding encrypted calls, everyone in the department was in deep shit.

Climbing into the Ferrari, she headed towards the town centre. The black van wouldn't follow her. They'd check the direction she headed in, then call up a tail parked on the main road.

She drove slowly, constantly checking the rear-view mirror. A big Ford was following. There was no mistaking it. Stopping at a row of shops, she made a couple of purchases, then continued on down urban streets, heading for the ring road. The Ford was always there, maintaining a discreet distance.

In the town she paid cash for a mobile phone, giving the name and Oxford address of Ling Prentice, then used it to call a motel at a motorway junction and book a room with two single beds for a Mrs Ling Prentice and her daughter, Wei. Ten minutes and some jumped lights later, she'd lost the tail and found a public call box built against the wall of a post office.

'Stationery and Equipment.' The young man sounded eager to please.

'I'd like an armchair.'

Music sounded faintly, then the line clicked

and a female voice said, 'Hullo?'

'Ulrick, the armourer?'

'This is Stationery and Equipment. What's your name?'

'Bathsheba.'

'And what's the first and last two digits of your security code?'

Samantha recited numbers, then listened to keys tapping.

'This is the armourer, Bathsheba. Long time no hear. What can I do?'

'I need a four-by-four: something big and strong; something powerful,' Samantha said.

'Got a Range Rover. Four-litre engine, tinted windows, back seats removed, armoured and strengthened. Been used for escorting royalty: a sort of getaway car in the event of trouble.'

'Don't they need escorting any more?'

Ulrick laughed. 'More than ever, but we renew the transport every year.'

'Sounds fine,' Samantha said. 'And I need a thousand rounds for a Heckler sub, and a dozen boxes of shells for a nine millimetre automatic.'

'No problem.'

'And some RPGs. American, with disposable launchers; not that heavy Russian gear.'

Samantha heard laughter. 'Whose war are you fighting in, honey? Can't do rocket-propelled grenades: very restricted.'

'They're for the Eden project.'

'And what would your second and fourth digits be?'

Samantha unfolded the tiny diary page Loretta Fallon had given her and gave the numbers.

'OK. How many?'

'Let me have a couple, with high-explosive grenades, something potent.' Samantha had plucked the figure out of the air. If she had to use the things, she probably wouldn't have a chance to let off more than one.

'Anything else?'

Samantha heard the beat of a rotor, stared up through the glass side of the booth and saw the machine hovering a few hundred feet above. They had resources and they were organized. When they'd lost her on the road, they'd called for back-up. 'I think that's it,' she said.

'When and where?'

'Tomorrow,' Samantha said. 'The Norris Motel at junction twenty-seven on the M62 near Leeds. There'll be a towel draped over the cill of a window overlooking the rear car-park. If it could be left as close as possible to that?'

'A tall blonde called Sharlene will make the delivery,' Ulrick said. 'She'll ask for the first and fifth digits of your Eden code. Have them ready or she'll walk off. Who's accepting delivery?'

'Tell Sharlene to ask at reception for Mrs Ling Prentice. There'll be a hire car she can use for the return journey.'

Samantha replaced the handset. The helicopter was still thudding overhead, but it had drifted out of view. Sidling out of the booth, she waited a few seconds, then climbed into the Ferrari and headed home.

★   ★   ★

The Minister for Internal Security gave the Home Secretary a knowing glance. The Prime Minister was looking grey and drawn. The deterioration over the past month had been dramatic. He'd even abandoned that strutting, elbows-out power walk he'd cultivated during his second term. It was only a matter of time.

'Did you talk to Marcus?' The Prime Minister glanced at Peter Clayton.

'Yes, Charles. He took Quest off the Prentice search three days ago. Fallon must have told him to deal with it immediately after the meeting.'

'Thought she might have reneged on it,' Saunders muttered. He unscrewed the cap of his pen, began to doodle over the cover of a report on emergency measures for the disposal of the dead.

'Who's replaced her?' the Prime Minister demanded.

'Marcus said he'd do his best to find out,' the Home Secretary said. 'Fallon told him she'd be instructing the other section head to assign an agent.'

'Looks like Fallon suspects Marcus.'

The Home Secretary shrugged. 'She's not stupid, Charles. It's more than likely.'

The Prime Minister glanced at Saunders. 'You still have Quest under surveillance?'

Saunders finished inking in the eye socket on the skull. 'I thought it best. Just in case Fallon's stringing us along.'

'We'd better keep it that way,' the Prime Minister muttered. He turned back to the Home Secretary. 'How much do you think Quest knows?'

'She kept telling Marcus she'd got nowhere, and we don't think she got to the Prentice house before Tim's people cleared it. Marcus did say Quest was cynical about the search, though; said she suspected Prentice was in-volved in racially targeted biological warfare.'

'What isn't the bitch cynical about?' Tim Saunders demanded. He began to sketch in the skull's lower jaw. He decided not to mention that someone, possibly the woman called Quest, might have checked out the laboratory at Porton Down. No point setting hares running when he didn't have any facts.

The Prime Minister frowned. 'Situation's even more fraught after that derailment. Two hundred reported dead now and God knows how many injured. And Fallon's budget allocation! Christ, you'd think they'd get the terrorists *before* they planted the bombs.'

'They've done pretty well,' the Home Secretary said defensively. 'If immigration control was half as efficient.'

Saunders bristled. 'The buggers are home-grown, Alan.'

'Not the ones who did the latest train job,' the Home Secretary retorted. 'They were Algerian agricultural workers: illegals.'

'Let's not argue amongst ourselves,' the Prime Minister said irritably. 'Who's rooting out the organizers of the train bombing?'

'Quest. Marcus moved her in when he took her off the Prentice search.'

The Prime Minister's face was lined and tired. On television, at the dispatch box, he managed to hide it, but here he was letting it show. He frowned and returned to the thing that was troubling him. 'How much do you think she really knows about Prentice and Porton Down?'

The Home Secretary shrugged.

'If that ever got out it would mean more than loss of office,' the Prime Minister said grimly. 'Did what's-his-name at the Ministry of Health arrange for us to be given expert advice to support the avian flu scenario?'

'It's in preparation. The usual report for us and a paper's going to be published in the *British Medical Journal*. Some professor at one of the red-bricks is doing it.'

'It wasn't difficult, then?'

'Difficult?'

'Finding an academic who'd support the avian flu story?'

The Home Secretary shook his head. 'Only Prentice realized the virus was engineered. Prentice was the only scientist looking at targeting it on other ethnic groups. It's just an avian flu variant as far as the scientific community is concerned.'

'What are they saying about it in Europe?'

'Same story.'

'And what are their security services saying?'

The Home Secretary smiled. 'That's a question best put to the Foreign Secretary. We could ask Stanley to hang back after the cabinet meeting.'

The Prime Minister nodded. Relief was softening his features a little. 'Provided we cover our tracks, it looks as if we're in the clear.'

Saunders glanced up. 'Cover our tracks?'

'We've got to have the widow and child killed; Quest, too. Who knows what that bitch has uncovered, and according to Marcus she's a pretty good idea what's been going on. Can you organize it, Tim?'

'If we can find the widow and the kid there shouldn't be any problem. Quest's under surveillance and we can take her out when we're ready.'

'You'd kill the child, Charles?' The Home Secretary seemed shocked.

'We're virtually in a war situation, Peter,' the Prime Minister reminded him irritably. 'Decisions we've taken to ensure the security of the state could be misconstrued. And I'll tell you again, I'm not prepared to be pulled down by a couple of women and a child.'

'But a child?'

'She's five years old and bright enough to take in what the mother tells her. Even if she can't absorb details, she'll be aware that something's very wrong. So, gentlemen, for our future peace of mind . . . '

★   ★   ★

Samantha drove through a sprawling council estate where a few well-tended houses were dotted amongst neglect and dereliction.

Determined to shake off anyone trying to follow her, she'd parked the Ferrari at Barfield Railway Station and transferred to a small hire car. On the journey to Leeds, she'd repeatedly checked the road behind and the air space above, but she'd seen nothing untoward.

A telephone call to the manager of the Blissful Moments massage parlour had got her the address of Ling Prentice's friend, Kwan Peng. Samantha, doing her best to sound like a Chinese woman struggling with English, had told him she was Kwan's sister. A broad Scottish voice had asked her to tell Kwan to get her scrawny arse back to the parlour because he was desperately short of girls.

Attlee Avenue, Morrison Walk; the street names dated the place. Samantha found Bevin Road, made a left and tried to count numbers on doors and gates. She stopped outside a semi-detached house that faced three or four boarded-up properties. An old car had been driven through a gap in the concrete fence and parked in the front garden. Dirty net curtains shrouded the windows, and no one had bothered to paint the new front door.

She picked her way down an uneven path between the parked car and an overgrown

210

lawn, then walked through a narrow passage between the gable wall and an outhouse. The gate at the end opened a few inches, then stuck. She wrapped her green satin coat over her dress, then squeezed through to a back garden that was even more untidy and overgrown than the front.

Pausing beside a window, she peered through. A black-haired child was kneeling on a chair in front of a cluttered table, spreading jam on slices of bread. Small for a five year old, she was engrossed in the task, the knife big and unwieldy in her tiny hand.

When the child glanced up and saw Samantha, her eyes widened and her face radiated joy. She dropped the knife, slid from the chair, and disappeared from view. A key scraped in a lock. When the back door opened the joy faded from the child's face like the sudden dimming of a bright light.

'It's Wei, isn't it?' Samantha spoke softly. 'Wei Prentice?'

'I thought you were my mummy.' The child was on the verge of tears.

Samantha realized what had happened. A black-haired woman in a jade-green oriental dress covered in embroidered dragons; the little girl's mistake was understandable.

'Where is your mummy? Isn't she here?'

The child stayed silent, just gazed up at

Samantha, her tiny mouth trembling.

'May I come in?'

'Kwan say no one to come in.'

'Your Aunt Alice sent me. Do you remember her, the lady with the big house?'

Wei Prentice nodded.

'Can I talk to Kwan?'

'She's asleep. She's been sick.'

Samantha bent down, took the child in her arms, and stepped up into the kitchen. Wei didn't resist. Her dress was grimy and crumpled, and she smelt as dirty as she looked.

The sink was full of dishes. Half-used packs of sliced bread, jars of jam, cereal packets, milk cartons and other domestic debris littered every surface.

Closing the door with her heel, Samantha brushed hair from the girl's face.

'Where's my mummy? Are you going to be my mummy now?'

A month is a long time in the life of a small child, Samantha reflected. 'I've come for you,' she said. 'I'm going to make you safe, then I'm going to find your mother and bring her to you.' She felt Wei's arm moving around her neck, and she held her close.

'Where's Kwan?'

'Asleep. I was making her dinner.'

'Is she upstairs?'

The child nodded.

Samantha passed through a door at the end of the kitchen, found herself in the hall, and began to climb uncarpeted stairs. 'Which room?'

Wei Prentice pointed to a door.

Samantha knocked gently, called the woman's name, then, leaving Wei on the landing, stepped inside.

The curtains were drawn and a table lamp was providing the only illumination. Plates of uneaten bread and jam and cups of water covered the bedside table and the top of a chest of drawers.

Samantha stepped closer to the bed. 'Miss Peng?' she said softly.

There was no answer.

She reached down and drew a vomit-stained sheet clear of the woman's face. Samantha guessed she'd been dead for two, possibly three days.

Replacing the sheet, she went back to the landing. 'You were right,' she said to the little girl. 'Kwan's still sick and she's having a nice long sleep. Where's your room?'

The child pointed, and they entered a bedroom that over-looked the back garden. The single bed was a tangled mess, and books and toys were strewn over the floor.

'Have you any clean clothes?'

Samantha ignored the shake of the head, searched through an airing cupboard and took out clean things. Some she laid in a suitcase she found on top of a wardrobe, the rest she took with her when she led Wei Prentice into the bathroom. When they emerged, Wei looked more like a five-year-old girl should.

Taking her back to her room, Samantha said, 'Put any books and toys you want to bring in the case while I go and tell Kwan we're leaving. Will you do that for me?'

The child nodded and began to pack her toys.

Samantha returned to the front bedroom. Kwan Peng would probably have brought any important papers up here with her. Flinching at the odours of stale vomit and bodily decay, she began to search through the chest of drawers, then checked inside a flimsy wardrobe and the bedside cabinet. Amongst the clothes and clutter, she found some cheap jewellery and about £200 in an envelope.

Reaching down into the gap between bed and bedside cabinet, she felt a handbag and lifted it up. It contained a driving licence, cosmetics, condoms, a substantial fold of banknotes, and a handful of small coins.

She drew down the sheet. Kwan Peng was huddled in a foetal position, her red satin underskirt rucked up around her waist exposing white cotton pants that were badly soiled. Nothing was concealed about the body, so Samantha slid her hand under the pillows, felt a leather wallet, and drew it out. She flipped it open, found about a hundred pounds in notes, some credit cards, Kwan Peng's identity card and social security documents.

There were no letters, no postcards, no jotted phone numbers; nothing that would lead her to Ling Prentice.

But Kwan could do her friend a final favour. Samantha reached for her own bag, found the documents she'd taken from beneath the lining paper in Ling's dressing-table drawer, and made a selection. She removed all trace of Kwan from the leather wallet, substituted Ling Prentice's marriage licence and Wei's christening photograph, then slid it half under the pillow, close to Kwan's cheek.

Samantha gazed down at the body. It had that unmistakable greeny-grey pallor. Opaque brown eyes were half closed, and she could see tiny wide-spaced teeth behind parted lips. Death had robbed the woman of all dignity. Samantha drew the sheet over Kwan's face, picked up her bag, and returned to the child's bedroom.

Wei Prentice was trying to cram a doll into an already over-full case.

'Shall we carry her?' Samantha asked.

The child nodded, lifted out the rag doll, and Samantha arranged the remaining books and toys so the case would shut.

Taking the little girl's hand, Samantha headed along the landing, her stiletto heels thudding on bare boards. She paused outside the half-open bedroom door.

'Say good-bye to Kwan.'

Wei Prentice clasped and unclasped a tiny hand in a kind of wave. 'Bye, Kwan.' The child's farewell was no more than a faint whisper; a desolate sound in the house of the dead.

12

Samantha made Wei Prentice comfortable in the red hire car, then fastened her seat belt. She glanced around. The road was deserted, and there were no helicopters droning across the watery grey sky.

Kwan Peng's house and the adjoining dwellings were the only ones showing signs of occupation. Others had recently been boarded up, and two had been reduced to fire-damaged shells. A dog began to howl behind one of the houses. Plague and crime; death and destruction.

She slid into the driving seat and slammed the door, then reached over and gave the little girl's hand a squeeze. 'Are you hungry?'

Wei took a firmer hold on her rag doll and blinked up at her.

Samantha smiled. 'How about a nice meal, then we'll go shopping; buy you lots of new clothes?'

The merest flicker of a smile passed over the child's lips. Samantha gave her hand another squeeze, then drove out of the council estate and began to cruise through riot-damaged inner suburbs, heading for the centre of Leeds.

After a meal Wei had been too tired to eat, and the briefest of shopping expeditions, Samantha was putting candy-striped bags into the boot of the car. Wei Prentice was strapped into her seat. Irregular hours, too little sleep, and little or no food, had left her pale-faced and dark around the eyes. She was sleepy now. When Samantha wound Wei's seat into a reclining position, her eyes finally closed.

There were phone calls she had to make: calls Wei Prentice couldn't be allowed to hear. The car park was deserted. Samantha shut the child inside the car, groped in her bag for Kwan Peng's mobile phone, checked its number, then called the Blissful Moments massage parlour.

'Mr Taggart. I want to talk to Mr Taggart.' Once again, Samantha did her best to raise the pitch of her voice and make it sound like a Chinese woman struggling with English.

'He's interviewing a girl. I can't — '

'Tell him it's Meiko: Kwan's sister. I got bad news about Kwan.'

'Bad news?' The woman sounded concerned.

'Very bad. She's dead. Got to speak to Mr Taggart.'

'Was it the flu epidemic?'

'Think so,' Samantha said. 'Can I talk to Mr Taggart?'

'That's four girls in a month. I'm sorry, love. Your sister, was it? God, I'm sorry. Hang on, I'll get Scotty for you.'

Samantha heard the phone clatter down, the faint sound of a woman's voice, then the rattle as the handset was picked up again.'

'Taggart.'

'Kwan won't be coming back. She's dead. Been sick with this flu thing.'

'Wendy's just told me,' came the Scottish voice. 'I'm sorry: real sorry. She was a good kid. When was it?'

'Two days ago, maybe more. She was looking after a little girl: Ling Prentice's child . . . '

'Prentice . . . Prentice?' Recognition suddenly sounded in his voice. 'You mean Ling Haifong. Prentice was her married name. She got off with one of the punters and married him. Be about six or seven years ago. Professional guy quite a bit older than her. What about the child?'

'She's not here. Has someone at the parlour taken her?'

'Not there? Just a minute.'

Samantha heard him yelling for the girl called Wendy, a muffled conversation, then he was back on the line.

'No one here's taken the kid. Perhaps one of the neighbours?'

219

'I try neighbours,' Samantha said. 'Can you get hold of the girl's mother: Ling Prentice who used to be Ling Haifong?'

'Don't have her number. Don't know where she's living. She phoned the parlour a few times and talked to Kwan. Is her number amongst Kwan's things?'

'I look. But I give you mine,' Samantha said, and recited the number of Kwan's phone. 'If she phones in would you get her to call me so I can talk to her about her little girl?'

'Sure. When's the funeral? Some of the girls might want to go.'

'Man say six, seven weeks, maybe more.'

'It's getting worse. And I'll soon have no girls. Might have to close the place. Phone me, love; phone me when you've got a date.'

'Date?'

'For the funeral.'

Samantha switched off Kwan's mobile and looked down into the car. Wei Prentice was sleeping. Her chin had sunk into her chest and her grip on a psychedelic rabbit they'd bought in Leeds had relaxed.

Still using Kwan's phone, she dialed 999 and asked for the police, then watched a man walk down the line of cars, climb into one, and start the engine. As he was driving past, a female voice said, 'Police. Can I have your name and address?'

'Want to report a dead body in a house.'

'Can I have your name and address?'

'Dead woman called Prentice. Ling Prentice.'

'No, not the name of the deceased. I must have your name and address.'

'I'm not dead. Dead woman called Prentice. Body at thirty-seven Bevin Avenue. It's a big council estate just outside Leeds.'

'And where are you, and what's your name? It's important I have your name and address.' The woman sounded irate now.

'Dead woman called Prentice. She at my sister's house.' Samantha repeated the address, then switched off the phone.

Sliding into the car, Samantha closed the door as gently as she could. The call to the massage parlour might bring her closer to Ling Prentice. The call to the police should stir muddy waters.

No one followed her on the journey out of Leeds, and she left the motorway at junction twenty-seven. The Norris Motel was signposted at the top of the access road. She drove on for a couple of hundred yards, then turned into the forecourt.

Wei Prentice was still asleep, but Samantha couldn't wait any longer. She had to book in and be ready to take delivery of the Range

Rover and her mini-arsenal. She slipped on her sunglasses, gathered the still sleepy child into her arms, took the shopping bags out of the boot, then went into the modest reception area.

'Prentice . . . Mrs Ling Prentice?' The young man dragged his eyes off the embroidered dragons writhing over the bodice of her dress and busied himself at a keyboard. 'Here we are: ground floor double, at the back, with two single beds. Just for the one night?'

'Could be two nights. I'll be able to let you know first thing tomorrow,' Samantha said.

He spun the register round and handed her a pen. Samantha entered Ling Prentice's name and Oxford address.

'May I see your identity cards?'

Samantha clicked open her green Ferreti bag, pushed the contents around, then gave him a radiant smile. 'Sorry. We're only up here for a couple of days, and I've walked out of the house without our papers.'

'They're getting pretty strict about identity checks.' He frowned. 'Have you a bill, a car licence or something?'

Samantha dipped into her bag again and groped amongst Ling Prentice's papers. She'd left the marriage licence beside Kwan's body, but she still had Wei's birth certificate.

'Would this do? It's my daughter's. It has both our names on it.'

He glanced at the strip of paper. 'That's fine, Mrs Prentice.' Then he muttered, 'ID child's birth cert',' as he tapped at the keyboard. Reaching into a drawer, he took out a magnetic card and handed it to her. 'Room twelve. Through those doors and down the corridor. It's on the left; about halfway down.'

Brown cord carpeting, magnolia walls, chintz curtains and matching bedspreads; it was basic, functional and clean. Dropping the bags on to one of the beds, Samantha sat Wei on the other and smiled down at her. Brown eyes, dark-rimmed and unblinking, gazed back at her out of a wan face.

'How about a nice warm bath, then we can put some of your new clothes on?'

Wei let the psychedelic rabbit drop and lifted up her arms.

Samantha took that as a yes, picked her up and started for the tiny bathroom. The phone on the table between the beds began to bleep.

'Mrs Prentice? Lady here to see you about a hire car? She said you're having problems with it?'

'I'll be right out.'

The young woman called Sharlene had very short blonde hair, blue eyes and a deep tan. She was almost six-feet tall.

'Mrs Prentice?'

Samantha nodded.

Sharlene beamed down at Wei. 'Aren't you a little cutie.' She glanced back at Samantha. 'You've got a problem with the hire car? Can we take a look?'

As they headed across the front car-park, Sharlene said, 'What's the first and fifth digits of your Eden code?'

Samantha recited the numbers.

'Range Rover's parked round the back.' Sharlene held out a set of keys. 'The stuff you requisitioned is behind the seats, sheeted over.'

'Thanks,' Samantha said, 'I'm grateful.' She handed Sharlene the keys and paperwork for the hire car.

'Where's the return depot?' Sharlene asked.

'Barfield Railway Station. The hire car office is in the entrance hall. When you hand it back, would you tell them I've died in Leeds: flu epidemic?'

'Will do.' Sharlene beamed down at Wei and ruffled her hair. 'Got your mummy's good looks, haven't you? How about a smile? No?' She laughed, then somehow managed to fold herself into the tiny car.

Samantha took Wei into her arms. As they

watched the red Fiat drive out of the car park and head off towards the motorway, she felt the child's arm curling around her neck. She turned and looked at her. Their faces were very close.

'The lady said you were my mummy. Are you going to be my mummy now?'

Samantha smoothed Wei's ruffled hair, kissed her cheek and held her more tightly. 'I'm going to find your mummy, and when I do I'm going to bring her to you. Crispin's going to take care of you while I'm searching.'

'Crispin?'

'My friend. He's nice. You'll like him.'

'Can't he search and you stay?'

Samantha thought the question was best evaded. 'Let's have that bath,' she said brightly. 'And you can choose which dress and shoes you want to wear. Then we'll go and see Crispin.'

*　　★　　★*

Samantha soon discovered that Wei Prentice was only aware of the most basic facts. Her father was working in America. She'd left home with her mother in the night, and Kwan was caring for her because her mother had to hide from bad men.

'Did your mummy say where she was

going?' Samantha took the Barfield exit from the motorway and headed up an incline to a roundabout on the ring road.

The child shook her head, then straightened her legs and wiggled her feet so she could admire her new white and yellow shoes.

'Do you think she went to your holiday home?'

'What's a holiday home?'

'A house where you go to spend your holidays.'

Wei allowed her legs to fall back and gave Samantha a puzzled look.

Samantha tried another approach. 'When Mummy and Daddy took you away on holiday, where did you go?'

Wei remained silent.

'Did you go in an aeroplane?'

She shook her head.

'Did you go on a train or a big ship?'

The little girl shook her head and the beginnings of a smile shaped her lips.

Samantha laughed huskily. 'You're playing games with me, Miss Prentice.'

The smile became more obvious. 'Have you hurt your throat?' Wei asked.

'Hurt my throat?'

'When you talk it's all soft and whispery.'

Samantha reached over and squeezed Wei's hand. 'It's just the way my voice is. I can't help it. Now, be serious for me, because it's important. Did you go in an aeroplane when you went on holiday?'

'No aeroplane.'

'Just Daddy's car?'

Wei nodded.

Recalling her conversation with Rachel Weaver, Samantha said, 'Lots of food and clothes packed into the car?'

The little girl nodded again. 'And toys and games.'

Samantha turned off the ring road and drove into one of Barfield's more exclusive suburbs. Here, big old houses fronted on to quiet streets that hadn't been scarred by the rioting. The Range Rover was handling like a tank compared to the Ferrari, but it made her feel secure.

'Was it a long ride in the car?'

'All day long. We had to stop for meals and things.'

'Things?'

Wei gave her a disdainful look. 'Wee-wees.'

'I'll bet this place was called Devon?' Samantha said.

Wei shook her head and her smile became cunning.

'I'll bet this place was called Scotland?'

Another shake of the head.

'I can't guess. You tell me.'

She chuckled. 'It was called Narnia.'

Samantha's heart sank. She'd thought she was getting somewhere. 'And you went through a wardrobe and found a lion and a witch?'

Wei nodded and laughed.

'Narnia's a make-believe place. It couldn't have been Narnia.'

'Daddy said it was Narnia.' Wei said airily, as if she was calling on the ultimate authority.

Samantha slowed, negotiated some massive concrete road blocks, then drove on down a tree-lined avenue where detached houses were set back behind deep gardens. Turning into a street of smart little shops, she cruised past a florist's, a couple of boutiques, a delicatessen, a wine merchant, and an antique dealer, then parked outside the hairdresser's. The interior behind the art deco design frosted on to the window was dark and empty, but a light was on in the flat above, challenging the gloom of the overcast evening.

No one had followed her, she was sure of it. She held the door open and listened to the after-closing-time silence for a few moments, then unstrapped Wei, gathered her into her arms, and climbed out of the four-by-four. The cloying fragrances of the hairdressing trade assailed her as she made her way through the shop to the staff room at the back, then climbed carpeted stairs to the flat above.

Crispin was waiting for them in the obsessively clean and tidy home he'd shared with his lover, Jeremy. He smiled as he took hold of Wei's hands. The little girl seemed unsure but captivated; responsive to the smile, the handsome features, the physical perfection of the man.

'Come through and sit down, sweetheart,' Crispin said.

Wei buried her face in Samantha's neck, suddenly shy, and the three of them moved into a living-room that had pale blue-grey walls, a carpet that matched the wall colour perfectly, and a sofa and easy chairs with white loose covers.

'Something smells good,' Samantha said. She gave him a searching look. Beneath the fatherly expression he seemed distraught.

Crispin sighed. 'Sausages, beans and chips.'

Samantha laughed. 'Hardly your style. I was expecting eggs Benedict, at least.'

'Fine cuisine's a waste of time, Sam. I know from my sister's kids.'

Samantha lowered Wei on to the sofa. 'Did you bring the syringe and the serum?' The child slipped her thumb into her mouth and began to watch a television programme.

Crispin nodded, took Samantha by the

229

hand, led her into a lavish little kitchen, then whispered, 'You can't do it, Sam. You can't stick needles into the kid.'

'She's got to be protected. The woman who was looking after her has just died in the epidemic.'

'Then find someone else to do it. She'll never forget it was you who hurt her with the needle.' He grabbed a fork and began to turn sausages over beneath the grill.

Samantha gave a resigned sigh. 'You're right. I'll have to find someone else.' Then she made her voice tender as she said, 'Tell me what's wrong, Crispin?'

'Can't bear the place, Sam. Too many memories. I've been sleeping on the sofa; I just couldn't get into the bed. And I've taken all his clothes and things to the Oxfam shop. Seeing them every time I opened the wardrobe or a drawer was crucifying me.' Close to tears now, he lifted a basket of chips from the fryer.

Samantha slid her arms around him, stood on tiptoe and kissed his cheek. 'It gets easier to bear, Crispin. It just takes time.'

He gave her a grateful look. 'You'd better go to her, Sam. We can't leave the kid alone.'

Back in the living-room, Samantha noticed that the collection of silver-framed photographs of Crispin and Jeremy had gone. They, too, had become unbearable reminders of a happiness lost. She sank into the sofa, lifted Wei on to her lap, and felt her snuggling into her as she sucked noisily on her thumb.

When Crispin had bustled in with the meal and begun to coax Wei to eat it, Samantha took Kwan Peng's phone into the bedroom. She found the telephone directory, chose a doctor's surgery at random, and dialled the number.

After a long wait, the phone clicked, and a voice said, 'Doctor Mahmood.'

'I'd like you to immunize a little girl against the flu epidemic.'

'Is she a patient of mine?' He sounded agitated.

'We're visitors to the town. We're driving south tomorrow, and I want her immunizing before we go,' Samantha said.

'I'm just leaving the surgery. Some idiots have been spreading a rumour that terrorists started the epidemic and targeted it on the whites. There's rioting in the old part of town; Sheldon Park's a battlefield. I've got to get home to my wife and family. Can't you find another — '

Samantha glanced at the directory and checked the address. 'I can be there in ten minutes.'

'The vaccine's not particulary effective. It's

almost a waste of time.' He was doing his best to get rid of her.

'Private patient, Doctor. Shall we say two hundred pounds?'

'Two hun — ! Very well, then.' His voice had brightened. 'But if you're not here in fifteen minutes, I'll have to close the surgery. I can't leave my family alone with these lunatics rampaging though the streets.'

★   ★   ★

The receptionist had gone. Samantha settled Wei Prentice in the waiting-room and went through a door marked Dr Mahmood. A bald, overweight man, his dark face heavily pockmarked, was sitting at a desk making a steeple with his fingers. Big eyes behind heavy horn-rimmed spectacles widened when she stepped through the door.

'Dr Mahmood?'

He nodded. 'And you're Mrs . . . ?'

Samantha ignored the question, took the ampoule of serum from her bag, laid it on his blotter, and said, 'I'd like her injecting with this.'

Dr Mahmood slid his spectacles to the end of his nose, picked up the glass container, and rotated it while he read the tiny print. He glanced up at her. 'I've heard whispers about this. Where did you get it?'

'Switzerland. Had it flown in this morning.'

'How is it that you can have vaccine flown in when a doctor can't obtain supplies for his family?'

'Maybe you should take that up with the BMA. I just want you to inoculate a little girl.'

'I don't think I'm prepared to. Perhaps I should keep this vaccine and raise the question of supplies with the health authority.' Dr Mahmood was scowling up at her defiantly.

Samantha felt a crushing wave of tiredness. Wei Prentice was exhausted. She couldn't leave her in the waiting room much longer. And this pompous bastard had agreed to do the job after she'd offered a more than generous fee. Clicking open her bag, she reached inside and drew out the pistol. She pushed it in his face, kept her husky voice low, as she said, 'This is a very powerful weapon, Doctor. If I pull the trigger, your brains are going to be all over the carpet. Now, are you going to immunize the child, as we agreed?'

He closed his mouth and swallowed hard. 'Who are you?'

'The child outside is the daughter of Shing Ziyang, a Birmingham Triad master. If you upset me, if you distress the child, he'll send men to find you and inflict pain and humiliation that's beyond all imagining. Then they'll go looking for your wife and kids. Are you following me?'

He ran the tip of a pink tongue around fleshy black lips, and nodded.

Samantha held out her free hand. 'Then give me the vial of serum before you drop it, and use this for the injection.' She reached inside her bag, pulled out one of the wrapped syringes she'd stolen from Dr Merril, and laid it on the desk.

'Where's your mobile?' she demanded.

'My mobile?'

'Give me your mobile phone.'

'Why should I give you my . . . ?'

Samantha leaned over the desk and pushed the muzzle of the gun against the tip of his nose. Perspiration was running down his cheeks now. She could smell his fear. Keeping her voice low so the child couldn't hear, she snarled, 'Give me your fucking mobile.'

He reached inside his jacket, pulled out a phone, and handed it over.

Samantha took it, dropped it in her bag, then tore the connecting lead out of his desk phone. 'I'm going to bring the little girl in now, Doctor, and I'm going to be watching you. All of the serum's got to be drawn into the syringe, and all of it's got to be injected into her arm. And I don't want to hear a moan or a whimper from the child. If you don't do this right, Doctor, if you cause any pain, you'll wish I'd shot you. Do we understand one another?'

He nodded. His flabby face was sheened with sweat, his huge brown eyes wide and locked on hers.

Sliding the gun back into her bag, Samantha collected Wei from the waiting-room and brought her through.

Dr Mahmood went into avuncular mode. 'Wei? That's a pretty name. Are you going to sit on this seat for me?'

Samantha lifted the child and settled her on the chair.

Dr Mahmood tugged open a desk drawer and lifted out a tin. 'How about a lollipop? I've got red, yellow and green. You choose.'

Wei frowned up at him, puzzled by his nervously effusive manner, then she peered into the box and took one of the sweets on a stick.

'Now, shall we put some medicine on your arm to make sure you don't become ill?' He tore open a pack, took out an antiseptic wipe, and gently rubbed Wei's upper arm. He looked at Samantha and said, 'The medicine?'

She handed him the vial of Swiss serum, watched him snap off the top and draw the fluid into the hypodermic.

Wei was sucking hard at the sweet.

'How's the lollipop? Good?' Dr Mahmood bent forward, pressed the needle through the skin, and slowly drove the plunger home.

Wei frowned, but didn't murmur.

Samantha held out her hand. 'The empty ampoule and the syringe; I want to take them.'

Limp with relief now, Dr Mahmood dropped the fragments of glass and the hypodermic into Samantha's palm.

Placing them in her bag, she took out an envelope containing banknotes she'd found in Kwan Peng's bedroom, and dropped it on the desk. 'You haven't seen me, Doctor, and you haven't seen the child. OK?'

He flopped down in his chair and nodded. 'Why me? Why pick on me?'

'Pure chance. Your name's at the top of a page in the phone book.' Samantha lifted Wei down from the chair. 'Say thank you and goodbye to Dr Mahmood.'

The tired child managed a smile and clasped and unclasped her hand in a wave.

Out in the yard, Samantha laid Dr Mahmood's mobile phone on the bonnet of what looked to be his car, then lifted Wei into the passenger seat of the Range Rover. She could hear distant shouting, the crash of breaking glass, sirens wailing and helicopters droning. Beyond the surrounding roof tops, closer to the town, a column of black smoke was rising, almost vertically, into the overcast sky.

'Why did that man prick my arm?'

'To make sure you don't catch flu.' Samantha slammed the door, circled the Range Rover and climbed up beside Wei.

'What's flu?'

'It's what made Kwan sick. We don't want you to be sick like that, do we?' Samantha keyed the ignition and the four-litre engine rumbled into life.

Wei stopped sucking the lollipop and fixed Samantha in a steady gaze. 'Is Kwan better now?'

Samantha leaned across and stroked her cheek. 'She's fine now, sweetheart. Nothing's going to hurt Kwan any more.'

⋆ ⋆ ⋆

Doctor Mahmood remained slumped in his chair, staring at the retreating form of the black-haired woman in the green silk dress. It might have been been painted on to her body; every curve, every movement, flowed and

237

melted beneath its sheen. And how could she walk in those ridiculous shoes? This was the way women of wealth proclaimed their status in this God-forsaken country, but to him she was dressed in the raiment of a whore. And with her painted eyes and scarlet lips, that's all she was: some Chinese gangster's whore.

He forced himself out of the chair and limped over to the wash basin. His face was bathed in sweat. He turned on the taps and began to splash water on to his brow and cheeks. When he reached for the towel, he shuddered. Such malevolent eyes. She was like the tigress he'd once seen when he was a boy, boldly prowling through his village; powerful, contemptuous, utterly indifferent to the shouting men with their sticks and guns.

13

A clever layout made the most of the limited space in the motel bedroom. The bathroom door faced the entrance, and a recess, formed in the partition between bathroom and bedroom, served as a clothes hanging space.

Samantha drew the curtains, snapped on the bedside lamps, and considered tactics. She'd made sure the receptionist had taken a good look at her and Wei when they'd called at the motel that afternoon. Later, while crossing town to visit Dr Mahmood, she'd used Kwan Peng's mobile to phone the motel and ask for the putative Mrs Prentice. If calls were being monitored, the watchers would soon be sending in the hunters and, if they were professionals, they'd arrive in the small hours.

Taking off her coat, she put it on a hanger and hung it at the end of a rail so it would partly screen the recess. She stood the suitcase just beneath it, forming a concealed space from which she could view the entire bedroom area.

The headboards of the two single beds abutted the far wall. Samantha pulled back and rumpled the sheets on the bed nearest the window, then scattered some of Wei's clothes on and around it.

Extra pillows and blankets were squeezed on to a shelf above the wardrobe recess. She arranged them in the other bed, doing her best to form the shapes of a mother and child, snuggling close and facing the wall. The polystyrene busts she'd brought from the hairdressing salon were featureless; the hair in the wigs they displayed European rather than Asian, brown rather than black. Darkness and a little care in the arrangement of the sheets would make such subtleties meaningless. She crumbled away some of the polystyrene from the shoulders of one of the manikins, making its proportions more childlike, then straightened the wigs and placed the busts in the bed.

Samantha switched off the lamps and plunged the bedroom area into darkness. Bright light, spilling from the open door of the bathroom, cast black shadows around and within the wardrobe recess. What little light reached the beds only made the huddled forms more convincing.

It was almost one. She screwed the silencer on to the gun and checked the magazine. As an afterthought, she switched off the three mobile phones in her bag, then slid it on to the shelf above the wardrobe. The wait could be a long one, and a towel, folded over the top of a trouser press, provided something soft to rest her haunches against. Kicking off her green satin shoes, she stepped into the wardrobe recess and glanced through the gap around the edge of her coat. She had a good view of the darkened area surrounding the beds. Satisfied, she closed her eyes and abandoned herself to the vigil.

Night sounds began to be audible over the steady beating of her heart: the whisper of water in pipes, faint voices, the distant closing of a door, a woman's laughter, and, on the threshold of sound, the deep rumble of traffic on the motorway.

Recollections of the past week began to drift, dreamlike, through her mind: Ella Remick squatting over a coffin in a grave, goat-headed gods, the naked and the dead in army freezer caskets, Kwan Peng's body curled up in the soiled bed. Samantha began to shake. Death and the stink of death. She was burned out; balanced on the edge. She was as ill and exhausted as she had been a year ago. Marcus was a suave bastard and Fallon didn't give a shit. She'd clear this Prentice business, then she'd resign if they didn't give her the leave she wanted. She'd survive OK with the private investigation business.

Footsteps were approaching along the corridor outside the room. She wrapped both hands around the grip of the gun and steadied herself. They were passing now. A woman was giggling helplessly; a man laughing. The footsteps moved on and ended in the distant sound of a door opening and closing.

Samantha had begun to relax her grip on the gun when she heard a card scraping into the lock, then subtle changes in the background of faint sounds, echoing in from the corridor, told her the door had opened.

A dark shape moved across her field of vision and divided to form two silhouettes. One gestured soundlessly towards the bed nearest the wall and guns were raised. Samantha straightened her arms and curled her finger around the trigger. Thuds from three silenced guns merged into a single sound, then one of the silhouettes fell into the deep shadow between the beds.

'Bas . . . Bas?' The survivor was bending over his accomplice.

Samantha stepped out of the recess. 'Put your gun down and face the wall. Don't turn round.'

'Hey! What is this? We're official: Special Crime Unit.'

'I said drop your gun on the floor. Face the

wall and put your hands on it. Spread your legs.'

Samantha stepped back a couple of paces, groped for the switch in the lobby, and flicked on the light.

His red hair had been cut short, almost shaved, and his hands were sheathed in surgical gloves. The black bomber-jacket, trousers and trainers were new-looking. When he turned and glanced towards the bed, saw the bewigged polystyrene heads, the crimson swathe of blood and brains across the sheets and up the wall, his legs began to tremble.

'Get your cuffs,' Samantha commanded.

'Cuffs? I don't carry cuffs.' He began to turn his head.

'Face the wall,' Samantha snapped, 'or your brains are going to be all over it. Now, very slowly, use one hand to unfasten your pants, and let them drop.'

She watched his shirt tail come into view as the waistband of his pants settled around trembling knees. 'Take your cuffs out of your jacket pocket and put them on.'

'I don't have — '

'If you're Special Crime, you've got cuffs, and if you don't put them on I'm going to have to kill you. So *do it*,' she hissed. 'And do it slowly.'

He pushed himself off the wall, metal

chinked on metal and a ratchet clicked.

'Behind your back,' Samantha demanded. 'Fasten them behind your back.'

Bright metal flashed in the light as he struggled to hook the bracelet over his right wrist. Eventually he managed it, and the other ratchet clicked home.

She was still holding the gun in both hands, arms outstretched, feet spread. 'Turn around now,' she said. 'Turn around and face me.'

'Jesus! Susie Wong!' Eyes wide, he took in the black hair, the flaming lipstick, the jade green dress with embroidered dragons writhing over the bodice, their tails swirling down the skirt.

'And what do they call you back at the mess? The Herod brothers?' Samantha demanded scathingly.

'Herod brothers?'

'Child killers. That's what you were trying to do, isn't it? Kill a little girl and her mother.'

'They're illegals,' he jeered.

'How do you know they're illegals? Anyway, the country's full of illegal immigrants. Why pick on this mother and child?'

'They're plague carriers. Avian flu. Brought it here from China. The dirty bitches have been spreading it.'

'Who told you that?' Samantha demanded.

'Scientist from the Ministry of Health. Gave us a talk during the briefings.'

'You've had briefings? How many people have you got on the job?'

'Six teams of two. We work three shifts, round the clock.'

'Searching for a woman and child?'

'Yeah. Bas and me were in the mess when the call came.'

Samantha studied the man. He had the white, heavily freckled skin that goes with red hair, and he was broad and powerfully built; obviously very fit. 'You're army, aren't you?'

'Army?' He let out a snickery little laugh. 'No, I told you: Special Crime Unit.'

'Army's written all over you,' Samantha insisted. 'And I'm getting tired holding this gun. Don't make me impatient, or you'll get the same as your friend. Which camp?'

'Catterick,' he muttered angrily. 'We're all from different regiments. We had to go through selection and training before we were seconded to the unit.'

'Seconded to kill little girls and their mothers?'

'We were told the order came from the top. Bloody illegals. They're plague carriers, for Christ's sake.'

'You're not wearing a biological suit. Aren't

you bothered about them infecting you?'

'We all had injections,' he said. 'Some Swiss vaccine. That was the deal: be trained for the special assignment and get an injection and more pay.'

'So, for an injection and some extra pay, you'd believe anything some snot-nosed little bureaucrat told you?'

'You don't argue when the order comes from the top,' he protested. 'In the army, you don't argue when it comes from the ruddy sergeant major.'

'Top? What do you mean, top?' Samantha demanded.

He shrugged. 'War Office, Government, Prime Minister: the top. They just said, *the top*.'

'Where's the other team?'

'Other team?'

'You said six pairs working three shifts. Where are your pals?'

His eyes brightened with understanding. 'Gone to a house in Leeds. Message came through that the woman had died there and her kid might be hanging around.'

'When did this message come through?'

'Dunno. The four of us came on duty at midnight and we got our orders then.'

'Who does surveillance?' Samantha asked.

'Special Crime Unit people. We just get

sent out on assignments.'

'Do you have any children?'

He smirked. 'None that I'm maintaining.'

'Maybe that's why you're so willing to murder other people's.'

'Murder!' The word had stung him and he began to snarl out his anger, 'The dirty bitches have given the bloody disease to half the kids in the country. Don't talk to me about murder.'

Her huge green eyes gazed at him down the barrel of the gun. He'd probably told her what little he knew, and he'd taken a good look at her. She said, 'Turn and face the wall again.'

His body tensed. She could feel his fear. 'Hey, what are you going — '

'Just turn around. I'm going to unlock the cuffs. They're standard key, aren't they?'

'As far as I know.' Pants around his ankles, he made a series of small shuffling movements, then held out his wrists.

The force of the bullet hurled his head against the wall, and blood smeared down magnolia paint as he slid to the floor.

★   ★   ★

The rooms in the flat above the hairdresser's were softly lit. Samantha removed her shoes

247

and wandered through the uncluttered spaces. It was almost four. Crispin was sleeping on the sofa in the living-room. Wei Prentice, resplendent in one of her new nightgowns and clutching the psychedelic rabbit, seemed a tiny figure in the king-sized double bed Crispin used to share with his lover.

She unzipped the embroidered dress, stepped out of it and draped it over a chair, then took her bag with the collection of mobile phones into the kitchen. She closed the door and began to check for calls. Marcus had tried to reach her on her own phone, probably wanting the usual progress report. There had been no calls to the phone she'd bought using Ling Prentice's name and address, and no calls had been made to the phone she'd taken from Kwan Peng's handbag. She scrolled through its memory and copied down numbers she ought to check at a more appropriate time.

Moving back to the bedroom, she slid between the sheets; heard Wei Prentice's breathing slow and deepen as she wrapped her arms around her.

* * *

Crispin looked her up and down with something close to envy. 'Who's a sexy little

248

thing, then?' he said.

Samantha drew the bootlace strap of her black silk slip over her shoulder, leaned against the kitchen door frame, and gave him a lazy smile. 'Looking pretty hot yourself, Crispin.'

He made a kissing shape with his lips. 'God, I'm glad you're here, Sam. I was ready to walk out and never come back.' He dropped the oranges he'd peeled into the juicer and switched it on. 'I keep expecting him to come up the stairs in that side-buttoned overall he used to wear. I can't believe he's gone.'

Samantha heard what might have been a sob, and when he turned and glanced at her, his eyes were very bright. 'You spent the night on the tiles,' he said. He looked her up and down again. 'A regular, was it?'

She laughed huskily, thankful he had this misconception about her. 'Just a little business,' she said.

He switched off the juicer and poured the liquid into a jug.

'Was Wei OK?' she asked.

'Better than I expected. Bit wary, but she'll come round.'

'I've rented a house just outside Scarborough. It's in the North Riding Forest Park: detached place, decent garden. It would be best if you took her there this morning.'

Crispin sighed. 'Can't be too soon for me, Sam.'

'I've got a money belt for you. Five thousand. Pay cash for everything; don't use cards. And I'll give you a mobile number to call me on; don't use either of my usual numbers, whatever you do, and don't phone me unless you absolutely have to.'

He dropped rashers into a pan. 'What's the problem with the little girl? Renting houses, paying cash, special phone numbers: there's something not right about it all.'

Samantha watched him reach into the fridge and bring out a carton of eggs. She couldn't tell him too much, but there were things he had to know. 'Her mother's upset some dangerous people. They might try and use the child to get to her. That's why it's best she disappears for a while. No one knows she's here. No one knows where you're going. You'll be OK, Crispin.'

He forked the sizzling rashers around, then started to crack eggs into a bowl. 'Last night she told me her father was a professor; at Oxford University, no less.'

'That's something she ought to forget. And it might be better if she forgets she's called Prentice and uses your surname.'

'I don't know how I let you talk me into

this, I really don't,' he said.

Samantha pushed herself off the door frame, sauntered over to him, then stood on tiptoe and whispered in his ear, 'It's because you're so sweet, Crispin.' Laughing huskily, she kissed him on the cheek.

'You're wasting your time, Sam,' he sighed. 'Even in that sexy little slip, you're wasting your time.' He pointed towards the bathroom with the fork. 'Go and put my robe on and get the kid up for her breakfast.'

Later, Samantha fastened Wei's shoes while Crispin carried cases down to his car. Just three decent meals and a good night's sleep had removed some of the darkness from around the child's eyes and put a little colour back into her cheeks.

Samantha folded down the collar of Wei's dress. 'Will you be good for Crispin?'

'He's not called Crispin; he's called Arthur. He said he wouldn't get work if people knew he was called Arthur.'

Samantha laughed. 'Then we'd better keep Arthur's secret and call him Crispin, hadn't we?'

Wei nodded gravely.

'And you're going to try and be good for him while you're on holiday?'

Wei gave another nod. She didn't seem to be paying attention. Her face was very close;

her gaze searching. She said, 'Why are your eyes so enormous and green?'

Samantha tweaked her nose. 'Why are yours so big and brown?'

'Can you tell what I'm thinking? Sometimes, when you look at me, I think you can tell what I'm thinking.'

'No,' Samantha said huskily. 'I can't tell what you're thinking.'

'Why aren't you coming on holiday?' Wei's voice was accusing.

'Because I've got to look for your mummy.'

'Will you find her?'

'I hope so.'

The little girl eyed her steadily. 'If you don't find her, will you be my mummy?'

The question was like a knife in her heart. Samantha stroked Wei's cheek with her thumb and returned her gaze. What did one say to a five-year-old child who'd lost her father, was missing her mother, and who'd spent two days trying to feed a dead woman?

She bent forward and kissed her, folded her in her arms, and said, 'If I can't find her, I'll be your mummy.'

'And when you get back you'll never, never, leave me again?'

'I'll never ever leave you again.'

14

The Minister for Internal Security opened the red leather-bound folder and glanced at the topmost report. *Population Changes in the United Kingdom: the Avian Flu Pandemic and the Acceleration of Demographic Trends.* He flicked it open, saw that Jessica, his researcher, had highlighted key paragraphs with a yellow marker and tucked a neatly typed single-sheet summary inside. Efficient little thing, he mused, as he scanned the text, but big in all the right places. Going to have a weight problem if she's not careful, but very sexy right now. Pretty face, too.

The occasional word registered, and he began to concentrate on the document. *In many towns and cities,* he read, *underlying trends over the next decade would have resulted in the majority of votes being of immigrant origin. The apparent vulnerability of the indigenous population to the current flu pandemic is, however, accelerating these changes, and in most major centres of population, peoples of immigrant origin already have significant voting majorities (actual figures are given in Appendix 6).*

*Political parties must, therefore, be ever more sensitive to their cultural and economic needs and aspirations. It is, moreover, inevitable that . . . .*He gave up. Academics! Twenty pages to tell him something any politician would instinctively know, all larded with patronizing guidance he didn't need.

He plucked his researcher's single-sheet summary from between the pages and eyed it bleakly. Merry bloody England! Old Ruttle at the Ministry of Defence was right: they'd gift wrapped the sodding country and given it away, that's what they'd done.

Thinking about it was an irritation. Blotting it from his mind, he directed his thoughts down more pleasant byways. It was about time he thanked Jessica for all her hard work. His wife was driving Susan back to university, so he'd have no problem staying on in town. Dinner at that elegant little Italian place should get the evening off to a good start. He contemplated Jessica's ample curves; the black, buttock-hugging skirts she wore and the way her breasts shaped blouses and sweaters. He smiled to himself. Avian flu, demographic shifts, riots, disposal of the dead: these things no longer loomed large on his agenda.

The sound of the door opening cut short his erotic reverie. Glancing round, he nodded an acknowledgment to the Prime Minister and the Home Secretary as they strode the length of the room and took their seats at the table.

'We've got ten minutes before the cabinet meeting starts,' the Prime Minister said. He turned towards the Home Secretary, 'Give me an update on the search for the widow.'

'I've had no reports,' Peter Clayton said. 'I think we should get Fallon in and give her a grilling.'

'Don't care to flatter the arrogant bitch by inviting her here after she walked out of the last meeting,' the Prime Minister muttered. 'We'll deal with her when we've drifted into calmer waters. Are we happy Quest's been taken off the job?'

'Marcus seems convinced. He's got her hunting for the organizers of the London train derailment; says she's too involved with that to get involved with anything else.'

The Prime Minister nodded, then turned and watched the Minister for Internal Security doodling on the cover of a report with his expensive-looking pen: two sets of initials intertwined with the party's logo. 'How about you, Tim? Have your people got anything to report?'

Tim Saunders went on doodling, adding a JH to a rather neat TS.

'Tim?' The Prime Minister didn't hide his irritation.

Tim Saunders glanced up. 'Sorry. I — '

'The search for the widow: have your people learned anything?'

'Looked hopeful a couple of days ago, but now I'm not so sure. Police went to a house in Leeds after a report that a woman called Ling Prentice had died there. The woman was an oriental and she'd had a child, a girl, staying with her. Problem is, we couldn't get a DNA match between the corpse and the kid's clothing.'

'You've got the child?'

'Child's gone. Can't be traced.'

'You've got photographs of Prentice's widow. Can't they be used to identify the woman?'

'Not that easy,' Saunders said. 'The hospital that took the corpse stored it in a refrigerated truck with about a hundred others. Refrigeration unit failed without them realizing it, and they'd a lorry load of decomposing plague corpses on their hands. A hospital manager gave the go-ahead for a mass burial during the night.'

'You've lost the body?'

'Not lost, exactly. The corpses were bagged and tagged and could be exhumed, but finding one body amongst a hundred wouldn't be easy.'

The Prime Minister rolled his eyes heavenwards. He was gripping the edge of the table. His knuckles were white.

Saunders laid down his pen, linked his fingers, and said, 'There's more.'

'More? I don't think I could bloody well bear any more.'

'Our people intercepted a mobile phone call; a woman called Ling Prentice booking a room for herself and a child at a motel near Leeds. Later there was a call to the hotel from someone called Kwan Peng, asking for Prentice. We waited a few hours, then sent a couple of Specials in.'

'And?'

The Minister for Internal Security reached into the leather-bound folder, tugged out a swatch of photographs, and slid them over the table.

The Prime Minister looked down at the images. 'What the devil's this?' he demanded.

'Dear God!' the Home Secretary gasped.

'It's what another team found when they went in the next morning.'

'They're wearing women's wigs and one's got his pants around his ankles,' the Prime Minister said.

'Looks like an explosion in an abattoir.' Shock and distaste mingled in the Home Secretary's voice. 'So much blood, up the walls, all over the bed.'

'Combat ammunition. The experts tell me that's what caused the mess,' Saunders explained. 'Bullets open out as they pass through the body, tear a wide passage and leave a big exit hole. Anyone who gets hit never gets up again. That's the idea.'

'What do you make of it, Tim?' the Prime Minister asked.

Saunders shrugged. 'It's all rather confusing. This event and finding the woman in the house occurred at about the same time. And surely the widow wouldn't be so stupid as to use her own name when she booked into a motel?'

'Perhaps the widow killed the men,' the Home Secretary said weakly. Seeing the glossy images had made him feel sick and faint.

'Killed two Specials?' Saunders was scathing.

'Mother defending her child. Who knows?'

'Has the woman who stayed at the motel been identified?' the Prime Minister asked.

'Receptionist's the only person who saw the woman and the child. The woman said they'd left home without their identity cards and he accepted the child's birth certificate as ID. He swears the certificate was made out for a Wei Prentice, and a Ling Prentice and

Nathaniel Prentice were listed as the parents. Said the woman and her child were black-haired and the woman was wearing some embroidered oriental dress. I gather that's the sort of thing Ling Prentice wears. When they showed him photographs he identified the child for sure, but wasn't so certain about the mother; seems she was wearing dark glasses. He said an Australian woman called about problems they were having with a hire car, but we've not been able to trace her.'

'My money's on the widow still being alive,' the Prime Minister muttered. 'We're got to reach closure on this, Tim. We've got to get her.'

'The house where the dead Chinese woman was found is being taken apart,' Tim Saunders said. 'And it's under constant surveillance. It's on a run down council estate where half the properties are boarded up. We've put a marksman in the house opposite. He's got photographs of the woman and her kid and instructions to kill.'

'Didn't we ought to arrest her?' the Home Secretary demanded nervously. 'I don't care to be a party to killing a mother and her child.'

The Prime Minister rounded on him angrily. 'You were a willing party to Prentice being instructed to re-target the virus on specific racial groups. And I can guarantee we're all named in his notes and all our voices are on his bloody tapes.' He tossed his pencil down. 'Dammit, Peter, we've been through this before. It wouldn't just be a case of losing office. We'd lose far more than that. We agreed we can't risk leaving the widow and her kid alive. We'd never sleep easy in our beds.'

'But if we get the papers and things, the widow no longer has proof.'

'And without the widow to swear provenance, the papers and tapes are virtually useless. We can say they're forgeries put together by detractors. If the widow and child live they'll always be able to point the accusing finger. They've got to be killed. If we get the papers, that's a bonus.' The Prime Minister turned to Saunders. 'Time's running out on us. We may have to agree to a coalition government if the situation deteriorates much more. And that won't make it any easier for us to deal with the widow. Get a grip on it, Tim. For God's sake, get a grip on it.'

★ ★ ★

Samantha sipped tea and watched the early morning news on Crispin's television. The enormous size of the set was doing nothing to distance her from the images on its screen.

Areas blighted by rioting were becoming battlefields now. She watched as cameras panned along street after street of burnt-out houses and shops, rafters and chimneys black and skeletal against a bright spring sky. The presence of troops was no longer being disguised. Infantrymen cruised the streets in armoured cars marked with regimental insignias and painted the usual camouflage green.

Presenters, their faces and voices expressionless, intoned a litany of government approved comment. 'Rumours that the avian flu epidemic has been spread by terrorists and racially targeted are completely unfounded. Last night's outbreaks of rioting and looting in towns and cities throughout the country mirror events in Germany, France, Belgium and Holland. The Government has appealed for calm, and will take all necessary measures to restore order and bring life back to normal. Meanwhile, the mass immunization programme is to be extended to the old and people of working age, and vaccination centres will be set up before the end of the week. This afternoon, the Prime Minister will . . . '

Samantha switched off the set and went

through to the bedroom to choose something to wear. She'd parked the four-by-four in the service area behind the shop and used taxis to ferry clothes from her house to Crispin's flat, always breaking the journey at least once. The Ferrari was locked in her garage. She'd not disturbed the radio trace they'd planted on it. It could stay there, bleeping out its signal until its batteries were exhausted.

The black van hadn't been parked in the cul-de-sac on her last two visits home, but men had been watching and waiting, in the big Ford car, close to the junction with the main road. It was only a matter of time before they found her hiding place; if they hadn't found it already.

Samantha flicked through the suits and dresses on the rail. Not much to choose from here, and for some she'd no matching shoes or bag. She might have to make another trip to the house. She glanced out of a window that overlooked the service area. The spring sunshine was strong, but it was probably cool. The black suit with the white piping around its lapels and cuffs was probably the best she could do. Crispin had sponged a mark off the sleeve and had it cleaned, and the Allesandro dell'Acqua shoes and bag would team with it nicely.

Her mobile began to bleep as she lifted the suit from the hanger. She reached for it across the bed.

'Quest?'

It was Fallon. Samantha didn't want calls on her mobile in this new location, encrypted or otherwise. She had to end the conversation fast. 'The house you were looking for?' she said quickly, 'we've found something you might like. If you'd care to meet me at the hotel near the corner shop, I could show you round it.'

'When?'

'In an hour.'

'Make it two,' Fallon snapped, and the line went dead.

★   ★   ★

Loretta Fallon wandered through the reception area and into the bar. Samantha Quest was relaxing in a leather armchair, legs crossed, reading *The Times*. Another smart little suit, Loretta thought. The white piping around the lapels and cuffs made it a bit dressy, but it was very very smart. And the fit! She sighed out her envy and crossed over.

Big green eyes swept up as she approached, crimson lips tugged into a smile, and that soft smoky voice said, 'Thought you were dead.'

'Me? Dead?' Loretta sank into the facing chair.

'The early morning London train derailed south of Peterborough: thought you might be on it.' Samantha gestured towards the low table. 'I got you a gin and tonic. That OK?'

'Thanks. Just what I need.' Loretta picked up the glass. 'I would have been, but I decided to take the taxi back to headquarters. Did a deal with the driver on the price while he was taking me to the station.' She took a sip. 'You couldn't speak on the phone this morning?'

'I'm still under surveillance, so I've changed houses for a while. I'm worried about them using intercepted calls to locate me.'

Loretta frowned. 'They can't have believed me when I said I'd taken you off the search.'

'If finding the widow's so important, they daren't believe you.'

'You're still reporting to Marcus, as normal?' Loretta asked.

Samantha nodded. 'I'm supposed to be hunting for the organizers of the train derailment.'

'We've got them. French tip-off. Three Algerians travelling on French passports; picked them up at Heathrow.' She sipped at

264

her glass. 'The bodies you found at the Porton Down research centre: I had the names checked. Two agency nurses, both immigrants, and an unregistered Polish doctor, all hired from some place in London. There should have been a third nurse: they were working round the clock in eight-hour shifts.'

'The empty casket,' Samantha said. 'Maybe one survived and didn't need it.'

Loretta frowned. 'Do you think other people are still searching for Prentice's widow?'

'Someone's searching. I made a booking at a motel for Ling Prentice and her daughter, to see if I could smoke them out. Two Serious Crime men visited the room in the early hours. They'd been seconded from army units, given a pay rise, and immunized against the plague to make them keen.'

Loretta took a deep breath. It was as she'd feared: rival factions empowering themselves, bypassing the established organs of the state, preparing themselves for the final meltdown. When she said, 'Are you any closer to finding the widow and her child?' eyes, still and cold as death, began to probe hers.

Samantha wondered how much she could trust Fallon. Reuniting mother and child, protecting them, making them safe, were her overriding concerns. If she found Ling Prentice, she'd need all the support and influence this woman could bring to bear. She had to trust her. 'I've got the child,' Samantha said. 'She's safe. I've not located the mother.'

'The little girl: does she know anything?' Fallon asked.

'Nothing. Her mother left her with an old friend. The child thinks her father's in America, and she says her mother had to hide because bad men are chasing her.'

Fallon hadn't asked her where the child was. Samantha found that reassuring. It seemed the trust was mutual.

Loretta slid her empty glass on to the table and reached for her bag. 'I've got something that might help. When we last spoke, I promised I'd send someone to Oxford to visit the Weavers again. He had the file with your notes, and he said he was from the same firm of solicitors. Seems the mother's been taken into psychiatric care, but the daughter gave him this to pass on to you.'

Samantha took the envelope, saw it had been opened, and shook the contents on to her lap. There was a note from Rachel Weaver and another envelope containing a letter and a photograph. Samantha unfolded the note, and read:

Dear Miss Quest
I found this in a book after you'd gone,
but you didn't leave an address so I couldn't
send it to you. It was a letter and photo-
graph, not a postcard, that Mrs Prentice
sent me that time they went on holiday,
and I hope it's some use to you.
  Sincerely
  Rachel Weaver

PS Mummy's been taken into hospital and
she's getting better. They're letting her come
home at the end of the month.

'The letter's from Ling Prentice,' Loretta
said. 'No address: she's just scribbled
Hope Lodge and the date at the top of the
sheet.'

'Does anyone else know I have this?'

'The agent Rachel Weaver gave it to, his
section head,' she laughed, 'me.'

'How about Marcus?'

'If he knows, then something's gone
seriously wrong with the system. The two
sections are watertight for security reasons.
Communication's through me. Anyway, I've
got Marcus under surveillance, and I'm
pretty sure he's convinced things have gone
cold since you were taken off the case.'

'You've got Marcus under surveillance?'

Samantha didn't try to hide the surprise in her voice.

Loretta Fallon gave her a slow smile. 'I've taken him as a lover. I can't keep him under much closer surveillance than that.'

Samantha laughed softly, with amazement rather than amusement, then said, 'I'd consider that above and beyond the call of duty.'

'I've had a lot worse,' Loretta Fallon retorted. 'Marcus is quite a catch. And you won't always look like that, Miss Quest. Gorgeous young men won't always be at your beck and call.'

Samantha raised an eyebrow.

'I saw the photograph of you with your arms around that fabulously handsome creature.'

'That's my Man Friday,' Samantha explained. 'He cleans the house, does my washing and ironing, shops, takes stuff to the cleaners. He's gay. His partner's just died in the plague.'

'God, what an awful waste,' Loretta whispered.

'Too right. They were very close. I've never — '

'No; what a waste him being gay. Just think about it; wrapping your legs around him all night, watching him clean and polish all day. Heaven!'

Samantha laughed at Fallon's frankness, then brought the conversation back to business. 'Did you know about the raid on the motel?'

Loretta shook her head. 'No, and I'm pretty sure Marcus didn't either. If he'd known he'd have briefed me.'

'I contacted the police about the body of an oriental woman in a house in Leeds. I told them it was Ling Prentice. Did you hear about that?'

'Not a whisper. Was there a response?'

'I drive over and check the place out every day,' Samantha said. 'They've put yellow barrier tape around the house, and yesterday they were emptying it, bagging everything up and loading it into black army-style trucks.'

'Sounds like Special Crime are handling it.'

'Police systems must be programmed to respond to the word 'Prentice',' Samantha suggested. 'They're probably monitoring phone networks, too. I used a mobile registered in Ling Prentice's name to make the hotel booking, then used her friend's phone to call the hotel and ask for her.'

'You certainly laid down the markers. Does the little girl know about any documents or papers?'

'Nothing,' Samantha said. 'The child knows nothing. She's only five, going on six, and pining for her mother.'

'How about lunch?' Loretta suggested. 'May as well while we're here. It's almost twelve.'

'Sounds good,' Samantha said.

Loretta caught the eye of a youth in a white jacket and brought him over with an imperious stare. 'Could you fetch the lunch menus and some more drinks. Same again?'

When he'd ambled off, Samantha said, 'You seem pretty confident about Marcus; what he knows and what he doesn't know.'

Loretta smiled. 'He's become very confiding in the bedroom. Deep down, he's still the lonely little boy sent away from home to public school. With me he thinks he's found nanny and matron again. And he can be quite passionate. I find that flattering.'

'Bit kinky,' Samantha said, 'getting passionate with nanny.'

'That's just my analysis of the relationship. He won't realize it's like that. And if I had your face and figure, I don't imagine for a moment I'd be a nanny substitute.' She laughed. 'I never realized he was quite so obsessive about royalty. He keeps reminding me he's in line for the throne.'

'Tell me about it,' Samantha said wryly. 'Ninety-ninth at the last count.'

'I've given him special responsibility for

protecting the royal family: places of safety, escape routes, evacuation plans. He's been dashing all over the country, chatting to relatives and old school chums, dining with lord lieutenants.'

They eyed one another in silence for a few seconds, then burst out laughing.

'That should suit the old related-to-royalty arsehole right down to the ground,' Samantha said. 'What are you going to do about him breaking ranks?'

'Watch, listen, and wait for an opportunity. I'm in no hurry: he can be quite charming in that public-school, ex-Guards-officer kind of way.'

'Could you arrange new identities for the child and the mother if I find her? Birth certs, ID cards, social security numbers and all that stuff.'

'No problem,' Loretta said. 'But the widow inherits her husband's pension, and there's a decent house. If I can get my hands on the professor's papers, fresh ID might not be necessary. Let's leave that one in abeyance.'

The white-jacketed youth returned with drinks on a tray and a couple of tiny hand-written menus. Samantha stifled a yawn as she took her copy.

'Too much night duty?' Fallon asked.

'Mmm, partly that, but mostly I have

difficulty sleeping. A few whiskies usually do the trick.'

'Why do you think you have difficulty sleeping?'

Samantha glanced up from the menu and looked across at Loretta Fallon, wondering how much she ought to reveal. 'It's the men,' she said presently. 'All the men I've killed. I used to remember how many, but now I can't. But I remember some of their faces. When I'm sinking into sleep, they flicker into view, like an old black-and-white movie. Angry faces, terrified faces, faces made ugly by fear; young men, old men; hirsute and clean-shaven. Now I make them turn around before the kill. That way I don't get to look into their eyes at the instant the life's ripped out of their bodies.'

Loretta took a deep breath. What could she say? Marcus was right. Too much killing had left Quest tottering on the edge. He knew his agent better than she'd given him credit for.

'And when I kill, Miss Fallon,' the huskily hypnotic voice went on, 'it's not for the state, not for queen and sodding country; it's to protect the helpless and avenge the innocent dead.'

15

Samantha turned the old three-litre Citroën into the council estate and began to cruise down the wide main avenue. Driving past Kwan Peng's house in the same car two days running was unwise, and around here something old was less eye-catching than a nearly-new hire car.

'I'm giving it away, Miss Temple,' the unshaven salesman had said. 'Plague deaths are flooding the market with motors and cutting down the customers. What's your first name? Shirley? Shirley Temple. That's a cute name. Listen, Shirley, it's a gift at this price. Hey, I'll throw in a tankful of juice. How's that?'

She turned into Bevin Road, saw the yellow barrier tape fluttering across the front of Kwan Peng's home as she drove past, then parked a dozen houses further on. Reaching up, she tugged at a handle, unfolded it, and tried to wind the sun roof open. Rust showered down and the panel stuck when it had moved a few inches. She shook the debris from her hair, then flicked at her jacket and dress with a handkerchief, scattering flakes of rust from the flouncy skirt.

Thudding rotors, beating the air, were louder now, but there was nothing to be seen through the gap in the roof or the car's windows. The helicopter was probably circling just beyond the line of the rooftops.

Samantha turned and looked back towards Kwan Peng's house. No parked cars, no people, just three habitable dwellings amongst the dereliction. She studied the house facing Kwan's. Boarding had been removed from a first-floor window. How long ago? Two days, three, four? It had been there when she'd looked across from Kwan Peng's death-bed.

Coaxing the old car back into life, she turned it across the road and bumped over the kerb into an overgrown garden. She climbed out, headed round the back of the empty house, then moved through rear yards towards the property that faced Kwan Peng's. The helicopter was still droning above the estate. She looked up, squinting against the brightness of the sky, but couldn't see it.

Fragments of glass from boarded windows were strewn over pavings behind the house. The boards had been removed from the door, and a recently fitted padlock had been unfastened and hooked over a bright metal bar. Treading carefully to avoid crunching the glass, Samantha pushed at the door, stepped inside, and peered into near darkness. She could make out the dim shapes of discarded furniture and, as her eyes adjusted to the gloom, clothing, toys and magazines strewn over the floor. Perhaps the family had been touched by the plague, the children taken into care, and the remnants of their life together made secure against looters.

Samantha moved across tiles and carpet, then through a doorway, and found herself at the foot of the stairs. She could hear voices now, faint but distinct in the silence.

'She's heading down the street, on foot.' Click.

'You're sure it's the Prentice woman?' Click.

'Yeah, we're sure. Edmund got a good sighting as she stepped off the bus. Plenty of black hair all gathered up, thirties, oriental, bit of a looker. You've got her picture. Confirm when you get her face in the 'scope.' Click.

Samantha stepped out of her shoes and began to creep up the stairs. Sliding her hand under her jacket, she unfastened the strap on the holster, withdrew the gun and eased the safety catch over.

'Might not get her face in the scope if she's staring at the Chink's house.' Click.

Samantha moved into a pool of light on the

landing. She could hear the hiss of the two-way radio now. Three more paces and she was looking into the room with the unboarded window.

'Don't start nit-picking,' came the metallic voice. 'We've spent a lot of time on this. Just do the job. You should be able to see her now. I'll sign off and leave you to it.' Click.

Dressed in black jeans, black trainers and a black bomber jacket, he was kneeling beside the window, concentrating on the view through the telescopic sight of a rifle. Over his broad shoulders and shaved head, Samantha could see Kwan Peng's house, the yellow barrier tape fluttering in the bright sunshine.

The drone of the helicopter grew louder. It was cruising fairly low, some distance beyond the houses on the far side of the street. And then the woman appeared. She was wearing a bright-red belted coat and taking quick steps in her white high-heeled shoes. Her black hair was piled up and secured by combs.

The marksman adjusted the telescopic sight, all the time keeping the gun trained on the woman in red. She stopped at the gate, took hold of the barrier tape and stared down at it, as if uncertain what to do. The man's finger curled around the trigger.

'Don't even think about it,' Samantha

murmured huskily.

His head jerked round.

'Don't speak. Just rest the rifle against the window cill, then stand up and put your hands behind your head. Do it slowly.' Samantha edged into the room, kicked aside the remains of a take-away meal, then took up her feet-apart, arms-outstretched, two-hands-on-the-gun stance.

Alert eyes looked her up and down, first appraising, then challenging. It was obvious he was wondering how he could overpower her.

'Do it!' Samantha hissed, gesturing with the gun.

He began to rise to his feet.

She hadn't fitted the silencer. It was in her bag in the car. She was overlooking little things, but it was often the little things that made the difference. The sound of a gunshot would alarm the woman; probably make her run. He had to be taken downstairs, into a back room where the boarding was intact. Eyes locked on his, she said, 'Go and stand on the landing. Stay where I can see you.'

He remained by the window, staring at her with the cunning desperation of a cornered animal. Older than the men at the motel, he looked more capable. He'd have worked out that she intended to kill him; that he'd nothing to lose by resisting.

'Out of the room.' She jerked the barrel of the gun. 'Get out and move towards the stairs.'

'Slag,' he muttered. 'You're the dirty slag who killed Terry and Bas.' He half-turned towards the door, feigning compliance, then hunched his shoulders and sprang at her.

Samantha squeezed the trigger and stepped aside; saw a bright eye become a dark hole as he dropped to the floor where she'd been standing.

Heart pounding, she looked through the window. The woman in the red coat was glancing around, trying to work out where the gunfire had come from. The helicopter was drifting over rooftops towards the street. The thud of its rotors, the whine of its turbines, was reverberating through the house now. Above the din, she heard the radio click and an urgent voice said, 'What are you waiting for? Kill the bitch. We're going to lose her. Kill the bitch.'

Samantha ran down the stairs, grabbed her shoes and pushed her feet into them as she hopped towards the back door. Looking down a gap between the houses, she saw the woman half-running, half-walking along the street, all the time glancing back over her shoulder.

Returning through back gardens, Samantha made her way to the car and climbed inside. The starter let out a tired groan. She keyed it again and again, frantically pumping the accelerator pedal until the old engine faltered into life. Crashing it into gear, she lurched out of the garden and across the pavement. A car turned into the street from a junction up ahead and began to speed towards the woman. Samantha pressed the pedal to the floor, felt the big Citroën surge across the road as she turned it into the path of the oncoming car.

She hit it on the driver's door. Three tons of fast-moving metal; crushing it, heaving it over the road, forcing it to mount the pavement.

The woman in the red coat was looking back, alarmed by the noise. Samantha swung the Citroën round and headed towards her. Drawing alongside, she reached over, flung the passenger door open and yelled, 'Get in. For Christ's sake, get in.'

Terrified eyes stared at her, then glanced back at the wrecked car. A man in a black bomber jacket was struggling with a door that was too close to a wall to open. And then the helicopter roared into view, low over the rooftops, and a voice that was loud despite the howling turbines bellowed: 'Stay where you are. You are under arrest. If you attempt to move, you will be shot. Just stay where . . . '

Samantha reached out, grabbed the arm of the petrified woman, dragged her into the car and rumbled off down the street, coaxing the old Citroën to deliver all the performance it could.

Crash-damaged, exhaust rumbling, she bounced over traffic calmers as she swept through the shopping area on the estate, then jumped lights and headed towards Leeds along the Otley Road. They wouldn't land or open fire in a crowded place, she reasoned.

Through the gap in the sun roof, she could see the helicopter, drifting from side to side; hear the amplified voice endlessly repeating the command to stop.

Past a park and the university, and then they were closing on the city centre. Keeping her hand on the horn, she ignored traffic lights, forcing her way through the congestion as they swept on down the hill.

The drone of the helicopter was less intrusive now. Leaning forward, Samantha glanced through the windscreen. It was still there, but its altitude had increased, and the voice was no longer calling on them to stop.

Horns blared and pedestrians scattered as they rumbled across the Headrow and plunged into a narrow street. A neon sign on a multi-storey car-park said, *FULL*. Samantha made a left through its entrance, urged the old Citroën up a steep incline and stopped at the barrier. Gathering up her bag, she climbed out, went to the passenger door and tugged it open. The terrified woman gazed up at her. Samantha saw her face clearly for the first time then. The oriental features were almost beautiful, in a fragile kind of way, but they didn't belong to Ling Prentice.

'Why are they chasing us? And who are you?' demanded the woman. Her voice was shaking.

The drone of the helicopter began to echo through the cavernous spaces of the car-park.

Ignoring her question, Samantha took the woman's hand as she would a child's, dragged her out of the car, and led her, stumbling, past payment machines, down steps, and into a passageway. They had to stay under cover: two black-haired women could easily be spotted by observers hovering low above the city. They moved through a small shopping precinct, then kept within elegant Victorian shopping arcades as they ran down towards the market area.

Stopping at a stall, Samantha bought cabbages, had them put into carrier bags, then handed them to the woman. 'Take these. They're not looking for someone carrying shopping.'

At a kiosk, she purchased a silk scarf. 'Put this over your head to hide your black hair. And take that red coat off and put it in one of the bags.'

'Why were they looking for me? Is it because I'm here illegally? Because I work in a massage parlour?'

'They mistook you for someone else. So did I. Why were you going to Kwan Peng's house?'

'She had money for me.'

'But you knew she was dead?'

The woman nodded. 'Scotty told us.' She tied the scarf over her hair, then unbelted her coat, slipped it off and bundled it into one of the bags.

They stepped out into Vicar Lane. Traffic, shoppers; no droning helicopters, no wailing police cars: the city seemed to be just as a city should be on a weekday morning.

'Why go to the house if she was no longer there?' Samantha said.

'I thought someone might have gone in to sort things out. Kwan had friends. And I had a key.'

Samantha remembered the banknotes she'd discovered in the house. She'd included them with the cash she'd given Crispin to fund Wei Prentice's holiday near the coast. 'Why did she have money for you?' she asked.

'She kept the books for Scotty. If Scotty wasn't at the parlour, she'd give me a bigger share of what the men paid when it was busy. She used to hand it over at the end of the week, after Scotty had checked the books.'

'How much?'

'More than three hundred.'

'Four hundred cover it?'

The woman nodded.

Samantha shielded herself in a recess in a wall, opened her bag, counted out the notes and passed them to her.

'Who are you?' the woman asked again.

The sound of a helicopter was becoming audible above the rumble of the traffic. Suddenly it appeared over the dome of the Corn Exchange and drifted slowly across the city. Samantha touched the woman's arm, turned her, and they began to walk towards Boar Lane and the railway station.

The woman needed an explanation. When the noise had faded, Samantha offered a half-truth to protect herself and Wei Prentice. 'Kwan was taking care of a child. The child's vanished. I'm searching for her. Did you know she had a child living with her?'

The woman shook her head. 'She said

nothing to me about it.'

'The child was called Prentice. Did anyone called Ling Prentice ever phone or visit the parlour?'

The woman gave her a blank look.

'How about a woman called Ling Haifong?' she asked, giving her Ling Prentice's stolen maiden name. 'She used to work at the parlour.'

'I don't know anyone called Prentice or Haifong. I've only been with Scotty for six or seven months. Maybe the child and the mother died in the epidemic. So many people die. Half the girls at the parlour are sick or dead.'

'Thanks anyway,' Samantha said. 'Take a taxi home. Get out of the city as quickly as you can. And if anyone asks, you've never been to Kwan Peng's house, and you've never seen me, OK? Admit that you have, and you could end up dead yourself.'

★ ★ ★

Lulled by the hum of wheels on rails, Samantha watched sunlit fields and hedge-rows gliding past the window. The morning hadn't been a complete waste of time. She'd confirmed she wasn't on her own in the search for Ling Prentice, and she'd learned that instructions had been given for the widow to be shot on sight.

She unfastened her bag, took out the letter Ling Prentice had sent with the photograph to Rachel Weaver, and read it for the tenth time:

Dear Rachel
How are you? Keeping your promise and working hard, I hope. I wish you'd been able to come. Wei misses you.

There's a big old wardrobe in one of the rooms, and Nat told Wei it's the doorway to Narnia. She was happy about it during the day, but became scared at night. Even the cleverest of men can be quite lacking in common sense!

Could you babysit for me next Thursday? Nat wants me to attend some function with him. I'm already dreading the journey back: it seems endless. That and the weather are the only bad things about taking a holiday here.
Sincerely
Ling Prentice.

Here? Where was here? Samantha studied the photograph of a grey stone house. Tall sash windows were arranged on either side of a six-panel door, and three dormer windows rose out of its steeply sloping roof. Ornamental pots on squat chimneys were stark against a sky that loured over bleak hills.

She turned the photograph over. A neatly printed *Hope Lodge* had been crossed out and a childish hand had written *Narnia*.

Scotty, the proprietor of the Blissful Moments Massage Parlour, hadn't reported any calls from Ling Prentice, and no calls had been made to Kwan Peng's mobile phone. The house in Leeds had been kept under surveillance for almost a week. All that had achieved for the watchers was a dead marksman, a wrecked car, and the mistaken notion that Ling Prentice had been there and escaped.

Samantha slid the letter and photograph into her bag. If the men in the car had got a good look at her they'd know for sure she was still searching for Ling Prentice, and they'd be convinced she'd spirited her away. That thought gave her no pleasure.

Hope Lodge was, perhaps, her last and only hope. But where was Hope Lodge?'

★ ★ ★

The Prime Minister reached inside his pyjama jacket and scratched his chest. 'You've woken me up to tell me that, Tim?'

'You asked me to keep you posted, day or night, Charles, and a sighting of Prentice's widow in Leeds is a cause for concern. Christ, I was beginning to think the epidemic had seen her off and we were in the clear.'

'It's not the sighting, Tim, it's the bungling: the endless bloody bungling. Marksman shot dead, another man gets his legs crushed, a car written off, and the woman rides into Leeds and fades into the crowd.'

'We can hardly open fire above city streets,' the Minister for Internal Security protested.

'Precisely. She should have been shot before she left the house. Who was driving the escape car?'

'They didn't see the driver.'

'Didn't see?' The Prime Minister's tone was scathing.

'One man had been crushed, the other was trapped, and they were concentrating on the widow, not the car.'

'And you're going to tell me the car was stolen?'

'Purchased that day,' Tim Saunders said. 'Second-hand car pitch just outside Leeds. Sold to a woman called Temple: a Miss Shirley Temple.'

'It's Quest,' the Prime Minister said bitterly. 'Using that precocious brat of a child film star's name. She's mocking us.'

'Can't see her driving a clapped-out old Citroën.'

'It's Quest, Tim. I can feel it. She's running rings round us. It wouldn't surprise me to hear she has the widow.'

'Christ,' Saunders breathed. 'I bloody well hope not.'

'Has Peter been able to get hold of Fallon?'

'He's been trying for days. Just gets told she's out or unavailable.'

'When we drift into calmer waters, I'm going to dismiss that woman,' the Prime Minister fumed. 'I don't care what they throw at me in the House, I'm getting rid.'

'We'd better intensify surveillance on Quest,' Saunders said. 'If she's got the widow she'll have to keep her somewhere until they make their move. We might be able to deal with them both.'

'Tell Serious Crime to put a decent search and surveillance team together,' the Prime Minister snapped. 'And find some experienced men to go in for the final kill: some hard ruthless bastards who'll enjoy the job. Tell them Quest and the widow are the terrorists who've spread the epidemic. Everyone's lost friends and family, so that should psyche the buggers up and make them keen.'

'We've taken that line with the men we've already recruited,' Saunders retorted, then added under his breath, 'Didn't do much good. The poor devils still got nowhere and ended up dead.'

'And the tapes and papers, Tim. Don't forget the evidence. It's got to be brought here, in sealed boxes.'

16

Major Trantham blinked. His eye was smarting behind the black eye-patch. He blinked again, rapidly this time, trying to ease the soreness. Ruddy mowing machines. Flinging stones all over the place. Nearly damn-well blinded him.

Looking over the twenty men crammed into the tiny briefing room, he felt a rush of pride. Britain's finest: intelligent, alert, vigorous, at the very peak of physical condition. Selection chaps had done a good job and done it damn quickly, too.

He took a deep breath, stiffened his shoulders, then rapped on the desk. The men instantly fell silent.

'All present now, so I'll press on,' he barked. 'You've been found decent quarters?'

There was a rumble of assent.

'Good, good, that's the spirit.' Hardly needed to ask, he reflected. Swing 'em in a hammock over some rain-drenched swamp and they'd be happy. They were hard: iron hard.

'Terrorists,' he began, injecting contempt into his voice. 'Two terrorists, both women, both murdering whores. Brought the epidemic that some people are calling the new plague into the country a couple of months ago, and they've been dispersing the virus ever since. Deaths in every family. Every white-skinned family, that is. Virus was engineered by terrorists, targeted on north Europeans, and these murdering bitches have been travelling the country spreading it.'

He looked over the heads of the men to an aide standing at the back of the room. 'We'll have the slide show now, Sergeant.'

A brisk, 'Sir', rang back, the lights went out, and the major turned towards a square of brightness on a screen. The projector mechanism clicked and an image of an oriental woman in a blue silk dress appeared. The sergeant adjusted lenses, sharpened the focus, and beautiful features suddenly became vividly clear.

'Prentice,' the major snapped. 'Ling Prentice. Chinese woman, married a British national about seven years ago. Terrorist sleeper. Became active in March when she started spreading the toxin in large towns and cities, working northwards. Sighted in Leeds less than forty-eight hours ago, but she gave our people the slip. Next.'

The projector clicked and a waist-up image of a black-haired woman wearing a pinstripe suit moved on to the screen. The intake of breath was audible.

'Quest: Samantha Quest,' announced the major. 'And don't be fooled by the looks. She's an evil bitch. Utterly ruthless and absolutely deadly. Killed every operative that's managed to get close to her. Probably crippled and killed the men who were searching for Prentice in Leeds, then spirited her away. Run them through now, Sergeant.'

Surveillance had been working hard. A dozen images of Samantha Quest processed across the screen: front, side and rear views; head and shoulders and full body shots; wearing dresses and suits, some with tight skirts, some with full skirts.

'Ruddy fashion model!' exclaimed a voice in the darkness.

'Just look at the body on it,' whispered another.

The atmosphere in the darkened room had suddenly become electric.

'I told you, don't be fooled by the glamour,' warned the major. 'She's deadly. Kill without a second thought. Thanks, Sergeant. Let's have the lights back on.' His uncovered eye ranged over the room. Twenty pairs of alert, eager eyes gazed back. 'Any questions?' he barked.

'Have the women been located?'

'Quest's based in a small town in South Yorkshire: a place called Barfield. She's given the surveillance team the slip for more than a week, but they're increasing cover. They're pretty sure Quest and Prentice are currently working together in the Sheffield, Leeds, Bradford triangle and gradually moving north. That's why you've been based here, at Catterick.'

'Who's handling surveillance?' came a voice.

'Serious Crime Unit for now. If they don't get a result within a few days it'll be passed on to someone else.'

'And what's our role?'

'Hunt and kill as soon as we get a lead. Until then, all leave cancelled, confined to base. Wear fatigues in barracks; stealth dress when you go out on an assignment. And don't wear tags or carry any form of ID.'

'Kill not capture?' came a voice from the back.

'Instructions from *the very top*' — the major ran his one good eye over the men while he paused for effect — 'are to kill on sight. These women represent a major threat to the security of the state. Thousands have died. Every man in this room has lost family and friends to the plague. There's to be no capture and trial. This is a covert operation to hunt down and kill the evil bitches.'

He studied the grim silent faces. He'd got the message across. They were good chaps. Damned good chaps. He cleared his throat. 'One final thing,' — he reached over and tapped a large black metal box that had the House of Commons portcullis stencilled on its side — 'any documents, vials of toxin, personal possessions; anything they're carrying, must be sealed inside one of these, brought back to base, and handed over to me personally. Got that?'

The murmur said they had.

'Let's hope we don't have to wait too long for the word from surveillance,' the major muttered. 'The sooner we get this cleared up, the better.'

★ ★ ★

Samantha jerked upright, roused from a shallow sleep by the chirping phone. The tone told her it was the one she'd purchased using Ling Prentice's name. She groped for it, switched it on, said nothing, just sat in the darkness, listening to the silence.

After a long pause, a cultivated male voice said, 'Mrs Prentice? Mrs Ling Prentice?'

Samantha switched the mobile off. They must have been searching phone company records, and even though she hadn't spoken, they'd be able to locate her from the contact. It was time now. She'd waited long enough for a message from the widow. She had to clutch at her last straw.

Black woollen knee-highs, black jeans, thick-soled army boots, black roll-neck sweater: her clothes were all within arm's reach, and she dressed quickly.

Taking the pistol from beneath her pillow, she slid it into a shoulder holster and strapped it on, tugged it down until the grip nestled beneath her left breast, then concealed it with a black leather-and-velvet Balmain jacket.

She slid the phones, her bag, her laptop, into a leather hold-all, then went down to the salon. Groping her way past chairs and dryers, she moved through the darkness to the display window and checked the street. There were no parked vans or cars, no people, not even litter in this exclusive little suburb. She headed back, went through the staff room, and stepped out into the rear yard. After stowing her things in the Range Rover, she cast her eye over the contents: rocket-propelled grenades under a canvas sheet, water, fuel in jerry cans, the Heckler sub-machine-gun, ammunition.

About to close the rear door, she paused,

reached into the holdall, and took out an electronic sniffer. Keeping its stubby aerial below chassis level, she circled the four-by-four. There were no warning bleeps, and the meter pointer didn't flicker. They hadn't planted a radio trace.

Samantha got behind the wheel and started the engine, moved out into the street, then headed for the ring road and the motorway.

★　★　★

Major Trantham pressed a couple of tablets from the blister pack, reached for the glass of water, and swallowed them. Damned eye. Ached more at night, and that gritty soreness was lingering. He'd get the MO to take a look at it tomorrow if it didn't feel any better.

Red biro, black biro, A4 pad, all neatly arranged on a pristine blotter. Together with a red phone, a black phone, and his discarded eye-patch, they were the only items on the government-issue beechwood desk.

He glanced at the clock above the door to his office; watched the second hand pulsing round. A quarter-to-four. Groping in his uniform pocket, he pulled out a handkerchief and dabbed his eye. What the devil were the Serious Crime Johnnies playing at? They should know by now. He needed a steady stream of intelligence if he was to direct operations. They were turning out to be . . .

The red phone began to ring. He snatched it up. 'Major Trantham.'

'She's moved out, sir. The call on Prentice's mobile did the trick.'

'Thought it would,' the major said smugly. 'Was she alone?'

'Yes, there's no sign of the widow. We went over the flat yesterday. Found a man's things and one woman's things. Nothing to indicate that two women have been staying there.'

'She's living with the man?'

'Can't be. He's dead. Gay hairdresser who went down with the plague a couple of weeks ago. Looks as if she knew him and just took the place over when he died. So many deaths. It's happening everywhere.'

'Which way is she heading?'

'Towards the main road. That's all we can see from the house opposite the shop. Your people should be picking up the radio locator about now.'

The major chuckled. 'She didn't find it, then?'

'Her detector wouldn't respond to the new bug, its frequency's too high. Not got the same range as the old devices though. Your people can't lag too far behind in built-up areas.'

Impudent blighter, the major fumed to himself. He didn't need to be told that. Out loud he said, 'Everything's covered. Six cars: using them in rotation so she doesn't realize she's being followed. Did you search the Range Rover when you went over the flat?'

'Couldn't. Home Office vehicle that's been used on royal protection. Very secure. She'd have known we'd tampered with it and found some other transport. Rear seats have been taken out and there's quite a bit of stuff packed in the back. She was obviously getting ready to leave. When are you taking her out?'

'When she joins up with the widow. It's the widow they're really worried about. We're hoping Quest's going to lead us to her.'

'We think the widow's dead.'

'Possibly. We'll just give Quest a few days. If she doesn't find her, we'll pick our time and place and move in.'

'Well, good luck.' Laughter came down the line. 'She's a cunning little madam. I think you're going to need it.'

★ ★ ★

Traffic was sparse on the motorway: mostly lorries and the occasional convoy of army trucks, but hardly any cars during the hour before dawn. Samantha repeatedly checked the mirrors, and slowed to compel cars to overtake. Just north of Wetherby, she pulled into a lay-by, turned off the ignition, wound down the window, and listened in the silences between the rumble and roar of passing lorries, straining for the drone of a helicopter on aerial surveillance. Hearing nothing, she continued her journey northwards.

Beyond Scotch Corner, a car seemed to be holding back no matter how much she reduced her speed. Spending the past ten days staring into rear-view mirrors, constantly checking for tails, may have made her paranoid, but a car moving this slowly along an almost deserted motorway wasn't normal.

She studied the area of grass and vegetation adjoining the road. Up ahead, earth had been mounded to give a high vantage point for police vehicles. Switching off her lights, she drifted across the hard shoulder, then bounced over tussocky grass until the four-by-four was hidden behind the ramp. She climbed out, ran ahead, and crouched amongst a group of immature trees.

The sound of the car's engine grew louder. A halo of light blazed around the mound of earth and a red Vauxhall Vectra swept by. Samantha moved out across the grass, read the registration number, then climbed into the Range Rover and lurched back on to the hard shoulder. She crept along it for almost a mile. A couple of lorries rumbled past, closely followed by a silver Peugeot estate, and then she moved back on to the road.

The sky was becoming lighter as she closed on Newcastle. Up ahead, the red Vauxhall and silver Peugeot were still moving slowly, occasionally coming into view as the traffic climbed hills and snaked around bends. Behind her, a dark-blue Ford was keeping its distance, despite her modest speed. Samantha grew more uneasy. No vehicles had been parked in the street outside the salon. There had been nothing untoward when she'd circled the town and moved on to the motorway. The roads had been silent and empty. And it had been more than the usual pre-dawn silence: it had been that deathly stillness that had settled on places since the plague took hold.

Instead of skirting Newcastle, she plunged into the city, meandered through its empty streets, ignoring one-way signs, jumping lights, using every trick she knew to throw off a following car. She parked, lowered the window, waited and listened. There was no sign of the cars that had accompanied her up the motorway; no sign of airborne surveillance.

She watched yellow-jacketed street cleaners

picking up litter and emptying bins. When they'd almost reached her, she keyed the ignition and moved off. The low early-morning sun was casting long shadows, its watery light flashing through gaps between buildings as she motored along city streets, heading for the Tyne bridge and the motorway.

Traffic was heavier now. Samantha checked the cars in front and behind as it flowed around gentle bends. A dark-blue Ford was wedged between lorries a few hundred yards ahead. A red Vauxhall seemed to be maintaining a steady distance at the rear; it was too far behind for her to read the plates. She moved more slowly. Even lorries were overtaking her, but the Vauxhall maintained its distance and the dark-blue Ford remained in view.

She wasn't being paranoid. A team of drivers was stalking her, waiting for her to lead them to Ling Prentice. Her erratic journey through Newcastle should have shaken them off. There had to be a radio trace on the car.

Leaving the motorway at the next exit, she turned into a small industrial estate and parked behind a derelict factory. Another sweep with the electronic sniffer revealed nothing. She got down on her back and wriggled beneath the high floor of the car. Armour plating had made its underside smooth; hiding wires and pipes and the ribs and channels that strengthened the metal deck. They'd even extended the sheeting beneath the engine and behind wheel arches, robbing her stalkers of all the usual hiding places for a radio trace.

And then she found them: two small plastic boxes held in place behind the front and rear bumpers by black tape. She pulled them free. New devices, they had no identification marks and probably operated in a way that made them difficult to detect.

Climbing back into the car, she laid them on top of the dash, then returned to the motorway and drove on. Her stalkers fell into place before she reached Berwick: the red Vauxhall in front, the dark-blue Ford behind.

Minutes later, she pulled into a services complex, walked over the foot-bridge to the south-bound side of the motorway, and planted the radio traces on a French lorry.

Returning to the north-bound side, she found a restaurant and ate the full English breakfast.

* * *

Major Trantham reached over his uncluttered desk and picked up the bleeping phone.

'We've lost her, sir.'

'I don't understand. You can't have lost her.'

'She kept pulling off the road. The lads thought she was stopping to relieve herself, but she must have known she was being followed and had a good search for the radio locators. She pulled into a service station this side of Berwick and attached them to a lorry heading south. Team followed it back to Catterick before they realized something was wrong.'

Major Trantham drummed on the blotter with thick fingers and held his breath while he counted the throbs of pain stabbing through his eye. He got to ten, then exhaled and muttered, 'Resourceful little filly. She's probably still heading north.'

'Could be anywhere, sir.'

'And we've got to find her, Maitland. Call the other two teams and get them to space out along the motorway north of Edinburgh, as far up as Perth. And put someone from the team that's driven back on board a chopper, and send him up the motorway. I want a report every thirty minutes from now on. Got that, Maitland?'

'Got it, sir. Will do.'

★ ★ ★

Who'd said the hills of Scotland are like the flanks of slaughtered horses? Samantha pondered. Auden: the poet with a face like a bleached prune. It was one of the bits he'd left out of *Night Mail*.

Tired now, she was trying to stay alert. She'd left the motorway and driven westward out of Berwick, moving up the country through Galashiels and Peebles, staying on minor roads all the way to the Highlands.

This was a place of desolation. Heather, bracken, and a monotony of dark and sombre pine plantations that rolled over hills fissured by shadowy glens.

It was almost noon. She'd been on the road for more than eight hours. Up ahead, a break in the dry stone walling gave on to a trail that rose to the forest. She turned off, hid the Range Rover beneath sweeping branches, brewed coffee, ate sandwiches she'd purchased at the service station, then slept with her hand on her gun.

No aeroplanes, no ships, no trains, Wei Prentice had said, and her mother had complained about the weather and the endless journey. It had to be Scotland, and Hope Lodge, with its backdrop of purple hills, probably overlooked Loch Hope.

304

Samantha left what passed for a main road and headed through Strath More, lurching over bridges that spanned streams feeding a river that flowed down to the loch. The skyline was spectacular. Ridge beyond ridge, crest beyond crest; green fading into brown and then into shades of blue that merged with the evening sky. To the east, high peaks were golden in the last of the sun.

The loch touched the road, then swept away to encircle a plantation of birches and pines. Around a bend, almost hidden by trees, stone pillars flanked an opening and wrought-iron gates were pegged back. Samantha left the road, followed a track between trees for a hundred yards, and found herself in a clearing where heather was encroaching on coarse grass.

The house was set behind a tiny walled garden, its grey stones spotted with yellow lichen. A central doorway was flanked by tall windows, and dormers and chimneys rose out of a roof of purple slates. It was the house in the photograph: the house Wei Prentice had called Narnia.

She parked the Range Rover alongside a new-looking car and a small van, then headed down the garden path.

'Can I be of any help to you?'

Samantha turned, saw a short middle-aged

man in brown overalls peering at her around the corner of the house. She began to move towards him.

'Don't come any closer.' There was fear in his voice. 'If you're from the south, keep your distance. We've had none of the plague here, and I'm not wanting to be catching it now.'

She smiled reassuringly. 'I've been immunized. I couldn't infect you.'

He let out a derisory laugh. 'I've relatives in Birmingham. Three dead and they were all injected. The Government's been fooling you. Please,' he held up his hands, 'just stay there and tell me what you want.'

'I'm looking for Mrs Prentice. Is she here?'

'Left. More than a week ago.' His eyes narrowed. 'And why would you be wanting the professor's wife?'

'I'm caring for her little girl. She's missing her mother. I need to talk to her about coming back to England.'

Fearful of contagion, he was eyeing Samantha warily. 'She's gone,' he repeated. 'I can't help you.'

'I've travelled a long way. Could I rest in the house for a while; perhaps make a meal?'

'I've secured the place. I wouldn't want to be opening it up again. And there's the plague to be thinking about. Mrs Prentice wouldn't thank me for letting disease into her home.' He stared at Samantha for a few moments, then explained, 'I'm the handyman-caretaker. The professor set me on. He's in America and she's gone.' He sighed. 'Looks like I've lost the wee job.'

'The car in the clearing; is it Mrs Prentice's?'

'Aye.'

'She left on foot, then?' Samantha said.

'Seems so.'

'And where would she go on foot from here?'

He rubbed the side of his nose with his thumb. 'Towards An Lean-Charn, maybe. That's the peak beyond the loch. The family often used to walk up beside the stream to the lakes. There's a wee house there. Derelict. Laird Kilmuir used to have food and drink served to his shooting parties in the kitchen of the place. That ended when I was a bairn.'

'Is there anywhere else she might have gone?'

'Not on foot.'

'She's been gone a week,' Samantha said. 'Aren't you worried about her? Have you contacted the police?'

'The day she left she told me to say nothing. And she knows the hills. I don't interfere, missy.' He nodded towards the Rover. 'The river's unseasonally low. The four-by-four would get you across the rapids at the head of the loch. And if you're careful you can drive around the far shore until you come to the stream. It's three miles or more.' He seemed to want her to go.

'Thanks,' Samantha said. 'I'll give it a try. If anyone comes asking, don't tell them I called. Mrs Prentice wouldn't like it.' She turned and headed for the car.

He called after her, 'If you find the professor's wife, tell her I've fixed the broken sash; tell her I'm still watching over the house for her.'

★　★　★

Samantha followed the stream up the side of the glen to a ruin of a house that overlooked small lakes of dark water. The air was cold and clear, and stars were beginning to glitter in a sky not yet completely dark.

She settled the strap of her bag on her shoulder, felt for the grip of the gun beneath her coat, then made her way up the remains of a path to the house. It was no more than a dark shape in the gloom; the opening where the door had been, a rectangle of blackness. She stepped closer, stared up at some sacking that had been stretched across an upstairs window, then moved through the doorway.

Keeping her voice low, she called, 'Mrs Prentice?'

She held her breath, listened for a while to the stream cascading down the glen and the beating of the blood in her ears. Dropping her bag beside the door, she took out a torch and probed the darkness of the large, low-ceilinged room. An iron cooking range had been built into a chimney breast, stone flags covered the floor, and a stone stair rose steeply against the far wall.

Samantha drew the pistol from its holster; kept it under her coat while she climbed to the upper floor and shone the torch around. Laths grinned through decaying plaster, and stars glittered between rafters that were like black bars against the sky.

One of the two rooms seemed more intact. Rounding the stairwell, she shone her torch through the door opening, saw a sleeping bag, a radio, a gas lamp, a couple of books and a haversack that had been propped against the wall. She stepped inside, sensed a presence, turned and directed the light on an oriental woman, huddling beside the door-way.

'Ma Weihma?' Samantha whispered Ling Prentice's real maiden name.

The cowering woman squinted up into the brightness. 'Who are you?'

'Light the lamp so you can see me.'

Samantha followed her with the beam of the torch as she shuffled across the floor on her hands and knees; watched her shake a match from a box, strike it, then hold the flame to gas hissing through a mantle. It flared, and the decrepit room was filled with soft white light.

Ling Prentice crouched on the sleeping bag; small and slender. She stared up into Samantha's face for a dozen heart-beats, then said, 'Such eyes: such terrifying eyes. And you speak in my tongue and call me by my true name. Only the dead know my true name.' Her voice dropped to a whisper. 'Are you the dark angel? Have you come to take me?'

Samantha remained silent, not sure how to respond to the woman's fear. Deciding to ignore it, she murmured, 'Alice, your sister-in-law, sent me. I have your child.'

'My child is dead,' Ling Prentice snapped bitterly. 'The man who called me said my child is dead.'

'Man who called?'

'About a week ago. A man kept phoning me. He phoned me all day. He kept saying, 'Mrs Prentice, your child is dead'. I was scared. Nat had warned me they would search for me. The next day I left the lodge and came up here.'

'You used your mobile phone?'

'Of course. There's no phone in the lodge. I called Kwan a couple of times to check on Wei. Next day I got the calls from the man. I didn't use the phone after that.'

'They were trying to use the signal to locate you. That's why they kept phoning.'

'He said my daughter die in the plague; the plague my husband created.'

'He was lying,' Samantha said. 'On both counts. Where are your husband's tapes and papers?'

'I have the important ones here. Nat got a message to me before he died; told me what to destroy, what to keep.'

'They implicate powerful men in grave crimes, Mrs Prentice. They must be used wisely to protect you and your child.'

Samantha gazed down at the unkempt figure. The forces the state would unleash to ensure her death would be awesome. She might not live to see her child. Samantha said softly, 'What do you want me to do?'

Ling Prentice began to weep. Anguish was making her beautiful face ugly, and her small body was shaking. 'Take me to my child,' she moaned. 'Please, take me to my child.'

17

The sun was driving away the mist when they made the river crossing and emerged on to the narrow road that wound through the glen.

'Watch the sky,' Samantha said, to a more presentable Ling Prentice. The widow had pinned up her hair and changed into a black sweater and crimson skirt.

'What am I watching for?'

'Helicopters, planes: that's how they'll be searching for us.'

'Those things in the back, the tube things you were sliding together before we set off; what are they?' Ling Prentice asked.

'Rocket-propelled grenades. If they locate us, they'll send in a platoon.'

'A platoon?' Ling whispered.

'A team of men. They'll want to be certain of killing us both and seizing your husband's papers.'

Ling shivered. 'You are the dark angel. I think I am going to die.'

Samantha smiled wryly. Ling Prentice seemed unable to widen her concern to include them both. 'Surely it's worth any risk to hold your child in your arms again?'

'They told me my child is dead. I was safely hidden. I could have stuck it out.'

'Wei isn't dead,' Samantha insisted. 'And it's the papers and tapes you have, and the things they think you know, that put you at risk. You can't hide for ever.'

'But the plague,' Ling Prentice moaned. 'We're driving into plague towns.'

'You can't catch the plague,' Samantha snapped, beginning to lose patience. 'The injection I gave you prevents it. Now, watch the sky. That's how they'll search for us.'

★   ★   ★

Showered, shaved, clean linen, decent breakfast; the pain in his eye almost completely gone: Major Trantham was feeling optimistic. The chaps would come through. Hand picked, dammit. Nation's finest.

The red phone began its half-hourly bleeping. He reached for the handset.

'We've located them, Major.'

'Them?'

'Two women in a Range Rover, heading across the Highlands. They're moving south right now, towards Lairg.'

'How do you know there's two women in the car?'

'Base at Craigmoss put four battlefield

drones up for us. The women have got the sun roof open and the cameras are picking them up, sharp and clear.'

'They'll hear the damned things. That's what they've got the sun roof open for. You'll put them on their guard.'

'Drones are circling at two-thousand feet, Major. Can't be seen, can't be heard.'

'Move in, sharp as you can, while they're in the middle of nowhere. Use a big chopper and send a dozen men. We've got to get 'em this time.'

'Will do, sir.'

'And Maitland . . . '

'Sir?'

'Make sure the drones are grounded before the chopper goes in. We don't want other eyes prying. Most of all, we don't want a souvenir video.'

★　★　★

Turbines screaming, rotor blades thrashing the air, the huge machine came up from the rear and swept ahead. It was low enough for them to see lines of rivets and old identity numbers ghosting through hastily applied black paint.

'Stop or be killed. Stop or be killed.' A powerful amplifying system turned the

314

commands into blows.

Samantha braked hard, the helicopter cruised on, then swung round and settled on the narrow road, presenting its impressive bulk to the car. Howling engines calmed to a moan, and rotor blades began to idle. In a high cockpit, the pilot turned to get a better look at them, then pressed a hand to the mouthpiece of his helmet.

'Get out of the car. Put your hands above your heads and stand still. If you move, you'll be killed.'

Ling Prentice was clinging to the edge of the seat, her body shaking. Samantha reached over, pushed open the passenger door and snapped, 'Get out. And when the shooting starts, crawl under the car.'

The widow didn't move; just stared, wide-eyed, at the black machine, straddling the road like a gigantic insect, fifty yards ahead.

'Do as they say,' Samantha yelled, then shoved her out and climbed down herself. Moving a couple of paces back, she positioned herself close to the rear door of the Range Rover, and raised her hands.

'Throw down any small arms.' The command was painfully loud.

Samantha reached inside her coat, tugged the pistol from its holster and tossed it into the bracken.

'You are to be taken into custody. Do not move. Just stand where you are and await your arrest. If you move, you will be killed . . . Killed . . . Killed.' The message echoed down the glen, words chasing words.

A hatch at the rear of the craft began to lower. Above its slowly descending upper edge, Samantha could see the barrels of assault rifles, and then a dozen determined faces came into view. There would be no arrests. They were going to be killed. There was so little time.

She ducked behind the Range Rover, opened the door and gathered up one of the rocket-propelled grenades. Dropping to her knees, she swung the launcher over her shoulder and sighted on the opening hatchway. The men's expressions suddenly changed, and the pilot turned back to the controls.

There was hardly any recoil when she squeezed the trigger, just the roar of burning fuel as the rocket surged from its launching tube. The hatch was still lowering. When the finger of flame stabbed it, the explosion was body-shaking, the rumbling echoes endless.

The turbines were silent now; the drooping rotors almost motionless above the helicopter's shattered flank. Bodies were strewn behind the twisted remains of the hatch, and the pilot and co-pilot were no longer visible. Protected by the bulkhead, they might still be alive and reporting back to base.

Dragging the second launcher from the car, Samantha knelt and unleashed another grenade; then flinched, deafened by the blast as it ripped open the black metal skin and exposed the intricate entrails of the machine.

After heaving a traumatized Ling Prentice back into her seat, Samantha retrieved her pistol, then turned the four-by-four off the road and ploughed through the bracken. Ears ringing, she watched for movement as she circled the wrecked helicopter. There was no sign of life, and no sign, as yet, of another pursuer in the sky.

★ ★ ★

The major grabbed the phone at the first bleep. 'How's it going, Maitland?'

'Everything seems OK, sir. They located the car just south of Altnaharra and the last message we received said they were going down to give the command to stop.'

'Last message? What do you mean, last message?' Alarm was sounding in the major's voice.

'Strath Bagastie's a deep cut through the mountains. If they've landed on the road they might not be able to get a signal out, especially with the radio gear installed in that big old chopper.'

'Are the drones down?'

'Landed the drones just as the team went in.'

'I don't like losing contact, Maitland.'

'It happens, sir. It's the terrain. They're probably tidying up. I told them to bag the bodies and bring them back in the chopper; detailed Butler and Sloane to drive the Range Rover to Catterick and hand it over to you. No stops. Should be here mid-afternoon.'

'They understand that nothing has to be touched?'

'They understand, sir.'

★ ★ ★

Samantha swung the three-litre Jaguar off the York-to-Scarborough road and began to search Forest Park for the house she'd rented for Wei Prentice and Crispin.

She'd hired the car in Inverness after leaving the Range Rover in a dark corner of a municipal car park. In Edinburgh, she'd bought clothes for Ling Prentice and herself, then taken a hotel room where they'd rested until dawn.

While Ling Prentice slept, Loretta Fallon collected the briefcase stuffed with Nathaniel Prentice's notebooks and tapes, and promised to protect his widow and child. Samantha had to trust her. The deal that had to be brokered, the pressures that had to be brought to bear, were things only Fallon could deal with.

Samantha drove slowly down narrow lanes green with spring foliage. Eventually she found it. *Braemar*: the name of the house was gilded on to a slab of slate set beside a gap in a high beech hedge. She manoeuvred the car around a swathe of tarmac, then parked in front of a pebble-dashed house that had recently been painted white.

High fencing closed off the rear garden. Samantha led Ling Prentice through a gate and down the side of the house as far as the kitchen door. In the middle of a well-tended lawn, Wei Prentice was rocking on a swing. She had her back to them, and the movement was fluttering the skirt of her blue gingham dress. Samantha touched Ling Prentice's arm, urged her forward, then stepped through the open doorway.

A meal was cooking in the family-size kitchen. Crispin was whisking batter, the basin held against the bib of his blue-striped apron. He had his back to her and his gaze was fixed on the screen of a portable television.

Samantha looked through the big picture window. Ling Prentice was close behind her daughter now. She must have spoken, because the child turned and her face was suddenly radiant. Samantha saw her mouth form the word, 'Mother', then she slid from the swing and held up her arms. Ling Prentice stooped down and gathered her up.

'Sam! Didn't hear you come in.' Crispin followed her gaze through the window. 'You've found her, then? Thank God for that. Day and night, it's all the kid's talked about: 'When will Sam bring Mummy home?''

Samantha gazed at the unbelievably handsome man holding a Pyrex bowl and a whisk. She didn't speak. She was drawing comfort from the normality of it all: the washing on the line, a little girl in a gingham dress, the smell of cooking.

Crispin gave his whisk a flick. 'Yorkshire puddings. The kid adores Yorkshire puddings.' He frowned. 'You're looking a bit jaded, Sam.'

'Feel a bit jaded, Crispin.' Samantha looked down the garden at the ecstatic little girl in her mother's arms. Her body was shaking and her eyes were filling with tears she didn't want him to see.

'It's all been happening this morning,' Crispin said. 'Prime Minister and half the cabinet resigned. Forming a coalition to govern through the emergency. Things might get better now.'

'Don't hold your breath,' Samantha muttered. Her mascara was running. She couldn't hold back the tears. She'd reunited mother and child, but at what cost?

'Hey! What's wrong, Sam?' Crispin slid the bowl on to the worktop and put his arm around her shoulders.

She didn't answer. She was picturing the young men in the motel, the marksman in the boarded-up house, the men in the helicopter. Chance instruments of the malign political will; duped and dead; slaughtered so a child could greet her mother with a smile.

Crispin turned her to face him, began to wipe the black smudges from her cheeks with the hem of his apron. 'What if I run you a hot bath, get you a whisky, wash your hair, and give it a blow dry?' He squeezed her shoulders. 'What would you say to that?'

She treated him to the vivid blaze of her green eyes. 'I'd say you were the dog's bollocks, Crispin.'